SICK GIRL

A PSYCHOLOGICAL THRILLER

RACHEL HARGROVE

DEDICATION

For the doctors who saved me.

1

AUBREY

I'll KILL her after yoga class.

Everything I need to end Melissa's life is tucked in my gym bag, next to the damp towel I forgot to dry and a leaking bottle of Vitamin Water.

I've got it all figured out. The only thing Melissa loves more than her yuppie hobbies is her tall non-fat lattes at Starbucks, which she always buys after an hour of Cow Pose and Proud Warrior II. The last image she'll see is the bottom of a mediocre cup of coffee. Her heart will gallop, her body will seize, and she'll be *gone*.

And I'll be a murderer.

Guilt clenches my stomach as I smooth the yoga mat pockmarked with holes on the polished, cream floor. Several feet away, a bright pink blur slaps the ground. A woman in galaxy leggings and a white T-shirt crouches beside me, a ringed red planet stretched across her thighs. "Hey," she grunts. "You ready for this?"

"Not really."

"Thank Jesus. Someone in here is sane. I have to remind myself how good yoga is for my health."

God bless Emma. She's fat and doesn't give a fuck. She joined a month after I did and comes to class wearing spandex and semi-sheer T-shirts emblazoned with phrases such as THICK CHICK in gaudy lettering. The only reason she's here is to exercise. Weight loss is a bonus for Emma, and that's why I like her. She's in no hurry to change herself.

Emma glowers at the doors leading outside. "The weather's crazy."

A cool mist had dusted my cheeks while I walked to the studio, but the fog burned away. A bright strip of sunlight sears the asphalt beyond the doors. "The forecast said eighties."

"Which is way too hot for SF."

"I guess, yeah."

Emma lies on the mat, stretching her hamstrings. "Hey, I've been meaning to ask you something." She chews her lip. "What's your secret?"

The hell is she talking about?

Emma's gaze runs up and down my body. "You know what I mean. How do you stay so thin? Nothing in the world will stop my weekly Dynamo donuts fix, but my doctor says I need to make healthier choices." She rolls her eyes at the very suggestion.

Perhaps I should tell her I survive on apple slices and lemon juice. That kombucha changed my life. I intentionally contracted a parasite. My organic vegan, gluten-free, certified humane lifestyle makes food options sparse.

The truth is too depressing.

Growing impatient, she nudges me with her elbow. "Swear to God I won't judge. How do you do it?"

I meet her gaze. "Cancer."

Emma stares at me until a sound wheezes from her closed lips. It takes me a moment to realize she's laughing. At me.

She playfully hits my shoulder. "You're too *funny*."

Screw it. I won't set her straight. At least someone here has a sense of humor, unlike the dozen women flittering into the studio. They talk in hushed tones as they unwrap their yoga mats and kneel as though the mirrors are an altar. New Age music tinkles through a built-in stereo, which is surrounded by glowing candles and questionable Buddha statues. Getting a membership cost me a fortune, but it was worth it because she's here.

A straight-backed woman in Lululemon yoga pants sits in front of a wall-to-wall mirror, the logo on her thigh a dead giveaway for wealth. Her white-blonde mane is tied into a dense ponytail. The pink band pulls her hair so tight her eyebrows rise in a permanently shocked expression. All I see is the back of her head, but I know it's her. No one carries themselves like Melissa. She never hunches, even when she thinks she's alone. Every morning, she applies a thick coat of makeup on her golden skin, which she maintains with a weekly airbrush spray tan. When she's in a hurry, she doesn't run. It wouldn't be dignified, and Melissa Daughtry is the picture of class. Her *name* sounds like money.

Melissa takes her sweater off, the light dancing on her back muscles as she pulls it over her head. She's in that good phase of cancer. Still attractive. Not too thin. She has a dancer's body. It's as though she went on a sixty-day kale juice cleanse.

I'm in the wasting away stage. If this were the nineties, I'd be the poster girl for heroin chic. Ribs push against my skin in ghastly white lumps. Hollowed cheeks replace the chubby baby fat I used to hate. My hair hangs limp at my shoulders, but I refuse to wince at my reflection. After a while, you deal with it. People walking the street don't. They stop and gape at me.

"Okay, ladies! Five-minute warning!" an overly chipper voice chimes. "We're doing the Sun Salutation today!"

A murmur of excitement rolls through the yoga class, and I spot my hopeful face in the mirrors.

Beside me, Emma frowns. "Damn."

Judging from the smiles in the mirror, Emma's the only one who'd rather be somewhere else. I don't hate yoga. It can be meditative. Once in a while, I'll close my eyes and allow the mystical music to pull me into a trance, and it feels good. But I can count the number of times exercise wasn't painful on my hand. Standing is a struggle, and Sun Salutation always starts with a twenty-second hold of the tree pose.

Ignoring Emma's jealous stare, I yank the hoodie from my head.

"Whoa, you've lost weight." Her smile twitches. "You're not really sick, are you?"

"Sort of. I swam in a lake and contracted a parasite."

Her nose wrinkles. "Ew."

"Yeah. I spent six weeks wasting away before I went to a doctor, who told me I had giardiasis. It turns out if parasites live in your gut long enough, they can destroy the surface of your intestines and make it impossible to absorb food."

"Well," she says, apparently at a loss for words. "You look good."

Not according to the instructor. A few weeks ago she recommended I increase my core strength and suggested that perhaps this wasn't the right class for me.

No kidding.

I wouldn't be at this overpriced yoga studio if Melissa didn't spend every Monday and Wednesday here. I need exercise like I need more masses in my colon. My doctor's orders were simple. Bed rest. Lots of calories. I'm sure they were the same for Melissa, but damn it if she takes one day off exercise. Does she think she'll beat cancer with barre? I watch her through the windows in her house. She spends hours on that goddamn bike, cycling away. Sometimes after her doctor appointments.

How does she do it?

Would it kill her before I got the chance?

"You know, you could just talk to her."

Emma's sly voice yanks me from my thoughts. Her smirk carves deep dimples into her cheeks.

My spine zips straight. "What do you mean?"

Her grin widens. "Aubrey, you're always watching her."

Heat rises to my face. Am I that transparent?

"It's fine. You don't have to be embarrassed." She glances at Melissa, shrugging. "If I were gay, I'd probably find her hot, too."

"I have a boyfriend."

"Yeah, okay."

I open my mouth and close it. Why tell her the truth? It's better if she thinks I'm harmless.

Growing impatient at my silence, she sighs. "Aubrey, come on. This is San Francisco. Do you think I care who you date?" Emma snorts with laughter, turning her attention to the front of the class.

I swing my gaze to Melissa, who stretches her quads and hops on one foot. It's hard to imagine her body lying lifeless on the ground. There's so much resilience in her. The girl never stops.

I've got the method and delivery all figured out. After yoga, she goes to the café and drinks a latte—I fished her cup from the trash a few weeks ago. I'll spike her drink with nitroglycerin, which won't show in tox screens, at which point everyone will blame Starbucks. Or cancer. And I'll—we'll be free. Once she's gone, I won't have to come to class anymore, but I think I'll continue. I like what it's done to my legs.

A crack splits the air as the instructor for the class, Lucy, claps her hands. Lucy shines like a topaz gem with a thousand lights pointed at it. Her round face beams with positivity. It wouldn't bother me if it weren't for her constant, not-so-subtle suggestions that I load up on more fat and protein before coming to yoga. Everybody thinks they're an expert these days.

Lucy walks across the mirrors in fuchsia leggings and a green tank top, bending to push a button on the stereo. "All right, ladies. It's time to start!"

Suppressing a groan, I stand and assume Tree pose as hippie music washes over the studio. My foot slips down my left leg, and I stumble. I'm the only person in the class who still can't master this, and, for some stupid reason, it grates at me. I try again. Holding Tree for more than ten seconds saps what little energy I have. After three aborted attempts, I give up.

Lucy's stare finds me across the room. Her lips purse into a small show of disapproval.

My hands and knees slap the floor as everyone switches from Cat to Cow.

Lucy focuses her smoky eyes on me. "The next position

will be hard, but I know you can do it!" Both palms planted down, she flips herself and rests her legs on her elbows.

There's no way my sticks for arms will hold my body like that. Lucy's ombré hair falls in a curtain behind her head as she glares at me between her thighs. Bent over, she waddles forward, her upside-down frown a grotesque smirk. I find Melissa, whose biceps tremble as she attempts the pose. She takes a few tries but manages it, her face frozen in stoic concentration.

For the rest of the class I make sure to half-ass the poses whenever Lucy glances in my direction, and when she shuts off that god-awful music, I take my time rolling my mat.

Breathless, Emma gets up on a shuddering knee and waves a wordless goodbye as she heads for the showers. The studio gradually empties as I pretend to tie my shoelaces. Lucy chats with stragglers as Melissa pulls a silver cashmere sweater over her damp body.

What's it like to be rich enough to use expensive wool as an after-workout sweat absorbent?

A throb of envy pulses in my hollowed stomach as she grabs her mat and stands. She's on her way to the locker room, and then to Starbucks.

This is my chance.

2

MELISSA

I'm dying for Starbucks. Twelve ounces of cheap, fast, *good* stamped on cardboard with a green-and-white logo. When I was working, that coffee chain was my sanctuary. Now it's the only thing getting me through my twice-weekly yoga classes. In an hour, I'll have my cup in hand.

The domed space of the Tesla echoes with my sigh. A cool breeze blows through the ventilation as soft indie rock warps the air. I peer out the windshield at the sidewalk blanketed with sunlight and try not to burn with envy.

I wanted to be just like them. The women with perfect smiles who use filters on Instagram photos. Bloggers who take selfies in overcrowded cafés, their posts filled with enough keywords in their hashtags to be the first Google search result. The ones who belong in this coveted zip code. They line outside the studio, wearing designer yoga pants and shirts in varying shades of pastels. Whole Foods is where they shop, and Starbucks is what they drink. Cold-pressed juice stocks their refrigerators and every few months, they go on a lemon water cleanse to clear the toxins from their bodies. Weekdays are a rolling schedule of maids, cooks, and gardeners tending to their various needs. Summers are all-inclusive resorts in Cabo. Winters are weekends in Tahoe.

Dyeing my hair blonde wasn't a conscious decision to imitate them, but the matcha green tea enema was. Only tried it once.

A broad hand grasps mine. Squeezes. I tear my gaze from the women, meeting my husband's quiet stare. God, I forgot he was here.

"You don't have to wait with me," I say.

The leather squeaks as he leans closer. "I want to."

All my hairs stand on end as Tom kisses the shell of my ear, his unshaven cheek stinging my skin. He pulls back with a glowing look I do not deserve, the one that says I'm everything he could ever hope for. That I'm perfect.

He's the one who should be standing on a pedestal. I bought this overpriced car because Tom wanted it, and I can't say no to him. Distant Swedish ancestry gave him a tall, broad-shouldered figure and blond hair with natural highlights that most women would kill for. *Striking* would be a good word to describe him.

Through the windshield, a woman in the line steals glances at my husband when she thinks I'm not looking.

Tom doesn't notice—he's never realized how attractive he is. "You should mingle with them."

"What for?" I spent months trying to make friends in this neighborhood. No dice. "All they want to talk about is the importance of co-sleeping and the next diet fad."

He grimaces. "You need friends other than cancer survivors."

"I have nothing in common with these people. Just look at them."

He does. "And?"

"The biggest decision they have to make tonight is pot roast or baked salmon."

Laughing, he turns toward me. "Oh, come on."

"It's true!"

"Don't be so judgy." He gestures at a stocky brunette at the end of the line. "What about her? She seems nice."

That's my Tom. He always sees the best in people, unlike most tech bros glutting this city.

"Sure," I say. "I'm just not big on conversation unless it's about software."

"One of these days you'll have to learn how to socialize. That skill can come in handy quite often when dealing with humans."

"I managed to get you without it."

"That's because I did all the talking." Tom gives me a shadow of a wink and smile.

We met in a dive of all places. He stood head and shoulders above the crowded bar. I saw him before he noticed me, but when he did, he excused himself from the redhead at the counter and made a beeline for me. From the moment we met, I was hooked. There was no resistance, nothing but the soft wing beats of butterflies when our lips touched. Something about him held my attention and simmered my blood like nobody else. It was a fairytale romance from the beginning; a rare, instantaneous connection you feel humming in your body.

A flurry of warmth replaces the dread in my stomach. It's moments like this I can almost forget the hell raging inside me. Six months ago our picture-perfect marriage was turned on its head by an unwelcome visitor.

Pancreatic cancer.

Tom drums the steering wheel. "Can I get you anything special for supper?"

Fat and salt. "Barbecue pork sandwiches from 4505? The kids would love that."

"I'm sure they would, but is that a good idea? The diet plan says to avoid trans fats."

"Well, get whatever you want. I'll make myself a salad."

He blows a frustrated sigh. "You need to keep up your strength."

I wave at the line of women outside. "What do you think this is?"

"Meditation?"

Leave it to a former college football player to dismiss yoga as physical activity. "Exercise. I'm not sitting on my ass while this disease takes over my body."

"Okay, but you should put more thought into what you have every day. Eating healthy is the most important thing you can do right now."

This is what our conversations have become. Debates about my stupid diet. I drag my nails across my legs. "Did you have anything?"

"Yeah," he says. "Took me ten minutes to bolt down a sandwich before I picked you up."

"Your boss won't like you taking fifty-minute lunches."

"He understands."

I doubt that. Tom's a software engineer. If his supervisor thinks he's had one too many long breaks, we're screwed. Losing his job would be catastrophic because I need the health insurance. The tech community isn't forgiving, and Tom's always taken things for granted.

When my career was booming, I encouraged Tom to buy himself nice things. And he did. The extra expense wasn't a big deal while I was raking in cash, but we're not doing so well anymore. I'll have to rein in his fancies even though it saddles me with crippling guilt. I want him to have things.

"I'll take an Uber next time," I say. "Finding parking is always a pain."

"Really, I don't mind. I'm where I need to be." A smile hitches on his face as his fingers tiptoe down my thighs, spreading heat over my skin.

I grab him before he can stroke the sensitive patch between my legs. "*Tom.*"

"What? You're sexy in those tight leggings." He grasps my chin, brushing his lips against mine. "It's been so long."

I wait for an answering rush of blood, something to prove I'm still alive, but this damned illness takes everything away. Cancer is a hurricane, leaving nothing but devastation and pain in its path. I can't feel anymore. Anxiety numbs the swell of passion that used to rise inside me. Joy, desire, excitement—they're all gone. He kisses me, and I close my eyes, willing myself to experience something other than dread. *Feel*, damn it.

I try. I trace his collarbone. Roll my palms over his chest. I'm lucky to have him—so lucky. He grinds his mouth against mine, and all I feel is the roughness of his beard against my chin.

Tom pulls back, eyes softened. "Sorry."

"No, I'm sorry." He's not the one who should apologize. "I'm not myself. It's not you, babe. I swear to God it isn't."

"I know," he says.

Does he? How often does he long for the days when I wanted him?

Tom wraps his arm around my shoulder, pulling me into his chest to stroke my head. "I love you."

"I love you, too."

I used to mean those words with every fiber of my being. They resonated through my soul. I could reach down and find a well of affection for him. It's there, I think. Buried under the constant roar pounding through my brain, the question keeping me up at night.

If the cancer was gone, would I still love him?

I can't let myself answer. The weight of this disease crushes everything, and my heart is dust.

3

AUBREY

MELISSA'S PONYTAIL swings from side to side like a pendulum. I count the seconds I have until she's out the door. Five, *maybe* six.

My knees pop as I struggle to my feet and follow her. Ear to the phone, she's oblivious. Women like her always are. They don't notice the little people scurrying around them.

She halts as a loud group gathers in front of the exit. Nearly there, I shove the rolled mat on the pile beside the weights.

"Au-brey!" a singsong voice exclaims, stopping me in my tracks.

Lucy bounces on her soles. "Come here! Just wanna chat for a sec."

Another pep talk? "I don't have time, sorry."

Her smile widens. "It'll only take a minute."

I glance at Melissa, who makes a lazy circle around the studio, the rose-gold iPhone mashed against her cheek. My cell is two generations removed, and a horrible crack runs down the screen. Melissa's is pristine. She swipes it with a finger painted in brilliant teal.

I envy her. Every detail about Melissa is perfect: her manicured fingertips, the Nike soles, and even the way her golden skin complements the pink of her iPhone. I listen to her frustrated sighs and try to muster the courage to strike up a conversation.

Planning her murder was easy. Going through with it? Not so much.

It's natural to feel close to Melissa. I've followed her for weeks and studied her schedule. Spent hours waiting outside buildings. All that time following Tom's wife gave me insight into that blonde head. I fucking *know* her. She's not just some rich bitch I need to take out—she's the mother of his kids. A good person who is in my damn way.

Lucy blocks my stare. I want to smack the smile off her face. "What is it?"

She doesn't flinch. "Hon, I wanted to ask if everything was all right. I've noticed you having issues with some of the more difficult poses."

Yeah, I have cancer. "I'm doing my best."

"I understand that, sweetie, but I'm wondering if you're a good fit for this program. Perhaps you'd be more comfortable in Beginner Yoga. Or you could...take a break."

"You mean stop coming?"

She looks grateful that I mentioned it. "This course is too advanced for you."

"No, it's not."

Her laughter is like wind chimes—hollow. "I'm afraid I disagree, and I will not spend any more time helping you catch up."

She'll kick me out because I can't balance on my head for ten seconds? "I paid for the class. It's important to me." I blink rapidly, laying it on thick. "To be honest, this is the one day of my week when I feel good."

"I'm so happy to hear that!" Lucy bursts. Her voice carries to where Melissa is still engaged in her phone conversation. "But I think it'd be better if you joined the beginner's group."

"For you, maybe, but I am not going anywhere."

"As instructor, it's my job to make sure everyone is at ease. And I've received complaints."

"Is my outfit not up to code? Does this class have a Lululemon requirement?"

She sneers. "Your presence is a distraction. Some of the girls aren't comfortable around you."

"I'm not following. Did I do something wrong?"

"No, it's nothing like that." Chewing her lip, she pauses for a second. "They're concerned about your health."

"Don't these women want to be thin?"

"Of course—everybody wants that—but I'm getting daily comments from women in the class who are worried."

"If they're so upset, why haven't they told me themselves?"

It's wonderful to watch Lucy struggle with these dilemmas. She chews her lipstick and lets out a frustrated sigh as though I'm being unreasonably difficult. Behind Lucy, Melissa pulls the phone from her ear, her features frozen in disgust.

She turns it off and marches toward us. "What's going on?"

For a second I'm paralyzed.

We've never talked, but I've imagined her voice. Thought it'd be delicate, feminine, like the gold necklaces dangling from her neck.

17

Lucy beams at Melissa. "Oh, it's nothing to worry about."

Melissa crosses her arms. "I must have heard wrong. You said she couldn't come anymore, right?"

Delicate? She's a *whip*.

"I think another group would be a better fit for Aubrey." Lucy's positive energy seems manic now. "There were concerns voiced by several of your classmates."

"Excuse me?"

"I hate to bring this up, but last class someone was *triggered* by Aubrey's appearance." Lucy faces me, her voice hushed. "A few of the girls have eating disorders."

"Triggered," Melissa repeats.

"People who've experienced traumatic events can relive them when they see or hear—"

"—I know what it means. So what happened? A girl ate a donut and vomited it up?"

"It's not a joke, Miss Daughtry. And a person in Aubrey's condition"—a pin could drop in the damn studio—"should not be exercising anyway."

Bright patches of fury burn on Melissa's cheeks. "What the hell did you say?"

"Okay," Lucy says, wide-eyed. "There's no need for profanity."

"Don't take it personally," I mutter to Melissa. "She doesn't understand."

"Yes, I do!" Lucy bursts. "I have a BA in Nutrition. This is what I do. I recognize signs of eating disorders."

Flames stroke Melissa's face in vibrant red. "She doesn't have a disorder. She has cancer."

The air in the studio disappears as though it was torched by Melissa's rage.

For a second Lucy stares at her in disbelief, shock blossoming over her face. "Oh...I-I didn't know. I'm sorry."

Melissa crosses her arms. "Why are you apologizing to me?"

I bury my smile as Lucy turns to me, shamefaced. "Sorry."

A frustrated sigh hits the air as Melissa gives Lucy one last look of deep disgust before sweeping from the studio.

I follow her into the damp locker room, my words caught in my throat. "Thank you."

But I still need to murder you.

Melissa nods, ripping open a locker to grab her white Coach purse. "You're in the Thursday group."

She's talking about our Meetup for people with end-stage cancer. "Yeah."

"Lucy was way out of line. I know what it's like to be told to eat more." She lets out an angry sound. "As if that'll help."

I'm in love with her lilting voice. "Thanks again." I retrieve my bag. "I owe you a coffee. The look on her face...that was priceless."

A cool fog descends over Melissa. She stiffens. "I was on my way to Starbucks."

"Perfect. I'll treat you."

A second passes before she speaks again. "You don't have to."

"I want to."

She cracks under my beam. "Okay."

The locker door slams shut. Melissa shoulders the purse, the straps digging into her bone. Giving me a nod, she heads out.

God, this is it.

My heart clenches as I follow her into the gym, which

reeks of the sharp scent of unwashed bodies. Every step closer to those gleaming doors jolts into my chest.

I'm going to do this.

Melissa glances at me. "You okay?"

"I'm still shocked, I guess."

"Don't let her get to you," she says in a firm voice. "My doctors are always trying to tell me what I can and can't do. It doesn't bother me because they're paid to give me their professional opinion. But Lucy can go fuck herself."

"Yeah, it grates on you after a while." I clutch the bottle in my purse, silencing the rattle. My supplier charged me a premium for the nitro. I could hardly afford a few doses, but one or two will suffice. He was clear about that. Two pills. A quick death.

Melissa holds the door open for me, and we stroll into a dense chill that freezes my damp clothes against my skin.

"I'm a Starbucks slave through and through," she says with a sigh. "When I first moved here I tried all the local businesses but kept coming back here."

The Starbucks next door is packed to the gills with tech employees working from home. They look the same with their identical laptops, their wan faces lit by the screens. Glowing apple icons fill the store with soft light. Melissa works in tech. I looked her up ages ago and examined her LinkedIn, feeling more diminished as I read each line. CEO of Mission Digital. Harvard MBA graduate. Two kids.

I understand why Tom married her. Looking at her, you'd think she had success written in her DNA. Natural blonde. Fine-boned features. Wide shoulders. She's at least a C cup— or she would be if she weren't sick. By all appearances, she won the genetic lottery.

Then maybe one day, she finally had the persistent ache in her stomach checked. The blood work wasn't alarming, but the doctor ordered an MRI, and then a biopsy of the suspicious lumps. Her doctor called. Told her to come in. He broke the news to her in his office, a box of tissues within arm's reach. Turned out, she had a year or two left. That's how it went for me.

The café is packed, but the line is short. I never enjoyed the smell of roasting coffee. Over the years, my taste buds have died, and I can tolerate the bitterness without screwing up my face in disgust. Now I pretend to be into pumpkin-spice lattes every fall. It's the trendy thing to do.

Melissa excuses herself to the bathroom. "Oh, and I'll have a tall non-fat latte."

Of course she will. "Sure. How many sugars?"

"Two stevia," she says with a swish of her blonde ponytail.

She whisks away as I place the order. An employee dressed in a green smock hands me the drink. I touch the sides and burn my fingers. Ignoring the pain, I carry it to the sugar and milk station, popping open the lid. A flurry of activity surrounds me. Not one person would suspect anything suspicious.

My hand dives into my purse, searching for the bottle. I rifle through countless receipts, lipstick tubes, and business cards before my fingers touch plastic.

Is it murder if I kill someone who's already dying?

Carefully, I press the lid. It twists open. I shake the two pills into my palm and break them.

Is anyone watching me?

Fear is like a thousand needles pricking my exposed skin. I expect a man to glance over my shoulder and shout for the police. The guy pouring a diabetic coma's worth of sugar into his coffee won't leave. Someone must notice my wide eyes, the sweat running down my neck, but no. Behind me, they're all focused on their smartphones and laptops. I could have bombs strapped to my chest, and they wouldn't flinch.

Just to be safe, I palm a couple packets of that stevia crap and shake their contents into the cup as I pour the nitroglycerin tablets inside. The white powder sinks into the foamy latte, and I give it a quick stir. Then I replace the lid.

It's done.

All I have to do is pass the drink, watch the liquid slide down her throat, feign distress when her heart stops working, and try not to hate myself for the rest of my life.

My hands wrapped around the scorching cardboard, I carry it to an empty table. Steam rises from the small hole.

I tense as Melissa's golden figure emerges from the bathroom. Her blonde head swivels, and she finds me. Without smiling, Melissa makes a beeline for me and sits, grabbing the cup. "Thanks. You didn't get anything?"

Am I crazy or do I hear a note of suspicion? "Caffeine is too harsh on my stomach. I had to stop drinking it months ago."

She gives me a grim smile. "I don't tolerate it much either, but I can't stand taking away one more thing for this disease."

Drink it. "I have nothing left to give up."

"Yoga," she says, lips touching the rim. "Why did you join?"

I shrug. "It's meditative. My doctor tells me I need more hobbies to take my mind off the fact I'm dying. Maybe I should play chess instead."

She laughs, tipping the cup.

I hold my breath. This is the moment that'll change my life forever. I'll move into his house. Her children will call me Mom. Tom and I will be together. I won't be alone anymore.

An ear-splitting ring crashes the silence.

Melissa pulls back with a curse, coffee dripping down her lips. "Damn it." She snatches the shrieking phone in her purse and frowns at the name.

His face fills the screen. Tom.

The air squeezes from my lungs.

She answers the call with a scowl. "I'm inside. Having a cup of—fine. Fine, I'll be right there." Stabbing the phone, she ends the call. "I have to go. My husband is looking for me."

"I understand." I force a smile as a tall man appears behind the glass, his handsome features recognizable from this distance.

A jolt slams into my chest as his gaze sweeps over the café. If he sees me with his wife, he'll know I had something to do with it. Tom will never forgive me.

She can't die. Not now.

Melissa reaches with a smooth arm as I lunge, spilling twelve ounces of boiling coffee. She jumps backward, narrowly avoiding the splash that soaks into a tech bro's backpack.

Indignant, he rips out his earphones and glares at me. "Dude."

Melissa gapes at her brown shoes. "Damn it!"

A Starbucks employee hurries to the table as I stammer an apology. A wave of despair crashes into me as I meet Melissa's widened gaze. Five minutes ago we were joking. Now she looks at me like I'm an idiot.

The bell tinkles as Tom walks inside. He can't see me with her.

"Where are you going?" The tech bro stands beside an indignant Melissa, who watches me flee into the restroom.

In the bathroom, I find a stall and slam the door. My T-shirt flutters with my heartbeat.

Did he recognize me?

If he did, the only good thing in my life is gone.

I grab the phone from my pocket, swiping it open. I expect a text from him telling me it's over. That he warned me. His wife was off-limits, and I went too far.

I stare at the cracked Messages screen for several minutes. My lips go numb with the effort of keeping my scream inside because if he ends us, my world ends. The light in my universe ceases to exist. I can't live without sunshine.

No texts from him.

Maybe he didn't see me. Or perhaps he's waiting until he can slip from his wife and ask me, What the hell?

I blink away the mist, the hard plastic digging into my palm as I squeeze and grit my teeth. He's the only thing going for me, and I probably lost him. She'll describe me to Tom. He'll know.

What am I supposed to do?

4

MELISSA

Tom was supposed to be here an hour ago. It's been way longer than that, and my patience is whittled to a thread. I'm tired of his disappearing act—leaving me with the kids at a moment's notice while I'm stuck at home. After a week of watching the kids nonstop, the last thing I want is more time in the house.

My skin is cracked and raw from hours of kneading dough. An ache pounds between my temples and through my lower back, but I ignore it. I'll sit when I get this damned pie crust to flatten.

A beige mound sits on a dusty white countertop. I reshape it, sprinkling the rolling pin with more flour and try again, pressing down and forward. The ball oozes outward.

Finally.

I roll the dough, stretching it out, and a fist-sized circle tears from the center. It wraps around the wood.

Rage floods my brain. "Fuck."

In the living room, a small voice pipes up. "You said a bad word."

I gaze over the mountain of failed baking attempts on the kitchen island to meet my five-year-old daughter's scowl. A mess of golden curls tumbles down her head, framing a chubby face that is at odds with the heat blazing from her eyes. Her father's eyes. None of my children inherited my dishwater blonde hair—thank God—but she has a streak of stubbornness that rivals my own.

"Yes, I did. Sorry, honey."

Her frown deepens. "Daddy says people go to jail for using bad words."

"Hopefully that won't happen to me." I return my attention to the marble island, where sticks of butter thaw next to a carton of eggs. I've probably wasted ten pounds of dough.

For the hundredth time, I scrape the piece off the rolling pin and dust everything with more flour, balling the pie crust into a sticky ball. Maybe I've used too much butter. I try again. For a moment it looks like the excess flour worked until deep cracks splinter throughout the crust. Past attempts taught me that once it gets to this state, there's no saving the dough. It's overworked and useless.

I lower my voice. "Fuck, fuck, *fuck*."

I've been at this for hours. It was my only task for the day. All I wanted was to make a pie for the next-door neighbors who just moved in, but apparently, I'm a failure in everything domestic. The stew I made yesterday sucked, and it hurt my feelings more than I cared to admit when I saw Tom's portion in the garbage.

Grabbing the bin, I sweep the mess from the counter inside. The burnt pie shells join the balled dough—I count at least ten. The remaining twelve eggs should be fine, but screw it all. I hurl them one by one. They splatter over half-eaten oatmeal and lumps of raw, buttered flour whose shapes remind me of tumors. Then I grab the *Simply Pie* recipe book Tom bought and throw it away. I'm tempted to seize the Cuisinart mixer that cost me four hundred dollars, but the trash isn't big enough. Eventually, I'll get rid of it. I have no business baking.

The garbage is full. I take the bag, tie the ends, and lift. The heaviness strains my biceps. That's my fault, too. If I'd spent less time on cardiovascular health and more on upper-body strength, I wouldn't be this weak.

Stacy yells from the living room, "Mommy, can I watch *Frozen*?"

I want to moan. *Not again.* "Sure thing, sweetie. I'll be right back."

Ignoring the warning pumping through my veins, I walk onto the sun-bleached concrete outside. This unnatural heat must be sapping my energy because I can't move a few steps without my heart punching my ribs.

My feet crunch dead grass, and I turn my gaze at the brown lawn. The sight of it sinks a lump in my throat all the way to my stomach. The gardener was the first we let go. We couldn't afford him anymore, and with my illness and Tom's work schedule, we don't have the energy to break out the lawnmower.

I can't look my neighbors in the eye. We're the eyesore of this community. Blankets of deep green grass cover every single lawn except ours. I have an excuse ready—that we have plans to redo the landscaping in favor of drought-resistant plants—even though we have no money for that either.

Music booming next door drags my gaze. Hugo, the landscaper for the Fairchilds, trims the rosebushes bordering their property, a beaten-up stereo at his feet. Pink petals litter the pavement as he works. He sees me and waves. I raise my hand half-heartedly, not daring to glance inside the Fairchilds' house where I imagine Barbara folding her thin arms over her small chest, clicking her tongue as she watches me stumble and mouths *nouveau riche* in her molasses-like Savannah accent.

Tom wanted to move here. He grew up idolizing Pacific Heights, with its gigantic homes and pristine lawns, a luxury in San Francisco. The moment I hit it big, he dragged me to open houses. Even with my success, I couldn't afford them. And then he found a foreclosure in the prestigious neighborhood. A *modest* six-bedroom house dwarfed by the giants on either side. It went to auction, and we bought it from a young couple who had to leave when their startup failed. Which is what's happening to us now.

How embarrassing.

Hugo shifts behind the branches, wiping his brow under the wide-brimmed hat. He bends, removing his gloves, and grabs a bottled water. Uncapping it, he raises it to his lips and tips his tanned head. My skin shivers with his satisfied sigh.

I duck out of sight, dragging the garbage. The bag is too damn heavy. My heart pounds as I heave it a few steps. My lungs scream. Only a bit further. God, I'm so weak. No doubt it's because of that meager salad I ate last night. Tom wouldn't let me eat the almonds—too much cyanide. Apparently everything causes cancer.

I focus on my feet. One after the other. The black plastic bin stands behind the gate in the alley between our houses. A metal shriek grates against my ears as I pull the gate open.

Then I bend to pick up the bag. Blackness spreads over my vision.

I'm going to faint.

The trash hits the ground. I breathe in the sweet smell of rot. I want to fall on my knees and suck down air, but I can't let them see. Keeping my mouth closed, I inhale through my nose. It's not fast enough to appease the searing pain in my lungs.

I double over and gasp.

A high-pitched whine echoes near me. Hugo's weed whacker shreds through overgrown patches of grass. Behind the twisted thorns of the roses, I watch his face. Can he see me?

Closing my eyes, I will myself to calm down. Five seconds pass before I open them. For God's sake, the bag is not that heavy. I lift it again, my lungs seizing. My hand releases its grip. Bottles inside clink together and smash as the white bag lands on the ground. Darkness crawls on the concrete.

The weed whacker's shriek fades. Hugo lifts his head over the rosebush and peers at me. "Hey, there."

Oh no.

My pulse gallops ahead. I claw myself to a respectable standing position, pretending to admire his work until I catch my breath. "Good morning," I squeeze out.

He points at the trash. "Spilled some wine?"

A crimson stain spreads over the driveway. I nudge the bag and discover the bottom is dripping wet, a foul odor emanating from the juice.

"Damn." I meet his worried gaze. "It slipped."

Hugo moves from the bush, his wiry mustache twisting

into a frown as he takes in my appearance. "Let me help you with that."

"No, it's fine!"

He hesitates, face full of concern. "You sure?"

"Yeah." Hands shaking, I grab the bag and yank it toward the bins, leaving a bloody streak on the ground. "Don't worry. I'll wash it right away."

I smile to let him know I'm not dismissing him as my strength evaporates in the sun. He gives me a long look, his bushy eyebrows narrowing. "Okay," he says, as though it's against his better judgment. "Take care of yourself."

I am, I want to scream to his back.

Every morning I fix myself a kale-lemon-cucumber concoction seasoned with celery salt. It smells and tastes disgusting, but I choke it down because I need nutrient-rich foods right now. I exercise daily, sometimes until I fall off the treadmill gagging. I keep my body hydrated so that it's in the best shape to fight the cancer.

But all anyone sees is the sickness, and it doesn't matter how hard I try. My ribs push against my chest in fine lines, which get deeper all the time. Mom pesters me with questions whenever she sees me—*Did you gain weight?*—and sends me articles from her Facebook feed. Every time Dad comes over, I pretend his comments don't get to me, never mind I spent my childhood ignoring his constant warnings that I'd get fat. Even Tom treats me like a fragile little girl. When we make love, it's as though he's trying his damnedest not to break me.

Once Hugo is out of sight, I open the lid to the trash and heave the bag. Using every ounce of stamina, I shove it inside and stagger toward my house. Tom will have to clean the mess for me—I can't. I can barely do anything anymore.

The brass doorknob burns my hand. I twist it, push, and sigh as I duck into the refreshing coolness. Dizzy, I shut the door and glance at the kitchen. It's in shambles and bags of flour sit on the counter. The sink is filled with murky spatulas and whisks.

The idea of spending the next hour cleaning my mess fills me with dread.

"Mo-om!" Stacy roars from the living room. "You said I could watch it!"

"Mommy needs to rest, darling. I'll get your brother to help you."

Stacy groans.

A nap won't cut it. I need to be dead to the world after that jaunt outside. Maybe I'll take two Percocets and wash them down with white wine. That ought to complete the initiation rite to Pac Heights social circles, which are damn near impossible to penetrate.

My headache builds like a swarm of angry bees, gnawing at my brain. I leave Stacy and walk across the hall—six bedrooms—what the hell were we thinking? Stopping at Grayson's room, I knock on the door before opening to four walls splashed with deep blue and black.

Grayson lounges among a pile of Legos, assembling a pirate ship with white sails. He rolls to his side and flicks his sandy hair from his face. "Hi, Mom."

Every time I'm in here I'm amazed at my eight-year-old son's tidiness. Since he was a toddler, he'd return his toys to their positions on shelves or tuck them in boxes, and the habit stuck with him. When I listen to other moms talk, they make it sound like getting their kids to pick up after themselves is an exercise in futility.

I smile at him. He doesn't smile back. "Sweetie, can you watch over your sister for a while? Mommy needs a break."

Without hesitation, he rolls to his feet. "Sure."

A twinge of unease hits my chest as he carefully scoops his toys and deposits them into the bucket filled with Legos. Grayson's never given me a reason to worry, but I do it anyway. A child his age should be more expressive. He should be boisterous and loud. Hell, if he smiled once in a while I wouldn't be so concerned, but Grayson's always been serious to a fault. He doesn't talk about his friends at school. As far as I know, he has none.

"I think she wants to watch *Frozen*. You remember how to work the DVD, right?"

Grayson nods.

I thread my fingers through his silky hair and brush his head. What did I do to ever deserve such a good kid?

He fixes me with a beady eye. "Mom, are you getting sicker?"

Even they're noticing. "I'll be fine, hon. Don't worry about it."

Grayson moves from under my hand, as though he's irritated by my touch. "Are you going to die?"

"Of course not."

"Are you sure?"

Did he see me outside? "Grayson, honey, why are you asking these questions?"

The fiery challenge in his gaze smolders. "I dunno. You look really sick."

He's not scared.

A chill spider-crawls down my spine. Sinking to my knees, I wrap my arms around my son's small body. "I'm doing the best I can, Grayson. I want to get better for you and Stacy."

He shrugs. "What'll happen if you're worse?"

"Don't worry, sweetie. That won't happen. Go play with your sister."

As always, he obeys. Grayson sweeps out with a robotic slowness as I walk through the hall and brace my hand on the bedroom door.

Am I dying?

The cool darkness of my room offers me zero comfort. I roll on the mattress and shut my eyes, but sleep doesn't come. A dull ache pounds in my head, which buzzes with unanswered questions. Fear clenches my jaw. Giving up, I leave the bed.

Things will turn around. I won't let myself spiral.

I return to the brightness in the hall, wincing as my vision adjusts. The soundtrack of *Frozen* plays. I slide into the laundry room, which is blissfully free of music. I open the washing machine and grab an armful of dirty towels, but there's already a mass of wet trousers stuck to the bottom. Annoying. I drop the bundle and yank out the small load. A pair of wrinkled jeans slides into my hands, along with one of Tom's button-up shirts and boxer briefs. I grope the machine's depths. There's nothing else. Just Tom's change of clothes from last night.

That's odd.

Tom rarely does the laundry, but when I ask he takes care of it without complaint. Washing a couple articles of clothing, though, was *not* what I meant. What a strange thing to do. Who comes home and immediately washes their pants and shirt?

A dark suspicion in my mind uncoils.

He came home late. Ducked into the shower without saying hello.

A frantic beat plays in my pulse.

No. No, that's not possible.

I search the pockets and find two waterlogged ticket stubs for a six o'clock showing at the Cinemark. It's the new Jennifer Aniston romantic comedy I wanted to see.

Oh my God. He took another woman instead.

My nails pierce the cardboard as the pieces come together in devastating blows—the smell clinging to his shirt, his distance, the hours spent running errands.

The wet clothes slap the floor.

5

AUBREY

Tom hasn't texted me. Three days now. My phone sits below the cash register, its screen dark and silent. I check Messages for a reply I might've accidentally missed.

Nothing.

A tight feeling constricts my chest, and I gaze at the fluorescent lights above. Maybe their eye-watering brightness will burn a hole in my brain and destroy the disgusting part of me that needs him to write back. Two emergency oxy pills beckon from their hiding place in my pocket. I took some this morning to soothe my nerves, but the questions pound my head with an ache that refuses to go away.

What if she told him my name?

Does he know?

A synthetic calm coats my brain in a brittle shell. Panic roars below the surface, like a thin sheen of ice over a raging river. Any moment, my phone will blink with a text from him, and it'll be done. I'll have nothing to live for. I won't be able to watch Melissa through her bay windows without pain.

But right now I am a robot. A happy, smiling machine who greets the next customer with an ear-to-ear grin. "Can I see your ID?"

The teen decked head to toe in European fashion meets my gaze, his pupils shrinking as though I've asked him to take off his clothes.

"Seriously?" he asks, reaching for his wallet.

A halo of radiating warmth throbs in my chest. Every negative emotion is absorbed in my perfect state of happiness, like specks of dust flying into the sun. But the longer I hold his vacant stare, the more my medicated coma fades. I gaze at the half dozen paint cans already bagged. Company policy states that we must ask the ID for anyone buying aerosol containers, and not because the little assholes graffiti businesses. It's to prevent our impressionable children from spraying into a Ziploc bag and huffing the fumes until they pass out.

Personally, I'm in favor of letting nature take its course. "I don't make the rules, kid."

A frown creases his forehead. "I'm not a kid."

Sure you aren't. He hands me his driver's license, which has a picture of a chubby-faced boy with shoulder-length, mousy hair and a cocky grin.

"That's me," he says unnecessarily.

"Yeah, I can tell. Thanks, Spenser." I hand the card back and take his plastic, inserting the chip into the reader.

He tosses his head to clear his vision; his bangs slide like a thick curtain. "I go by Spense."

I don't care. Spenser takes his receipt as I smile. "Have a nice day."

The moody teenager gives me one last glare through that

half-covered eye before grabbing his bag and shuffling out of the hardware store.

I reach under the register and grab a water bottle, taking a quick swig before ringing up the next man.

A grin staggers across his impish face. "Hey, you."

Not him again. "Hello."

Rick's a contractor with lots of work in the area. He's constantly buying supplies. I deal with men like him all day. Men with wandering eyes, whose hands are blackened with dirt, the only bright spot wrapped around their finger in a wedding band. I smile, scan their purchases, and send them on their damn way. After a few inappropriate comments, they blend together.

Except for Rick. He's fat, short, married, and stares at my tits like the rest of them. But he has mastered the art of the leer, which he uses on me even though I've brushed off his come-ons for years. The only redeeming quality about him is how striking his eyes are. They're a shocking blue, the most beautiful turquoise I've ever seen on a man. Too bad they belong to the most disgusting lech.

Rick coughs wetly into his grubby hands as I scan his two-by-fours. His gaze drags up and down my body. I brace myself for lewd questions about my sex life and suggestions I take a ride on the Rick Express if I'm not happy with my boyfriend.

But Rick says nothing of the sort. He frowns. "You all right, hon? You look like you'll keel over."

Not what I expected. "I'm fine. Really."

"You're sick."

A gold star for Rick. "I'm running a little ragged today, but I'll be okay."

The sparks from my medicated high fizzle into ash.

Will he miss me when I'm gone?

No. He'll hit on the next sweet young thing that'll replace me. I doubt it'll occur to him to ask what happened.

Rick doubles down on the fatherly concern, which is hilariously at odds with his advice. "Hon, being this thin isn't attractive. You need to gain weight." In other words: Eat more, and you'll be hot again. "Why's your manager making you run the cash register?"

The ice behind my stony facade cracks. "I know, right? Everyone knows you don't put the bruised fruit on display."

"Jesus, I didn't mean it like that. You're still sexy."

I'm sad.

I rarely dwell on sadness because it doesn't do me any good to wallow, but a miserable part of me must've looked forward to being hit on. And suddenly his only commentary is to tell me how sick I look. Should I be self-conscious about my stick-thin body?

Now I am. "Whatever. That'll be fifty seventy-nine."

Reaching into his dirty jeans, he grabs his leather wallet, and I complete the purchase with a ringing sense of loss. Tom doesn't make me feel anything less than beautiful. I wish I could say the same for everyone else. Apart from Tom, this place and its people are all I have. My parents died within years of each other before I grew out of my teenage shithead phase. At thirteen, I was an orphan. Aunt Cathy raised me. She did the best she could before I moved out and stuck with the first paying job I found. Never had big career aspirations.

A mediocre existence suited me fine until I was diagnosed with cancer in my colon. Tom gave me a taste of the sublime and Melissa showed me what life could be like. Days of watching her sip trendy lattes, float from one self-help class to another, and occasionally zip to Napa for wine tasting made my grueling forty-hour work week look pathetic by comparison. The highlight of my month is discount boxed rosé from Trader Joe's and an Arnold Schwarzenegger movie marathon.

At least I'm done for the evening. I flip the switch on my register, the light changing from green to red. When I finish the queue of customers, I log out and slip the vest from my shoulders. Then I head toward the back.

A teenage coworker opens the Employees Only door. Mike waits for me, smiling. The kid's uniform looks like it's never been washed and the ends of his jeans are ripped, but he doesn't complain and is always on time.

"Sup, Aubrey." He follows me inside the brightly lit room. "Have you seen the end caps for the new Coke display? They're legit."

This kid needs a better hobby. "What?"

"Dude, check it out." He brandishes his phone, and I glance at the photo, which is a semi-impressive exhibit of soda bottles mounted into a pyramid shape.

Mike's performance in academia probably wasn't stellar, and his parents don't pay him enough attention, so I smile and nod. "Wow, that's neat."

"Stayed up two hours after closing to do it," he says, puffing out his chest. "Hey, you wanna hang after my shift?"

I flash him a grin as I open my locker and stuff the green vest inside. "Sorry, I've got plans with Tom."

The mention of my lover draws long shadows on Mike's face. "Cool. Maybe another time."

He's a good kid, but I don't want an eighteen-year-old friend. What I need is more nitro pills, but Ross Hardware doesn't pay well enough. As much as I hate to admit it, this job wears on me. The ache in my lower back is rivaling the ones in my head and stomach. My feet are sore after every shift. It's hard to roll out of bed.

Eventually I won't be able to do it anymore.

And who will take care of me? Tom? He has his hands full with a sick wife and two kids. Until Melissa's out of the way, I can't quit.

I slam the locker shut after grabbing my purse, looking forward to getting out of this store, until Amit pokes out of his office. "Aubrey, can I have a word?"

Amit is the shift manager and a pain in my ass. His recent promotion went straight to his head and he spends his days micromanaging the dull activities of his boring, law-abiding employees. He adjusts his glasses on his bulbous nose and wipes a sheen of sweat on his forehead.

I step inside his office, narrowly avoiding his bulk as I take the seat in front of his desk. "What's up?"

Amit settles into his chair, his button-up shirt bursting at the seams. "I just wanted to see if everything was all right with you."

I tolerated Rick. Concern from my manager raises my hackles. "Everything's great, thanks."

"Really? Because you don't look good."

Hell no. I'm not giving him a reason to let me go. "What are you trying to say?"

"Aubrey, you're so thin I can count the ribs on your chest."

Maybe you should keep your eyes to yourself, perv. "Have I ever been late to work? Does anyone complain about my job performance?"

"No, not really."

"It's a simple question. Do they bitch about me or not?"

He rips off his round glasses, wiping the perspiration from his brow before fitting them back on. "Aubrey, in the last week I've had two customers approach me about your appearance. They think I'm running a sweat shop—that I'm forcing you to work when you obviously need—"

"A burger?"

He glares at me. "A doctor."

"I have cancer. Trust me, I'm seeing a team of doctors."

"Oh...Oh wow," he says, grimacing. "Um...How bad is it?"

It'll be easy for him to find a replacement. "I'll survive."

Not exactly a ringing endorsement for confidence, but it puts Amit in his place. He can't let me go without becoming the insensitive ass who fired the cancer-stricken girl.

"I need this job, Amit."

"I understand," he begins in a delicate voice. "But at some point, you'll have to quit. Right?"

"That will not happen."

He opens his mouth to say something and seems to think better of it. "Okay. But—in the meantime—can you wear long sleeves to work? To, er, cover your wrists."

"I'm not covering up my body."

Wincing, he shakes his head. "No one's asking you to change—just attempt to look presentable."

"I am not hiding that I'm sick because two people in the store can't handle a fucking human being with cancer."

"Aubrey, stop with the profanity."

"Tell me how to dress one more time, and I'll go straight to HR. You'll have to explain to them why you told your female employee to cover up."

Chuckling, he sits back in his chair. "Be serious. You know that's not what I meant."

I cross my arms over my chest, shrugging. "It sounds a lot like gender discrimination. How many stores did Ross Hardware close this year? I doubt they can afford a lawsuit."

Amit looks angry with himself. "There's no need for that kind of talk!"

"I agree. It's ninety degrees out, and I'm not wearing a stupid long sleeve."

"Fine."

Jerk.

I don't spare him a backward glance as I walk out of the office and break room. First Yoga Bitch, now Amit? Good thing I'm meeting someone who doesn't care how I look.

I exit the store and stroll under the harsh gaze of the cloudless sky. My car is parked at the end of the parking lot, where there's tons of shade, but when I touch the door, it singes my skin.

Never mind. He'll be waiting at Taco Bell.

I stride across the strip mall to the other side with chain restaurants and find Patrick sitting under a purple umbrella. He wears a pair of American flag short-shorts which are apparently all the rage among college boys, and a vintage Counterstrike T-shirt.

I hooked up with that guy.

Back during my brief stint with higher education, I wandered into a winter-themed party at a frat house. They had a snow blowing machine that blanketed the lawn in powdered ice, which resembled the black slush on sidewalks after a half hour. It was my first time at a party. I wanted to see what they were all about, so I drank jungle juice and danced with a passably cute guy. I woke in his bed and discovered we were in the same English 101 class.

He was known for selling Adderall to students right before finals. When I was diagnosed, he sold me oxy after doctors refused to write me a prescription. Since he graduated and got a job at Walgreens as a pharmacist, I've been buying pills from him.

Patrick's moon face widens with a grin when he notices me. "Hey, hey."

I sit across from him, hands balled into fists. "I need more nitro."

He swirls the straw in his drink. "Jesus. No 'Hi, how are you?'"

"The niceties can wait. This is important."

"I'll bet it is."

"What's that supposed to mean?"

This might be a problem. I told him I wanted a humane way to end things if my cancer worsened and made up some bull about how hard it is to get physician-assisted suicide in California. I don't care if he buys the story—I just need more pills.

His lips twitch into a smarmy grin. "What happened to the ones I gave you?"

"I fixed a cocktail to drink and lost my nerve."

Even to my ears, that sounds like a lie, but Patrick nods. Maybe he doesn't give a shit. "I understand. Offing yourself can't be easy."

"I decided to hang on for a little while, but I need more. Just in case."

Patrick heaves a great sigh and frowns as though he's concentrating. It looks hard. "I can get you a couple pills."

"Awesome."

"But it'll cost you double."

My jaw drops. "That's six hundred dollars."

"Yeah," he says with a shrug.

"Do you have any idea how much I make a month?"

"Not my problem." He leans back, smile evaporating. "You have cancer, and that sucks, but I'm putting my career on the line every time I swipe those pills for you."

"They're not a controlled substance!"

He chuckles, swiping a greasy strand of hair from his face. "So? You know how long it took to get my degree? I'm not jeopardizing that for you. Not without being paid well, at least."

"You're squeezing a dying woman." I gape at him.

His eyes shine with the faintest glimmer of guilt. "Aubrey, I'm sorry you're sick. The rest of us still have lives, though."

"Cocksucker." I rise from the bench, fury pounding in my head, made worse by the heat.

The straw pops from his mouth. "There's nothing wrong with sucking cock. Might get you a discount."

"Shut up."

"Bye, Aubrey!"

I walk away from the fumes of grease pouring from Taco Bell and glare at anyone who passes me as I head toward my car.

Maybe this is a sign from the universe that I'm not supposed to kill Melissa. That instead I should destroy the part of me that's in love with Tom. I'd have an easier time ripping off my arm. He's the reason I wake in the morning. I sleep because my dreams are filled with him. I think of him gliding under my hands, his smooth chest, the sting of his rough jaw grazing my cheek, and peace washes over me better than any painkiller.

The afternoon I met Tom was the best day of my life. I had nothing going for me but this disease—this cancer—that was ruining me. My body had a fixed expiration date—less than five years.

Tom was the ray of hope through the endless black. He stole my attention with a single touch. I fell for him the moment he pressed that rose in my hand and gave me his card. He was too beautiful to be real. His blue eyes were flecked with gold, and they burned with passion. I wanted that flame inside me. I called his number the second I returned home. We met later that night, at a five-star hotel. The first time we fucked I was sore all over, but the pain didn't return until he was gone. When we're together, I forget the damned disease.

He's perfect.

He's married.

I dive into my purse to find the keys. A glowing text from Tom catches my attention. It's a photo of a champagne bottle resting over a silk pillow, and on the label, he wrote my name. Aubrey.

I'm at the Hilton downtown. Come to me.

And like a helpless fool in love, I obey.

6

MELISSA

MY NAILS PIERCE RED FOAM.

Everything is fine.

I open my palm. The stress ball inflates with expanding white letters: Hang in there!

Reminds me of when I was first diagnosed. The tide of well-wishing cards was endless. Even now people I haven't talked to in decades post on my Facebook timeline, filling it with bullshit sentiments like "Get well soon," "Our thoughts and prayers are with you," or my favorite, "Speedy recovery!"

They used to make me feel warm inside, as though two hundred and forty-three comments would be enough good karma to summon a cure for my cancer. I would pull through; if not with the combined positive intentions of hundreds of people, then with a Kickstarter.

It's been setback after setback.

First, the doctors refused to believe me. My labs didn't indicate a need for an MRI. I was a hypochondriac. I had an eating disorder and needed therapy. The pounds shed from my waist, and still, they denied me until I paid for the test out of pocket and saw the scans.

The last oncologist said there was nothing he could do.

Nothing.

Well, Tom didn't accept that. If traditional medicine wouldn't help me, I'd try East Asian remedies. And I am, but the cancer is worse than ever. Everything in my life is spiraling out of control, and it happened faster than I could grasp. I keep waiting for my symptoms to plateau. My startup to stop struggling. The passion for my husband to return. And now he's keeping things from me.

Is he having an affair?

Breathe. Just Breathe.

A woman's voice echoes the mantra. "Take a deep breath and let it out."

The air catches in my chest. I can't relax. I keep thinking about those tickets—the woman he spent the evening with.

Who is she?

"Okay, let's do it again. This time I want you to imagine that ball of pain rising. All the way to your mouth. When you exhale, picture it shrinking with every breath."

The bitch made my husband toss aside his vows. I need her name.

"Visualize a sphere. Do you see it?"

Yeah, it's lodged in my throat. The damn thing isn't going anywhere. Neither is that image of my husband's wet clothes tucked in the washing machine. My eyes sting when I brush the movie ticket stubs in my pocket.

I can't focus.

I keep imagining my husband in the arms of another woman. The distance I sensed is real—I didn't imagine it. The gulf between us widens every day, and now he's lying by omission.

A sea of relaxed voices rise and fall.

"Good," Kylie says. "You're doing fantastic."

Screw this.

My eyelids flutter open to a semicircle of cancer victims in varying stages of decay. They're skeletons wrapped in fabric. Barely any skin or fat. Their eyes frighten me the most. They sit in shadowed holes surrounded by protruding bone.

I know these people. Every week I come here, listen to their darkest confessions and inane hopes, and try not to think about my company for one hour. Tom doesn't like me coming here. He thinks it makes me depressed. I wanted to have the best shot at beating cancer—and what better way to round off a cocktail of holistic medicine than with a group of supportive women going through the same thing?

Except it's far from cathartic. I look at these people and see myself in a few years. The reminder that I have a loving husband waiting for me at home doesn't work. The movie stubs burn a hole in my pocket.

Is he cheating?

Kylie's clear voice rings out. "All right. I'm going to ask you to open your eyes in a moment. When you do, you will feel relaxed and refreshed."

Not happening.

No one seems to have difficulty following Kylie's orders. I scan their tired faces, gaze falling on Aubrey. She sits on the far end, a pink tank top strapped to her flat chest. Her limbs remind me of a bird's hollow feet. Thin. Brittle. Dark chestnut hair grows shoulder-length, limp against her cheeks. Vestiges of great looks grace her fine-boned features. She's like Natalie

Portman at her thinnest. Aubrey dances on the edge of pretty and scary. Hell, looking at her is unpleasant.

Aubrey's eyes flicker open, her deep-set gaze meeting mine.

We haven't talked since the disaster at Starbucks until this morning. Aubrey approached me to mumble an apology which I had to accept. The whole incident was baffling, and her reaction even more so, but I'm used to socially awkward nerds making embarrassing faux pas. Tech is full of them.

Anxiety runs through me like a spear, and I glance at the friendlier sight of the moderator. Kylie's a mental health counselor in a post-grad program. She sits in the middle of the circle, wearing foundation that's too light for her skin. Pink blush smears her cheeks in two broad strokes. Her makeup drives me insane. Ever since I met her, I've wanted to grab the blending brush in my bag and attack her face.

"Open your eyes," she says.

The rows of skeletons obey, blinking slowly. I exhale through my nose, listening to the rattle of voices.

Kylie sighs. "That feels better, doesn't it?"

A few people nod.

"How about we get started? Does anyone have anything they'd like to share?" Beaming, she gazes at the circle.

"I do." A thin arm belonging to an emaciated man stretches toward the ceiling.

My nails gouge the foam so hard my knuckles whiten.

Kylie's smile refuses to crack. "Go ahead, Henry."

Henry's a sixty-something blue-collar worker with a sagging mustache. He leans forward, his loose-fitting shirt like a cape. "Lately I've been drinking a lot. And I don't mean a couple beers here and there. I wake up and reach for the bottle." He fidgets with his hands, scraping at a fingernail.

"When my doctor told me I had six months left, it was all I could think of every day. Now I have a handful of weeks, and I'm more worried about my wife cheating on me."

He pauses, smiling. "Can you believe that? I'm dying. It shouldn't matter, but it does. I don't know who the hell it is."

Henry's listless gaze sweeps the circle of sympathetic faces. I stop myself from seizing the tickets and examining them for the hundredth time.

"I wanted to hire one of those people to follow her. Private investigators? Is that what they're called?" He laughs, shaking his head. "This is ridiculous. In a few weeks, I won't be here. Maybe I should keep it to myself. I want her to move on. I just—I don't know. A part of me is hurt she wouldn't at least wait until I'm gone."

His voice grows softer until it's almost whisper-silent, but I hear every word as though they're projected from a stereo. "I hope he's a good man—that he treats her right."

A vision of my husband in a tuxedo taunts me. A young bride clutches his arm. She doesn't have marionette lines. Her face is round with baby fat, the wrinkles on her forehead nonexistent. She strokes his clean-shaven jaw. A devastating smile carves dimples into his cheeks.

I am forgotten.

"Sorry. I didn't want to get emotional." Henry coughs into a balled fist, sniffing. "The other day I found text messages on her phone. I wasn't snooping or anything. They glowed on her screen, almost as if she wanted me to see them. I guess that'd be fucking easier for her, wouldn't it?"

I brace myself against the storm of his words.

"It'd be so much better if I dumped her." Acid drips from his tone. "Bitch."

"All right! Thank you, Henry." Red-faced, Kylie searches the circle. "Who wants to speak?"

"I do." A dozen shocked people face me. They've never heard me talk. "I think my husband's having an affair too."

They glance at each other. My life isn't the peaches and ice cream sundae that everyone sees on Facebook. They don't know that I wake in the morning and my pillow is still damp.

No one says anything. They just stare.

"What happened?" Henry croaks.

"I found a small load in the washer, and it was all his clothes from last night. Which I thought was pretty strange. Then I went through his pockets and pulled out two movie ticket stubs." I didn't mean to blurt it out like that, but with all their eyes on me, my voice grows stronger. "It's not one thing. He comes home late and doesn't tell me where he's been. I don't know what to do about it."

"You should talk to him," Kylie urges. "He might be doing nothing wrong. Many spouses feel overwhelmed with their partner's diagnosis. Even they need a break sometimes."

"But why lie? He knew I wanted to see that movie and he took someone else. He washed his clothes."

"That doesn't mean he was cheating." Kylie gestures outside. "It's been hot lately. Maybe he was sweaty."

I stare at her. "He couldn't wait to wash them in the morning?"

A woman wearing a white bob wig crosses her arms. "Don't listen to Bo-Peep, honey. Your instincts are dead on."

Kylie frowns, abandoning her breathiness. "I choose to give him the benefit of the doubt. You should, too."

"Why? So she can feel better about herself every time her husband gives her a bullshit excuse for coming home late? I mean, Jesus. Some of you need to wake up." She glares at Henry. "You should kick your wife's ass out of the house. Or at least cut her from your life insurance plan."

Henry bristles. "My personal life is none of your goddamn business."

"You brought it up." Martha continues her tirade. "Marital vows are supposed to mean something. You don't fool around the second your spouse gets sick!"

Kylie's voice cracks like a whip. "Martha, this is a judgment-free zone."

Martha sinks into her seat, muttering as people shrink from her. A flutter of nerves begins in my chest, and I swallow hard when I meet Aubrey's stricken gaze.

"Right." Kylie clears her throat. "Why don't we take a ten-minute break to cool down?"

Fine with me.

My mind buzzes in a state of near panic as chairs scrape the floor. Cut him from the life insurance? That's extreme. Shouldn't I give Tom the benefit of the doubt, like Kylie suggested? I could ask him on the drive home. A thrill shoots into my chest at the thought of that conversation.

I stand and walk away from the group as chatter fills the room, whose blank walls are papered with motivational posters. A cat dangles on a tree branch, urging me to "Hang in there!"

Eventually I wander to the plastic table filled with snacks. Kylie brings in donuts every week from a posh bakery in the Mission, but I've never had them. I'm supposed to be avoiding saturated and trans fats.

A thin black woman reaches for a bacon-encrusted donut.

She tears off a small piece and pops it in her mouth. "Wow, that's good. You should try some."

I give the donuts a rueful look. "Wish I could."

"I'm Leaih."

"Melissa." I grasp her cool hand, shaking it.

She nods with a grim smile, picking at the pastry. "I'm sorry to hear about your husband."

My stomach clenches. "I don't know if anything's happened."

"Yes, you do," she says with a knowing look. "Listen to your gut. I wish I had. My boyfriend didn't stick around after he swore he could handle the disease. The fool actually said we'd fight it together. *We'll beat the cancer, Leaih.*"

Tom said those exact words. I swallow hard, burying my discomfort.

"Yeah," Leaih sighs. "As soon as shit got real, he left."

"I'm sorry to hear that."

"Whatever." Leaih shrugs, her voice all bile. She touches my arm, leaning close. I beat back waves of nausea as I meet her eyes—big, dark pools crystallized with misery. "We all die in our own arms."

She releases me and the tight ache lodges in my throat.

I regret my confession.

Tom and I are *nothing* like these people. They're as hopeless as ghosts floating in Limbo. They walk around half-alive, waiting to join the ranks of the dead.

And in a few months I'll look like them.

My world tilts on its axis as I seize the table for support, the breath knocked out of me.

"Hey, are you all right?"

A concerned face swims in front of me. "I'm fine."

Ignoring her, I walk toward the double doors and yank them open to brilliant sunshine, sucking the stifling air. I blink against the light, staring at the pavement as the world rights itself and my breathing calms.

A long shadow grows over me, stealing the warmth from the sun. Italian loafers scrape the ground, inches from my Pradas. Swallowing my gasps, I trace the hem of his dark jeans to an athletic waist covered by a blue polo. My gaze snaps to his Han Solo grin.

"Hey, babe. I thought the group wasn't done for another half hour." Tom's silky voice unknots my shoulders. "Are you okay?"

"N-no."

His smile fades as I choke with a sob. "What happened?"

"Nothing." I rub my eyes, past caring about my makeup. "Take me home."

Concern knits his eyebrows together as he holds me. His beard grazes my cheek as a harsh whisper blows across my lips. "I love you."

I search for the lie beneath his promise. In the shelter of his arms, I can't sense anything false. He's been nothing but supportive. He's driven me to countless doctor appointments. Tom puts up with me when I have no energy to cook or clean. When nausea grips my guts, he's there to tie my hair back.

My head tips, the dazzling sunshine blinding me before Tom blocks it, planting a soft kiss on my mouth that stifles my shuddered gasps.

He breaks away with a starry-eyed smile. "You forgot your meds this morning."

A plastic tube presses into my hand. The pills rattle as I

read its label. Pancreatic Enzymes. Fifty milligrams. Twice a day.

I twist open the cap, stomach roiling at the sight of the blue tubes. "They make me sick."

He strokes my arm. "That's the cancer, not the enzymes. I know it's hard, but you need to keep with the regimen. I'll cook something light for supper. Chicken soup?"

"Yeah. That'd be great."

"I'll do it from scratch." He kisses my forehead. "We'll have to stop by Safeway to pick up a rotisserie chicken on the way home."

Plain broth sounds amazing right now. Thinking about those golden rings of oil bubbling on the surface fills me with warmth. How many women can say their husband makes their own stock?

He's the kind of man who tracks me down when I forget my medication and cooks me soup because I trust nothing from a can. He loves me unconditionally.

I can't shake the doubt.

Shaking out two pills, I pop them in my mouth and swallow. Tom hands me a water bottle, and I drink. Then his hand curves around mine, tugging me toward the car. His shadow falls away, and the sun basks me in its balm.

7

AUBREY

SWEAT BLANKETS MY NAKED BODY. I don't dare wipe it away. The longer his damp warmth clings to my skin, the more I can pretend he's still here. Half an hour ago our limbs were tangled on this bed. I tasted his sigh. If I close my eyes, that moment freezes: his hands gripping my waist and the golden light pouring in.

It's the first morning we've spent together. My yoga class was at seven but I skipped it for Tom. A spot cleared on his schedule. There was no way I would pass him up, even if I'm enjoying endless reiterations of Tree pose.

A ping interrupts my erotic daydream and I search through the tangled sheets for my phone. He sent me a text— a heart emoji and *Love you, Babe*.

A memento from his visit sits in the stainless steel bucket by the bed, the sparkling apple juice we never got around to drinking. He's such a romantic, my Thomas. On his way here, he picked up the bottle as a throwback to our first date. I grab an ice cube and pretend Tom's the one trailing it over my breasts, making a line to the soreness between my legs. A pleasant coolness spreads on my raw skin. It'll take a while for everything to heal, because there's only so many hours to pack in a week's worth of desire. He always leaves me satisfied. My body hums for days as though it can still feel him.

Violent knocking jars me from my naughty daydream. I sit upright and look through the crack of my half-opened bedroom door.

The voice accompanying the deceptively loud knocks fills me with dread. "Aubrey! Are you home?"

She knows damn well I'm here. I rip back the sheets. The cold stings my skin. I throw open a window to air out the heady sex smell, and then I pull on cat pajamas.

The wood rattles with the force of her fists as I drag my feet toward the entrance and unlock the door to a sixty-year-old woman dressed in a hippie brown dress from Anthropologie and oversized glasses. Her pin-straight hair glows with an orange hue because she insists on using boxed dye. Two shopping bags are tucked under her thin arms.

"Hey, hon." June nudges the groceries. "These are for you."

"Thanks." I wince at the state of my apartment. "Sorry, I didn't know you were coming."

"Even though I'm here every Friday? Geez, Aubrey. Budge up so I can come in."

Grabbing a bag, I fight the impulse to reject them and send June on her way. It won't do any good. June doesn't take no for an answer, and I'm pretty sure that's why her children refuse to visit. She's invasive. Bossy. Sadly, I don't mind the hovering or the mothering.

We met at a neighborhood block party weeks ago. I wasn't planning on going, but I grabbed my canvas bag and wandered down the street. Ten feet from my door, there she was. June found me through the crowd gathering around the table filled with cupcakes and cookies. She took one look at my emaciated figure and dragged me toward the food. The next day I woke to a chime. When I went to investigate, I saw a pecan pie on my doorstep. I thought it was a trick until I spotted the note attached to the top. Who the hell leaves baked goods for their neighbors to find?

A do-gooder like June. She doesn't expect anything from me—she just wants to help. Thankfully, there's nothing fake about her. I can't say the same about the friends on my Facebook feed. They add their thoughts and prayers in a comment box but would rather light their house on fire than offer support beyond a twenty-dollar donation to a GoFundMe. June wakes up every morning at six to cook for the homeless shelter and still has time to smother me with semi-wanted affection.

Ever since that block party, she's treated me like a bird with a broken wing, as though all I need to get better again is love and attention. Maybe June is right. Sometimes I believe I'd be in my best health if I had Tom as a husband, not a lover.

I heave the groceries inside, fighting the stab of guilt whenever I see the mountain of food boxed in Tupperware. "You really don't have to do this."

June shuts the door and bustles to the kitchen, waving me off. "It's no trouble. No trouble at all, baby girl. You're sick and you need help. That's why I'm here."

I slide the prepared dinners into the freezer. "I'm twenty-five, June. I have a full-time job and an apartment I pay for. Do you think I'd starve without you?"

"You'd fill yourself with junk."

Probably. The last thing I feel like doing after a long day's work is cooking. "Oh, June."

June sets her purse on my kitchen table and sighs at the mound of dirty dishes. "I've seen how you eat when you have nobody to cook for you. McDonald's. Taco Bell."

"They're fast and affordable."

She clicks her tongue. "You can do better than that."

"Not really." She crosses her arms as I stick a lasagna dish into the fridge to defrost. "My cooking skills have never been very sophisticated. Using a can opener is about as complicated as it gets in this kitchen. Blame my mother."

The water shuts from the sink and June wrings her hands, drying them on a kitchen towel. "Oh, sure. It's always the mom's fault. What's stopping you from learning how to cook? There are YouTube channels."

"Lack of interest, I guess." I grin when she throws me a dirty look. "And you come here every week with a truckload of food already prepared for me, so…"

"Well, at least you admit you're lazy." Her fierce expression crumbles. "I can't say the same for my kids. That's the problem with your generation. It is *never* your fault."

I laugh, knowing how much it'll incense her. "Nothing about my life has been fair."

"Stop it," June snaps, wringing a rag. "You sound like a child."

My cheeks burn. "But it's true."

"Tell that to the people in the homeless shelter." She scrubs the bottom of a stainless steel pot. "Or the at-risk youth in Oakland. I used to teach those kids. Some of them have lost all their loved ones to gang violence."

"Well, I don't have anyone to lose." *Except Tom.* "I suppose if you died, I'd be screwed."

She rolls her eyes at me. "I'm touched."

I squeeze her shoulder. "That was a *joke.*"

She soaks a rag in hot water and scrubs a spot on a plate. "I pray to Him every night to spare your life."

I take the gleaming dish from her, drying it with the towel. "That's sweet of you, but I don't think he's listening."

"He is there, hon. Whether you like it or not. Oh, I almost forgot." June drops the rag and grabs a bag, shaking it in my face. "Here it is, as requested. Can't imagine why you enjoy these, but I figure the more calories the better."

"Thanks." Mom.

Pork rinds are my guilty pleasure food and they always have been. My earliest memory of them was my mother rolling a plastic bag, and the savory scent hitting my nose like the first line of coke. Pork rinds and uncooked ramen are my go-to comfort foods whenever I'm sad. Six packs for a dollar instead of a lifetime of Prozac? That's a bargain.

"I'll get this oven preheated for the lasagna."

"Don't bother. This will be enough." I pop one in my mouth, the savory taste exploding on my tongue.

She grabs a wineglass, frowning. "Did you have someone over?"

"Yeah, but those are from last week." June glances up from her cleaning, fixing me with a white-hot glare that pierces my soul. "What? I've been lazy."

"You know damn well that's not what pisses me off." June opens my fridge to shove a carton of eggs inside, tsking at my huge box of rosé wine. "And getting you drunk on top of that? What a guy."

My face heats. "He didn't get me drunk."

"Really? Every time you're with him he plies you with booze. You have one too many drinks, and I receive a panicked phone call from you hours later after the bastard is gone."

"That—was—*once!*"

"I don't like him, Aubrey," she says as though her opinion matters. "He's a nasty man who calls you whenever he's bored."

Not this again. "That's not how it is. He was here this morning."

"Where?" she snaps.

"In this apartment. His car was out front."

She shakes her head. "I didn't see him. If I had, I would've kicked his ass."

He probably parked down the street. "Too bad. That'd almost be worth it to watch."

"I know you love him, but he's disgusting."

I laugh as an unpleasant flush fills my cheeks. "Tom is the opposite of that."

"Your boyfriend is married."

And I couldn't care less.

Now would be the time to remind her my affair is none of her fucking business. She means well, but I'm the one who's dying. I walk to the couch and sink into its cushions, hand rustling through the bag's contents.

The memory of this morning makes me smile. Nothing else in this world does the same. "He said he's in love with me."

"Of course he did, you young fool."

I toss the chips on the coffee table. "Okay, maybe you should leave."

June didn't listen the first time I ordered her to get out. I don't know why I expect today to go any differently.

Her body sags as she abandons her cleaning to sit next to me. "I'm worried," she says in another voice. "This man—this Thomas—doesn't care about you."

My hands ball into fists as pain travels in an orb from the front of my skull to the back. "June, I'm tired of working forty-hour weeks while fighting the cancer. Most of all, I'm sick of doing it alone."

"Sorry, sweetheart, but this is important. He's a predator."

"Tom is the only good thing in my life. He's the reason I get up in the morning. I don't care if it's wrong. My days are numbered, and I want to enjoy them while they last. Can't you understand that?"

She folds her hands into steeples. "Yes, I do."

"Then why are you giving me a hard time?"

"Relationships should warm you like the sun. They should make you feel better about yourself. Do you?"

No. "It won't be like this forever. He'll divorce his wife."

June softens. "Aubrey, he'll never do that."

That's why I bought the pills. I can't wait for their marriage to collapse. "Maybe."

"You're hanging onto a fantasy, sweetie."

A dagger runs through my heart at the thought of Tom rejecting me. Pain slices through nerves in my head, radiating all the way to my kneecaps. Without him, there's nothing but agony.

Nobody understands what it's like to be expected to make a living while dealing with this monster of a disease. There are days I wish I were dead to be free of this gut-wrenching, nails-gouging-in-flesh pain. He's my only hope.

June's wrinkled hands squeeze mine. "It's okay, Aubrey."

She thinks I'm gearing for another massive meltdown where I throw glasses at the wall, scream my voice hoarse, and get the police called to my apartment yet again.

I am done feeling sorry for myself. What I want is in my sights, but there's no use in trying to explain my plan. June would never approve.

My cheeks are already wet. All I need to say are the magic words. "I don't want to die."

"I know, sweetheart." June wraps me in a bear hug as though she means to squeeze the life out of me. I tolerate it like a dog, sitting still.

It's easy to work up more tears and collapse over June's shoulder. She cries with me, sobbing so hard that I'm the one patting her back and smiling through a tearstained face.

"It's okay."

"No, it's not. God, I'm sorry. I know you hate it when people cry."

This disease is painful enough without everyone falling to pieces, but June's charity makes my monthly grocery bill an afterthought, which means more money dedicated to the Kill Melissa Fund.

"Don't worry about it." I rub her back, smiling. "Things will change. I have a plan."

8

MELISSA

I'M LOSING MY MIND. A high-pitched voice blares from the new stereo system Tom talked me into buying, which is now being wasted on the tenth showing of *Frozen*. My daughter sits close enough to the TV to cause seizures, and belts the lyrics to "Let It Go."

Take a cue from the song, Melissa. She's a child.

I search for a distraction. The phone rests in the middle of discarded onion peels. A black screen reflects my face as I touch the button with my stained fingers. A picture of my husband and me embracing flares into the tiny rectangle. I swipe through Yahoo business and find my company's code. White numbers surrounded by red fill me with horror.

MIDX - 24.09

This isn't happening.

It must be a nightmare.

I glance around my kitchen for evidence—a distortion in the clock, an appliance out of place, anything that'll prove this is in my head. I close my eyes, drifting into the fog of my near-constant fatigue, and open them.

Everything's the same.

The knife lies grinning on the table, slicked with orange. A little poke, and I'll know for sure if I'm dreaming. My vision clouds over in tiny dots. I clutch the white marble counter to steady myself. The blackness recedes, and I'm left with my failure.

Last week we were down a quarter point. Now it's another half. Shaking, I press the button to force the offensive numbers to vanish. I grasp for the things that make staying at home worth it. The rest is good for my health. More time with the kids. Saves money.

There's also nothing standing in the way of my obsession. Tom can't tell me to knock it off with the phone when he's not here, which is often. He spends his days at the office while I stay here to cook, clean, and count the ABCs. The children are happier without a sitter, but I was never meant for domestic life.

Stepping down was a colossal mistake. Nothing will diminish that.

"Mom?" Stacy leans against the wall next to the refrigerator, her rosebud mouth fixed into a slight frown. "What are we having for dinner?"

I used to say the company was my first baby, and Stacy was my third. "Beef stew."

My five-year-old is as stubborn as I am. Disappointment sags her tiny shoulders. "I want pizza."

I drag the knife to the cutting board. A pair of decapitated carrots roll under my fingers, the flesh knobby and rough like my grandfather's skin. "We're not eating junk for dinner."

Her face falls. "*Daddy* gets us whatever we want."

Not true, but I'm getting used to her lies. "Stacy."

"We had pizza last Friday!"

"No, we didn't," I snap. "We ate broccoli soup."

Stacy crosses her arms, her eyebrows narrowed in a show of disapproval. "You had that disgusting stuff. Daddy bought us Michelangelo's when you went to class."

I rest the knifepoint on the carrot. "He did?"

"Yeah," she gushes. "It was mushroom and pepperoni. My favorite."

I could imagine Tom grabbing the bowls and dumping them down the drain as soon as I left, his handsome face cracked wide with a grin as he promises something else for dinner. Then I picture them huddled around a grease-stained cardboard box, and my husband passing cans of soda to our children. "Don't tell Mommy, okay?"

That sounds like what he'd do.

I force my hands still. He fed them junk behind my back. I prepared a nutritious supper, and he gives them processed crap. My kids eat *homemade* as a rule. Cooking is exhausting, but we can't afford the meal subscriptions I used to have.

God, I don't want to think about money right now.

The peeler rakes a line of orange flesh in one swift movement. A pile of chopped carrots sit in a heap. At this rate, dinner won't be ready until nine.

I glance at the pouting, round face that reminds me of mine. "Stacy, go play with your brother."

Stacy whines, lip quivering. "My stomach hurts."

A ripple of guilt runs through me as I slice the carrot into one-inch knobs. She's been complaining of that a lot lately. "Would you like a fizzy drink?"

Stacy's voice, loud and insistent, rings in my ears. "I want pizza."

And I want peace. "Not happening."

"Why?"

"Because I said so."

Stacy's whine reverberates through the kitchen, and I glance at the clock because I can't stand another second without talking to an adult.

"Stacy," I say as her complaints rise to a high-pitched wail. "What did I tell you about whining?"

Tears slide down her fat cheeks. "Not fair. It's not fair!" Her face scrunches in a pint-sized version of malevolence. "I hate you!"

If she hadn't said it a thousand times before, it would hurt more. "Sit and be quiet."

My blonde mini-me's howls echo throughout the home as she stomps toward the kitchen table, making sure her punishment is heard loud and clear. Glorious silence basks me with peace for two seconds until a scream jars the air. When she runs out of breath, her screaming staggers. Then she fills her lungs, and a sonic-wave blast of five-year-old rage rips through the entire house.

I set the knife down and pick up my phone, ignoring Stacy's crying to click the Safari app. On average, I refresh my company's portfolio page three hundred times a day. That's once every five minutes—or it would be if I didn't sleep. I stare at my cell for hours and do everything one-handed, even though it's programmed to send an alert if the stock moves a quarter of a point. The numbers bleed into my dreams. They're my first thought in the morning. Most nights I fall asleep to the glow of the screen, my eyes so raw it hurts to blink.

Tom hates it. The light keeps him awake.

I find it hard to sleep, too. If he knew what I was dealing with—if he shared a fraction of my panic—he'd curl into a ball and scream.

I reach for the paper towels to clean the mess on the counter, only to discover the roll stripped of the last piece. There's more in the closet. I sweep from the room. Digging my hand into my jeans pocket, I grab my phone and swipe it. The bright screen deepens the burn, but I don't blink.

A loud crash sounds from the kitchen. Damn me for leaving her alone for one second.

I walk onto the tiles, glancing at the wide-open cabinet door. Stacy rifles through where I keep my spices and yanks on a bag of semi-sweet chips, ripping it. She plunges inside the pack and removes fistfuls of chocolate.

"What are you doing? Those are for baking!"

Stacy whirls around, dropping it and scattering tiny morsels all over my pristine floor. Hands sticky with the candy, she leans on the cabinet door, and a sound like a gunshot cracks through the room. The hinge breaks from the wood, and Stacy crashes to the ground, along with the slab of oak.

"Stacy! What the hell is wrong with you? Crying isn't enough. No, you have to destroy my house, too."

Stacy's already bawling—her response whenever she does something bad. "I-I'm sorry."

"Get up!" I yank her arm, and she cringes from my touch. "Go to your room and stay there!"

Sobbing, she races through the kitchen, kicking chocolate everywhere. "Not fair!" she moans. "Not fair!"

Not fair sums up the last six months quite well. A year ago I was the CEO of a successful tech startup; now I'm kneeling in Toll House chips. I could scream if I weren't so tired. I scoop the biggest pile in my hands, dumping it in the trash. Hunger pits my stomach, tinged with dull nausea.

A key scrapes the lock of the front door, and I listen to the thundering of feet. Tom's booming voice calls for me. "Melissa?"

His patent shoes crush a stray chip as he walks into the kitchen, eyes widening at the mess. "What happened?"

Tom's backpack drops as he surveys the damage. My gaze searches his gray sweatshirt and dark designer jeans. He unzips the hoodie, revealing a sweat-soaked button-up shirt. I don't know what the hell I'm searching for—a smear of lipstick on his collar?

"Stacy broke the cabinet." I lurch to my feet, desperate to leave the house. "I'm going out."

He's halfway between unknotting the tie at his neck. "What? Where?"

"I need to fix the door. I'll be back soon."

Tom's light eyes search the stove and counters for a steaming platter of food. "You made nothing? Again?"

"I didn't have time. I'll finish the prep when I get back and store it for tomorrow. There are chicken tenders you can defrost. That with a steamed crown of broccoli should be enough."

He gapes at me as I grab the Gucci purse from the counter. "The kids hate broccoli."

"I'm sure you'll think of something else." I head out the front door, ignoring Tom's look of stunned disbelief. "Won't be gone long."

The sun's still high in the sky when I step outside. My feet crush the dead grass as I walk to my Lexus.

Tom hurries to the window. His blanched face shines behind the glass like a dog watching his master leave. This morning, I found Tom's clothes from the wash dried and folded in his dresser. He has no idea I carry the tickets with me everywhere.

Let him fumble around the damn kitchen himself.

As I back out of the driveway, my neighbor waves. I nod at Barbara and drive from the neighborhood.

Palm trees line the hill on Dolores Street, their leaves a dull green with the drought parching the roots. I roll down, caught in a sea of red lights. For once, I don't care. It's a blessing to sit in my car in complete silence, with cool air blowing into my face.

The sign for Ross Hardware store looms ahead. I pull into the covered parking lot and kill the engine. I never go here. Martha used to mind all the household errands until I had to decide between my house and having a nanny, maid, and personal assistant. I thought moving the kids out of San Francisco would've been tough on them. Selling the home wasn't an option. We wouldn't be able to stay in the city with two children, and I'd worked way too hard to get here. But it's all falling apart, no matter what I do.

I enter the brightly lit store and stroll the aisles to pick a hinge to replace the one Stacy broke. The cabinet door was custom made. I'll have to order it online. More domestic chores for me to do. I should be glad.

I find the longest line and stand in between a contractor and a man with Raid tucked under his arm. A wedding band wraps around his finger, but that doesn't stop him from leering at the female cashier, who is small enough to be a teenager.

Wait—I'd recognize that bony face anywhere. Aubrey?

71

Her lips curve as he drops the spray bottle on the conveyor belt. "Hey, sweetie. Put it on the card."

"It's Aubrey, not sweetie." She taps the plastic badge above her heart.

Flustered, the man apologizes. She rolls her eyes, and I notice the smear of black on her upper lid. Maybe she woke up in yesterday's eyeliner. She seems the type.

"I don't see a ring on your finger," he croaks in his bullfrog voice.

Aubrey lets it roll off her shoulders. "Well, I'm only seventeen."

"Really? Get out of here."

She winks. "Almost legal, but not quite."

No way in hell she's that young.

Aubrey leans over the counter, arms crossed to push nonexistent cleavage together. The man looks down her neckline and blushes. He mutters something about his wife and grabs the plastic bag. Aubrey laughs at his back. "Idiot."

Interesting. What happened to the shy girl I met in yoga? She smirks as though waiting for the next moron to run afoul of her snark. I can hear her mind whirring behind those dark eyes. The windows shutter closed when she notices me.

"Hey."

Aubrey breaks my gaze, red patches rising to her cheeks.

"Wow, I didn't expect to see you here." She grabs the hinge and scans it.

"One of my kids busted a kitchen cabinet, so here I am."

"That'll be thirty-five cents."

I grin at the notion of something costing under a dollar. Digging into my purse, I find two quarters that I drop into Aubrey's hand. "So you work here, huh?"

Aubrey opens the cash register and scrapes the change. "Ever since I was eighteen," she says with a resigned sigh. "Went to college, but it wasn't for me. Good thing too. Could you imagine having to pay student loans on top of everything else we deal with?"

I could see her at a hipster coffee shop where part of the appeal would be the snide baristas. "Unfortunately, I can." I take the hinge and toss it in my purse, waving off the coins. "Keep it."

I drag my feet toward the door. I have no desire to go home.

"Melissa, wait!"

I turn, expecting Aubrey to tell me that I left my cell phone at the register, but there's nothing in her hands. "What's up?"

A shudder runs through Aubrey's body. She shakes it off with a laugh. "My shift is almost over. Want to hang out?"

"Hang out?"

"Yeah. My place is a few blocks from here."

Hope beams on Aubrey's wasted face. I'd be a monster to refuse her, even if all we have in common is our disease. I suppose that's enough. "Sure."

Aubrey grins. "Great. Five minutes, tops."

"Okay. I'll wait outside." My hand dives into my purse. I'm halfway between shooting Tom a text before I delete it. Let him worry for once.

I walk outdoors and lean against the store windows. Aubrey joins me moments later and walks toward her car. I climb in my Lexus and follow her, stomach turning as she carves a path through seedier neighborhoods, chain-linked fences, trash, and homeless encampments.

Luckily, there's enough street parking for both of us at her apartment building, which is a triplex. The lawn is bone-dry, littered with cigarette butts.

I swing the car door open. The sound of a couple arguing echoes across the road. Sirens blaze on the highway nearby. Dog feces stain the sidewalk. God, what a dump.

Aubrey seems unperturbed by the mess. She locks her dinky Toyota and kicks through the grass, pushing her key through the lock. My nose wrinkles in anticipation, but her place is spotless. A thick layer of carpet covers the living room and dining area, cutting into cheap linoleum that's cracked in several places. A couple of appliances sit on the kitchen counter, and a short hallway leads to her bedroom and an adjoining bathroom also lined with carpet. Mirrors on the wall to the left make the apartment seem larger. It's neat. Clean. Relatively quiet.

Aubrey takes off her shoes at the entrance, and I slip out of my Pradas.

She opens the fridge. "Want anything to drink? I've got Charles Shaw." The light illuminates her smirk. "Just kidding. I have some Coke and orange juice. Jesus, I need to go shopping."

"I'm not thirsty; it's fine."

"Suit yourself." Aubrey pours herself a glass of boxed rosé wine, the kind they sell at Trader Joe's for two dollars. She drops a few cubes in the round, short drink and I bite my lip to keep from laughing.

Good lord. "How does it taste?"

She sips, her eyes fluttering. "Awesome."

Aubrey sounds like she means it. She gestures toward the

couch, indicating that I should sit. The stuffing is ripped from the cushions in the floral-patterned sofa, but at least it's clean.

"How much do you pay for this place?"

Aubrey grabs a coaster and throws it on the coffee table, which is scored with dozens of marks. "Twelve-fifty."

"What?" I search her mocha eyes for a lie. "The median rent for a one-bedroom is three thousand. How the hell are you paying that little?"

"I got connections," she boasts. "Actually, it's cheap because they erected a homeless camp nearby."

"Aren't you worried they'll rob you?"

She looks around, shrugging. "And steal what, exactly? I keep my oxy on me at all times, and as for that"—she gestures toward the TV—"they can have it."

"Wow. Any children?"

"No kids. No boyfriend, either." She takes another long draught of her boxed wine and shudders. "It's just me."

I imagine a world where my only concern is a rent I could easily make every month with a retail job. Jealousy stings my tongue.

Aubrey sinks into the cushions, eyes closed. "I might get rid of my car. It's supposed to last ten more years, but what's the point? I won't be around to drive when her machine heart stops working."

"You'll sell it?"

"Yeah, figure I'll use the money for palliative care when things go south." Aubrey sits straighter and opens her eyes. "What about you? Any plans for the future?"

"I do have some, yeah." I examine the chips in my manicured nails. They've gone to hell. "This will make me sound so dull."

"Tell me."

She's going to laugh. "I want to start working again."

"Seriously?" Her drink lands with a thud on the table. "I'd give anything to be in your position."

"I know, but my job was my identity before I got sick. I don't know what to do with myself anymore." The corners of my mouth lift in an apologetic smile. "Sorry, I'm not trying to complain."

She waves off my concern with a brittle arm. "Vent away. I don't judge."

I doubt Aubrey understands the desire glowing inside my being. Aubrey's a cockroach. She'll survive anywhere. I'm not like that. "I don't feel fulfilled."

"Of course you don't." She takes another small sip. "You were forced to quit your job. You had to stop being *you*."

She's right.

Suddenly the wine looks appetizing. "Can I have some?"

"Be my guest."

I grab the almost full glass and take two big gulps, the alcohol washing over my brain before it's down my throat. At this rate, I'll never get well enough to work. Tom's holistic crap hasn't made a dent in my symptoms.

Boxed rosé never tasted so good.

"Not bad, eh?" Aubrey takes the drink from me, laughing. "I'm not supposed to have alcohol with my drugs, but whatever."

A pang hits my side and I slide the drink over the table. "Can I use the bathroom really quick?"

"Sure. It's right down the hall." Aubrey stands with me, heading for the kitchen. "I'll make you a drink."

"Okay." I stare at my growing reflection as I walk to the bathroom, which has a carpeted floor. *Gross.*

After I'm done, I wash my hands and return to the living room. Aubrey presses a glass tumbler filled with pearly pink wine into my hands. She beams at me. "I'm really glad we did this."

"Me too." If anything, it's an illuminating insight into Aubrey's existence. She drinks her boxed wine on her moth-eaten couch, and she's *happy*.

What am I doing with *my* life?

"How—uh—how has your husband reacted?" Aubrey fumbles over her words. "I mean, to your illness."

I follow the direction of her gaze to my wedding ring, which I cover with my hand. "He's concerned."

And possibly seeing another woman behind my back. I can't admit that out loud a second time.

She cocks her head. "Does he work?"

"Yes, he's a software engineer. He picked up the slack when I quit." A shiver runs down my spine.

"Must be nice to have someone there for you."

"Yeah, I guess. It's still hard with the kids." I raise the glass to my lips, ignoring the protest in my stomach. "He'd hate it if he saw me drinking."

She scoffs. "What, you're not allowed to take a load off?"

I smile at her. "Tom thinks it's a bad idea."

"Oh, *please*. The worst has already happened to us."

"That's a good point." Even Tom wouldn't be able to refute that.

Aubrey raises her glass, gently knocking against mine. "Cheers."

I toss my head back and drink a mouthful, the warmth burning the back of my throat. The heat spreads to my brain, and I bite my lip. My tolerance has taken a nosedive. Drinking was a terrible idea. Tom would be so angry.

Ignoring Aubrey's encouraging grin, I slide the rosé over the table. "It's good, but I really shouldn't."

"Don't be a stick in the mud." She sets her glass down, the sleeve lifting to expose a length of sinewy flesh wrapped around bone. The fat melted away, and soon her muscle will disappear, too.

That can't happen to me.

I'm behaving recklessly.

I stand, black spots crawling over my vision.

Alarmed, Aubrey half-rises from her seat. "You okay?"

No. "Yeah."

Reminiscing about the past and drinking? I'm better than this. Tom's disappointment echoes in my head in mournful tones. There's still hope for me, and I'm going to cling to it with everything I've got because without it—without it I have nothing. My children, my babies, *will* grow up with their mother in their lives. I have to believe that.

"I need to go." I march toward the entrance, stumbling as I slide into my shoes.

Concern shines on Aubrey's features. "You sure you're okay?"

I can't stand to look at her one more second. "Yeah, it's late. My kids are waiting for me. Thanks for having me over, it was...well...it was good talking to you."

Looking worried, she opens the door. "Drive safe."

My heart beats frantically, pure fire eating the alcohol in my system. I'm not drunk. Never been this sober.

I can do this.

An orange light burning into the skyline blinds me as I descend the steps.

The night is coming. I won't go gentle.

I.

I FUCKING HAD HER.

She was in my apartment, drinking from a glass I gave her. If I had the pills we'd be together by now.

I love you.

I don't say it enough, so I write it down even though you'll probably never read these letters. Maybe I'll show them to you. It'll take time for trust to grow—a few years after your wife is out of the way. When we've been together for a while, I will tell you everything. And you'll do the same because—let's be honest—we're both liars.

Melissa told me the truth.

You're not a neurologist. Turns out, the love of my life isn't a man of medicine. He's a software engineer at Inicorp. I looked it up. Decent biotech company—not in the same league as Genentech or McKesson—but it's respectable.

Did you think I'd care?

I adore you, Tom. Not your job or your house. You.

Last night, you told me about feeling like Atlas. The

weight of the world gouges your shoulders, but when you're with me, it disappears. When we fuck you don't feel pain.

It's the same for me.

I could bask in your light all day, smile at the warmth on my face, and be happy forever.

I couldn't care less about the size of your bank account, your low-six-figure salary, the fact you won't be able to afford the mortgage when your wife dies—none of it.

The air I breathe is for you. I'm convinced that if you weren't in my life, my heart would stop beating, my veins would dry up, and I'd collapse, dead.

You're the reason I'm trying so hard to kill Melissa. I admire her. Every day I watch her through your windows, and I search for something to justify this murder. I never find anything. She's a faithful spouse who dotes on her children. She's a decent human being, which makes all of this harder.

Couldn't you have picked someone less amazing?

And that bothers me because I'm not perfect. Far from it. Hell, I don't deserve to stand in Melissa's shadow. But you chose me. You want me. When she is gone, we'll be together.

That is what you keep saying, and that's why I'm worthy of you.

It might be weeks before I try again. I can't afford another mistake. Literally. My oxy habit will have to pause for a while. Buying these drugs isn't cheap, and my supplier is heartless.

I'm still here. Biding my time.

9

AUBREY

THERAPY IS A PRISON WITHOUT HANDCUFFS. Every week I'm forced to return to this dingy office cluttered with files, the walls covered with art prints that look like they were bought in a clearance sale. I sit in an unyielding leather lounge. I hate the stale scent and shuttered windows.

My gaze drags to the middle-aged woman in floral skirts. She sits behind a mahogany desk. I judged her the moment I saw the Krishna figurine standing next to a crystal ball. Rich people can't get enough of Asian culture and it drives me mental.

Dr. Singmaster moves from behind the desk and sits in the chair next to mine. "Aubrey, do you remember why you're here?"

Of course I do. "I have to come here."

"The courts gave you a second chance with a ninety-day mandated therapy program."

One of the few times my frail appearance worked in my favor. "Yeah. So?"

"If you refuse to cooperate, all it takes is a letter from me, and you'll be given a harsher sentence. Is that what you want?"

I study her clasped hands and stony face lined with tasteful makeup. Dr. Singmaster isn't a beautiful woman, but she's pleasant to look at. She also doesn't have a mean bone in her body. "You will not do that."

"And why not?"

"Because you know I'll die behind bars. You don't need that on your conscience."

Flustered, she pulls her skirt down her legs. "Despite that, I'm bound by the law."

"In the grand scheme of things, is one makeup tube from Sephora worth it?"

Dr. Singmaster flicks her iron-gray hair and clears her throat. She doesn't like to be out of control. "Let's keep this on you. What happened today?"

"Nothing. My boss is an ass, as usual." I return my gaze to the outdated ceiling.

She looks worried. "Something's got you on edge."

I suck in my bottom lip. "He hasn't contacted me in a week, almost."

Her sigh cuts at me. "Well, I'm not surprised. Didn't I warn you this would happen?"

Yes, she has. Over and over. "He wouldn't ditch me. We have plans."

"No, you do. Ron will not follow through with his promises, Aubrey. He uses women like you to make himself feel better."

I gave them fake names. It takes me a second to remember who she's talking about. "Women like me?"

She purses her lips. "Vulnerable. Insecure. *Lonely*. You're a magnet for predators."

God, now she's using the same words as June. "You don't approve because he's married—I get it."

"My job is not to judge you, Aubrey. It's to help you visualize truths about yourself and your environment. So far you've refused to acknowledge that your affair with Ron is toxic."

"Wow." I loop my feet around the lounge, sitting upright to glare at her. "That's not true at all."

"In what way?"

"He heals me. I'm not in pain. When we're together, the agony disappears. He's amazing."

"What about when he goes back to his wife?" she says coolly. "How do you feel then?"

When his warmth fades from my bed, nothing can disguise the gaping ache in my chest.

I hate this doctor. "It's only temporary. He'll leave her."

"He will never do that, Aubrey. That's what I've been trying to explain to you. Men like him don't leave their wives. You told me he wasn't truthful about being a neurologist. What else do you think he lied about?"

I stand from the lounge, heart hammering as Dr. Singmaster gazes at me. I want to shatter her calm with my fist. She doesn't understand us.

"Aubrey, I'm being hard on you right now because you need to ask yourself why you seek inappropriate relationships."

My fingers dive into my hair. "I didn't go looking for a married man to fuck. He chose me."

Tom chased me in that market and slipped his business card into my hand. How was I supposed to resist his gorgeous smile? I don't know how he found me in that crowd. When I've asked him, he said there was a light burning under my skin. I was beautiful.

Maybe he didn't see beauty. He saw a damaged little girl and thought—*Score.*

"This is a perfect example of self-destructive behavior," she says, tapping her pen against her notebook. "You just admitted you have a problem with seeing a married man, but you do it anyway."

I seize a *Time* magazine from the end table and hurl it so violently it crashes against the blinds. The doctor doesn't blink. She's used to my outbursts.

"You're wrong!"

"Aubrey, please stop yelling."

"Even if he refuses to go—she will divorce him. Felicia is not the type to be content with a man screwing around."

She purses her lips. "How would you know?"

I ball my hands into fists. "I Googled her. She's a Harvard alumnus and founded a successful tech startup in the Bay Area. She won't take his cheating lying down."

My therapist is a bloodhound for bullshit. "Are you still following her?"

"No."

Her brows narrow. "Aubrey, I can't do this if you're not honest with me."

"Sometimes," I admit. "Yeah. I'm in her yoga class, but I don't talk to her much."

"I see." Her lips whiten. "Is Ron aware that you follow his wife?"

He'd be outraged if he knew.

My lips are closed, but Dr. Singmaster guesses the worst from my face. "You need to disengage from them. It's not right to intrude on their lives like this."

She's never been this pushy. "I'm not doing anything wrong."

"Aubrey."

"*Doctor*." A deep frown creases her forehead at my mimicking tone. "I'm keeping a distance."

"Okay, signing up for the same yoga class is not what I would call establishing boundaries." A ragged sigh tears from her throat. "Let's say everything you want comes true. Ron leaves Felicia and you're together. He wasn't faithful to his wife. How do you know he won't cheat on you?"

"Christ, I'm dying. Nothing matters anymore except that I enjoy the time I've left on Earth. Staying away from Ron would make me miserable. That's all. I don't care about what-ifs. Dwelling on them isn't worth it."

"Why not find a single man instead?"

I glare at her. "Are you still harping on that?"

"I think it's significant."

How is this not sinking in? "I'm in love with Tom—*Ron*. I don't want to date other men."

"You haven't tried."

"That's because I want him. Do you understand what love is? I'd do anything for him. I'd—"

Kill for him.

The furious scrape of Dr. Singmaster's pen makes me swallow my next words. This is getting out of hand. Patient-doctor confidentiality doesn't cover murder plots.

I sink into the leather chair. "Sorry. I lost control."

"Apology accepted."

The ceiling blurs as I lie back, but I refuse to blink. I'm not going to cry even if she makes more sense than I want to admit. Damn it. She's wrong. I'll go outside, check my phone, and there will be a text from him. Tom has never backpedaled on a promise. He'll apologize and invite me to dinner.

But what if Tom ghosted me?

"Aubrey." Dr. Singmaster's clipped voice worms into my consciousness. "Aubrey, are you still with me?"

"Yeah. What was the question?"

She taps her notepad. "You have to stop following Felicia and Ron."

This again. "What do you think I'll do to them, exactly?"

"You need to work on constructive ways to deal with your obsession, Aubrey."

"It's not an obsession. I'm allowed to be interested in Ron's wife."

"Why did you watch her at home?"

She thinks I'm a psycho. "I'm sensing judgment in your tone, Doctor."

Her nostrils flare as she crosses her legs so tight they look unlikely to move ever again. I should be more careful around this chick. If I screw up and the cops suspect a homicide, the first person they'll call is my court-ordered psychologist.

This doctor doesn't need more fodder for the police. "My upbringing wasn't exactly ideal. I watch her like the candle girl watches those families eat fat turkeys on Christmas Day."

Eyes softening, she leans closer. "Can you talk about your family?"

There's nothing to discuss but the endless drip of solitude. "There's not much to tell."

"You told me your aunt kicked you out," she says, slowly. "When you were fifteen."

The memory makes my head pound. "I was a mouthy brat."

"You were homeless for weeks." Dr. Singmaster looks at me like I'm a lost puppy. "Do you think anyone deserves that?"

I should have never told her that sappy story. Glancing at the clock over her, I read the time. Four-fifty. "Look at that; it's five. My hour's up."

I swing my legs from the lounge and storm from the tiny office. Dr. Singmaster doesn't call me back. She's seen this enough times to know it's better to let me go. Common sense says I should suck it up and play along. Complete the therapy and leave my thieving past behind. It would be easier if my doctor didn't seize every session as an opportunity to guide me away from bliss.

I will not give up Tom until he tells me to get lost. He's the one who started this. If he wants to end it, he'll have to man up. No. I need to stop second-guessing myself. He doesn't want to break up with me. I shouldn't let the doctor needle me.

Outside the heavy double doors, I lean against the wall and check my messages with a shaking hand. My chest squeezes the last molecule of air.

Nothing from Tom.

Ignoring me isn't acceptable.

I stumble through the doctor's office, past the receptionist's window, and crash through the glass door. It swings open violently to the dense fog outside, rolling down the hills and Victorian houses.

My pocket chimes.

Finally.

The phone slips from my hand. I grab it midair.

Has to be him. Has to. He loves me. I love him.

I glance at the screen, heart pounding with hope.

Patrick: *Are we still on? GoT is tonite.*

A wave of disappointment buries my brief spark of happiness. I punch my response: *YES. Stop asking.*

He types back a surly reply: *OK. Keep your shirt on. Or don't. ;)*

Sighing, I gaze at the sky in the hopes a deity will swoop down and bestow me with patience to handle this idiot.

Me: *I have everything. Will b there soon.*

Patrick: *Make it fast plz. There's a sale on Steam.*

Six hundred dollars for six pills was the deal. I dig through my purse, expecting to touch a stiff envelope full of cash. Damn, I left the money at work.

I march to my car and open the door. Throwing my bag in the passenger seat, I slide in and start the ignition. My tires streak the pavement as I peel out of there, heading for Ross Hardware before it closes in fifteen minutes. Shouldn't matter if I punch in the code for the warehouse entrance, but I don't want to risk anything.

Fog clings to the cars in the sparse parking lot. Diffused light from the store spreads like fairy dust. The chill seeps through the car when I cut the engine. I grope for my hoodie —*fuck*—that's in the locker too. I walk outside and hurry toward the open doors, where one of the new kids stands behind a CLOSED sign.

He rakes his buzz-cut head. "Ma'am, we're closing. Oh, Aubrey."

"I need to get in really quick. Forgot my stuff." I glimpse his name tag as he allows me to pass. "Thanks, Zac."

The store hums with sedated music that usually drives me insane. I've learned to tune most of it out, but Amit likes to keep the volume at a "corporate-approved" level, and lately they've been playing Justin Bieber hits. The whine of a high-pitched tween follows me into the Employees Only area, booming from the mounted speakers.

I walk past a murmuring voice, recognizing Amit's bulk in the office window. Everyone's already gone. I stop in front of the lockers. I flip the switch, illuminating the room, and scan the row of numbers for the familiar gleam of stainless steel.

Light beams on the rows. The locks have disappeared. All of them.

I rip open number 75 and stare at the back of a metal hull. *Gone.*

Did I forget to secure it? Not possible. It was there this morning, the round lock with a red dial. I stuffed my jacket and the envelope inside.

The room echoes with my shriek and the slamming of doors. I search each one. Empty. Empty. Empty. "*Where is it?*"

They've all been cleaned out.

I double-check 75, a sick feeling gripping my stomach. My fingers grope the steel as though they'll penetrate through a layer of deception and reveal my money. Nope, it's gone. Six hundred dollars.

Whirling around, I search the room for a hint of what

happened. I seize the trash can as a line of nausea crawls up my throat. A broken piece of metal glimmers in plastic.

I grab my severed lock, swallowing my vomit. The jagged pieces sit in my hand. Someone broke in and robbed me blind.

My scream rebounds off the open lockers.

10

MELISSA

A BEAUTIFUL BAROQUE design papers the walls. My face reflects off the gilded mirror rising above the sink, surrounded by light bulbs. Pure kitsch, but I love it. People grab reservations for this restaurant to take pictures of the restroom. Might as well check one item off the bucket list. Who knows how long I'll have?

I lower my iPhone, my enthusiasm for the photo evaporating like smoke. I haven't slept in days, and my color correcting fluid won't wipe the fatigue away. Purple shadows darken my eyes. I trace the hollows under my lashes and my thinned cheeks, which need to be plumped with more fillers. I hide my imperfections. All of them. Even my shaky marriage.

This is the woman I've become. Soft. *Weak.*

I can't bring myself to ask Tom about the tickets. I pretend everything's fine, but my life is crumbling. My phone is the dying link to my former self. I check it constantly. A permanent red box surrounding decaying white numbers threatens my health every day.

I used to be unshakable. I got things done. Somehow, I let this disease take over everything and destroy my confidence. The old me would've interrogated Tom when those tickets fell out of his pocket. Instead I apply a fresh coat of HD foundation and conceal.

I still look like death.

Red lace sprawls over my chest in a sweetheart silhouette, hiding the faint shadows of bones. The straps of my Alexander McQueen dress are loose. It's not as snug as I remember. The fabric bunches at my hips.

Enough is enough. I'll ask him about the tickets tonight.

I reach into my bag for a matte lipstick. The top opens, revealing a shade of vibrant red. I draw, and then I blot my lips with a paper napkin.

Grabbing my clutch, I leave the bathroom and walk a narrow hall into a shoebox of a restaurant. Low-hanging lights glow over communal dining tables packed together. Noise blasts me as I stroll into the main room. With everybody crammed in a tight space, it's impossible to hold a private conversation. I squeeze between a concrete wall and the bar, walking to Tom. Passing waiters bump into me as I climb onto the stool. A couple shares the table with us. The man's elbows keep digging into my side. It's the opposite of intimate.

Usually I'm the one who makes reservations, but Tom surprised me with a date night at Beretta. My stomach clenched when I scanned the small plates menu, the universal code for expensive as hell.

Sitting straight is hard on my back, but I zip my spine and offer my husband a smile.

Tom puts his smartphone down and clasps my hand. "Maybe you should have one cocktail."

Should I be buzzed when I confront him? Probably not. "I'll have water."

His lips flatten. "Okay," he says, closing the drink menu. "Order one, Tom."

A waiter squeezes against Tom's chair as people fill the narrow passage. "Nah. It's all right."

I roll my eyes. "Don't do that."

"No. They're too expensive, anyway."

Grabbing the menu, I scan the list of thirty-dollar entrees for affordable meals. Tom always orders what he wants, but I add up the bill ahead of time. The glaring red numbers in my Mint account suggest I should follow a more frugal lifestyle, but Tom wanted to come here so badly.

He says something that's lost in the cacophony. "What?"

Tom leans forward. "I said, would you mind stopping at Horsefeather afterward? It's a trendy cocktail place I want to try."

I bite the inside of my lip. "We can't eat out and have cocktails. That doesn't fit in our budget."

God, I hate this conversation. Tom takes it in stride, nodding. "Okay. That's fine."

Nothing about our lives is in the realm of *fine*.

A throb pulses in my lower back and my feet keep slipping out of my pumps. The waiter squeezes between us and rattles off the specials, but I don't hear a word. I can't talk to him about the tickets here. There's barely enough silence to listen to my thoughts.

Tom listens to the server, nodding along with a broad smile as he orders a hibiscus infusion from the mocktail list. I stick to my tap water and ask for the beet salad.

A candle flickers between us, casting soft shadows on

Tom's face. His jacket brushes the plates beside him as he leans closer. "How do you like the place?"

There's not much of the restaurant I can see over the sea of heads. "It's a bit loud."

"I love it," Tom says, grinning. "It's awesome. Wow."

The waiter deposits Tom's fancy drink, which looks like seltzer with crushed flowers floating among ice cubes. He takes a picture of the glass and posts it on Instagram. Tom's always been about style over substance. I stare at my water and consider doing the same with a few hashtags: #ifeelold, #whatever, #datenight.

He smacks his lips in apparent appreciation of the mocktail. "Babe, I heard of this new experimental treatment you have to try."

Must our every conversation revolve around my illness? "I don't want to talk about it."

"Why not?"

"Because it's depressing, Tom. This is our night out. We finally get an evening without the kids to do something romantic."

He stirs the drink with the little black straw. "I know it's not fun, but we need to stay on top of the latest treatments."

I lose myself in pity spirals often, even though I don't like feeling sorry for myself. "What's the point? None of them work."

"They need more time, Melissa. I know it's frustrating, but you can't give up. The kids and I need you." Taking my hand, he squeezes. "Please. Do it for me."

My head spins when I count how many I've tried already —the weekly infusions, the crash diet, supplements, pills, powders. "Fine."

He knows damn well I don't believe in any of it. The only reason I took the stupid floral vitamins and all the other nonsense he pushed on me was to make him feel better. It makes him happy to know I'm taking something for the cancer. What harm could it do?

Tom sits back with a satisfied curve of his mouth. The sight of it digs at me. Everything—even this restaurant—is always his decision. Part of that's my fault. I was overwhelmed and wanted him to take over, and he did.

He cocks his head. "What?"

"Coming here was a mistake. We can't hear each other, and we're sharing a table with a bunch of strangers. My back's killing me."

The smile vanishes from his face. "I'm sorry."

Why won't I ask him about the damn tickets? "Don't apologize. I'm just—I don't know."

"It's a trendy spot. Reservations book weeks ahead. I thought you'd like it."

"We can't afford half the menu."

Tom picks at the table moodily, the silence between us dour.

"I'm doing the best I can," he says in a low voice. "You're not supposed to eat fast food, and everything has to be organic or gluten-free. There's a long list of vegetables you have to avoid. That will narrow choices for going out, honey."

He's right. "I'm sorry. Let's not talk about the disease, okay?"

A bitter smile staggers across his face. "Sure. You got it."

An edge grates in his voice. I'm not pressing the issue. The flickering candlelight lulls my body into a false sense of fatigue. All I want is to fall into my bed.

"Have you heard from Emily lately?"

Now he brings up the woman who replaced me at work? I smile at him vacantly and point at my ear, shrugging. He nods.

This night will go smoother if I pretend I can't hear him.

And it's not so bad when he takes my hand in his occasionally, bringing my knuckles to his lips. Reminds me of our first dates. He was smitten with me before I was. The random bouts of affection made me glow. Back then, everything was perfect.

I never worried about him. There was no doubt. Now I wake every morning and hope he'll find the two ticket stubs where I hid them and explain himself because I'm too much of a coward to confront him.

The waiter arrives, pushing a sad plate of wilted lettuce and shredded beets topped with walnuts. Tom's pork loin au jus medallions smothered in a fig sauce slide in front of him.

"You know what, I'll have the blood orange margarita," he says to the server.

The man scribbles a note in his pad. "Sure, you've got it."

My fork scrapes the ceramic. I push a couple leaves in my mouth and spread the rest across the plate to make it look like I ate more than I did—something I've been doing since I was a kid.

Tom digs into his meal with gusto, closing his eyes in ecstasy as he chews. "Wow. This is amazing."

"I'm glad you're enjoying it." I shove the candied walnuts to the side. Cholesterol is not my friend right now.

"You've got to try some."

"Oh, I'm good."

He slices a thick piece and reaches over the space between

us, dumping it on my plate. A rich juice seeps from the meat, staining my lettuce.

"I told you I don't want it." He's always done this. It's an irritating personality trait inherited from his mother. Eating dinner at his mom's house is a battle. I can never eat enough to satisfy them.

Tom backed down over the years, but occasionally he gets a gleam in his eyes. Like now. "Babe, you need more protein in your diet."

I should do this. I should do that. "What do you think the spinach smoothie I have every day is for?"

"Yeah, but come on. You'd rather drink that green crap than have the juiciest pork I've ever tasted?"

My smile flattens. "The strict meal plan was your idea, remember? I have no clue if that is antibiotic free."

He laughs mid-chew. "Mel, it's San Francisco. I'm pretty sure everything's safe."

I push the leaves away from the meat. "Can't be too careful."

Someone knocks into my chair. I scowl at the man, who follows his date into the restaurant. He turns, throwing an apology over his shoulder. Flickering light from the candles ripples on his young face.

"Melissa?"

My mind scans for a name—Brad—and his position—software developer. I'd hired him to help me develop more projects at Mission Digital when I had too much to code and too little time.

Brad does a double take as he takes me in, his unpleasant shock like acid in my guts. "Wow. You look...happy."

There's a slight pause before he says the word, as though he had to dig deep for an appropriate adjective.

I'd give anything in the world to disappear on the spot. "Thanks."

Tom waves him over, speech already thick with the cocktail. "You should join us. The more the merrier."

He pats the seat that a couple just vacated and Brad takes one next to me with a resigned smile. "Melissa, you've met my girlfriend Vicki, right?"

A petite woman dressed in a clingy black dress and a jean jacket steps around him. She reaches out with a tanned, smooth arm and I shake it, noticing how thin I look compared to her.

I'm jealous of her round cheeks and dark eyes. Every strand of her ebony hair pulls into a high ponytail. I smell the finish of her hairspray as she leans in close. "Nice to meet you!"

Before I let go she glances at my wrist, her smile faltering, and sits next to my husband.

Tom shoots me an unhappy look I ignore before turning to Brad. "So how's Mission Digital?"

Brad shrugs, sending a thrill of fear through me. "All right. We're making progress, but it's slow."

The glory days pass in front of my eyes like a montage to a pop star's rise to stardom. Promising at first, and then a quick downward spiral. "We had more money than we knew what to do with."

"At least you invested. Can't believe I trusted Bitcoin." He flags down the waiter, ordering a beer.

I stare at the bottom of my cup and wish it was filled with booze. "Anyway, there's still hope."

The server slides a brown ale to Brad. He accepts the glass, taking a deep drink. "Honestly, I'm not sure there's a future for Mission Digital."

The pain in my back throbs angrily. "What?"

He frowns. "I think she's going to sell the company."

"*What?*" A thrill hits my chest.

Tom slaps the table with a broad hand. "Guys, enough about work."

"Sorry," Brad mutters.

I find air in my lungs. "She's *selling* the company?"

Tom glowers at me. "Come on, Mel."

"I mean, what did you expect?" Brad traces a wet circle on the counter. "One software update bricked the devices. The refunds alone put us a few million in the hole."

It was hard enough stepping down and watching my replacement run the company into the ground, but if we sell all my hard work has been for nothing. "Yeah, but what about our investors for everything we've lined up?"

"They want their money." He shakes his head. "We had a good run, and we should be grateful for that."

I can't believe what I'm hearing. "Brad, you can't let her do this. We won't get anything. I didn't give her the job so she could tear it down!"

"Relax," Brad says, patting my shoulder. "You're not on the hook financially."

"It's not about that," I say in a hoarse voice. "You know how much time I've invested into this? How much I've sacrificed?"

"I know it sucks." Brad grimaces. "I'll hate to lose the patents, but we knew this might happen. A startup being sold is a tale as old as time. Besides, nothing's official yet."

Sounds like more than a rumor.

A stabbing pain hits my chest like a knife diving in and out. This was why Tom suggested I disengage from the company. It was too much of a strain on my health, but learning about this secondhand is worse.

"There must be something we could do." Brad meets my gaze reluctantly. "Maybe we should make one last appeal to—"

"Guys," Tom snaps. "Not tonight. Please."

The world dims as I process this latest blow. She wants to sell my company? My *baby*?

What the hell happened after I left?

My spine zips straight as Brad engages Tom in conversation. "So how are you? You both seem well."

"Yeah, we're hanging in there." A brave smile spreads across Tom's face.

Brad glances at me. "So things are better?"

"Not yet," Tom answers. "But they will be. Right, hon?"

My legacy is following me to the grave.

I glance over the sprawl of half-eaten dishes to my husband's beam. I cough, masking the tremor shaking my lips.

Oh no.

Eyes glistening, I bow my head. Tears slip from my lashes to glide down my cheeks.

I hear Vicki gasp. "She's crying."

Mortified, I grab a napkin and dab my face. Flames erupt under my skin as I open my mouth to reassure them, and all that comes out is a choked sob.

Tom takes my hand. "Melissa."

I don't respond to the gentle brush of Tom's fingers. Jesus, falling apart in public isn't me.

Brad pats my arm, sharing an awkward glance with his girlfriend. "It's okay to be upset."

"Sorry." I stare at Tom across the candlelight. "I-I can't act like everything's all right."

The rippling light casts shifting shadows over his face. "What are you talking about?"

Brad jerks his head to the bar. "We'll give you guys privacy."

Tom watches them disappear in disappointment. He sighs, turning back to me. "What's going on?"

I wipe my eyes. "Nothing. I'm stressed."

Insistent, he squeezes my hand. "Talk to me."

I meet his piercing blues. "I can't pretend anymore, Tom. Look at me."

He does, frowning. "What are you talking about? You're beautiful."

"I've lost a lot of weight. Even they noticed."

Frustrated, he waves off Brad and Vicki. "Sure, the dress is a little loose, but you're still amazing."

"Tom, I'm disappearing." I gather his fist in my hand, squeezing. "You can't see what's happening to me. I don't eat. I barely sleep. I exercise until I fall off the bike."

He pulls away from me. "That happened once. Don't exaggerate."

"I'm working myself to death trying to save my life—"

"That's ridiculous." An unpleasant frown sags his mouth. "You're drinking juiced vegetables every morning—you're doing everything to stay healthy."

"Come on. Those shakes are mostly ice, lemon juice, and kale."

"Baby, it was never supposed be easy. I need you to keep going for me. I'm not ready to let you throw in the towel."

Stung, I glower at him. "I'm not lazy."

"I didn't say that," he says in a calm voice. "You could try harder, though. I always remind you to take your meds. You forget them constantly, and that means they won't have enough time to build up in your system."

My teeth grind. "And what about you?"

I watch him straighten. "I don't understand."

"I found movie tickets and your clothes in the wash." It comes out of me in a wave of words. "You saw that romantic comedy I wanted to see. Who did you go with?"

"Melissa," he begins in a whisper. "It's not what it looks like."

"Then what is it?"

"A friend asked me to go with her." Tom's red-rimmed, unblinking gaze meets mine as a strange sensation hums throughout my limbs, as though I'm separating from my body.

I gouge my thighs to keep my voice from shaking. "A *friend*."

"Let me finish. You're not the only one who's in a bad way. It's hard to cope with the cancer. Once in a while, I need a break from watching my wife dying. Someone at work wanted to cheer me up. I told her you said it was okay."

"You lied."

"Nothing happened!" he hisses. "If you must know, she caught me crying over my desk. She felt bad for me. That's it —that's all it was."

"I see."

Tom hunches over the table. "I didn't tell you because I knew you'd react this way."

That stings. "What way?"

"Like *this*," he says emphatically. "I'm on your side, Melissa. For once I wish you'd give me the benefit of the doubt. I'm sorry if what I did made you upset."

He looks sincere.

I don't know what to believe anymore.

11

AUBREY

MY SCREAM CLASHES horribly with Justin Bieber's lovesick whine. I yell until the breath in my lungs is spent. Rage bounces off the bland walls and pierces my ears.

Nothing stirs in the darkness.

I hurl the broken lock. The pieces score the metal with a loud gong. I storm to the table and lift, dropping it with a frustrated sigh. There's not a single projectile in sight to vent my feelings, and I'm too weak to trash the place.

Weeks of picking up extra shifts. Wasted.

"Um, excuse me." Amit hangs from the door leading to his office, wearing a black polo and khakis. "Can I help you?" He offers aid in a condescending tone that says, "Shut the hell up, please."

I point at the locker. "Where's my shit?"

A line of contempt wrinkles his forehead. "I will not respond to profanity. When you're ready to stop screaming and talk like an adult, I'll tell you where I put your stuff."

This idiot thinks he's a high school guidance counselor. I'm two seconds from slamming my fist into his head. "Where. Is. It?"

He clicks his tongue. "Please would be nice."

"WHERE IS IT?"

Amit raises his eyebrows, refusing to be goaded. "I placed your belongings with everyone's things."

"You what?"

He points toward a cardboard box in the corner of his office. I spot my hoodie thrown inside and take it. The pockets are empty. I rifle through the contents, tossing aside makeup tubes and junk, searching for a flash of white. I snatch a piece of paper, but it's a receipt.

My envelope with six hundred dollars—it's not here. "Oh my God, I'm going to puke."

"Do it outside, please." Amit busies about his office, humming along with the teenybopper music. He looks everywhere but me, determined not to meet my gaze.

I stand. "You did this."

He glances at me. "I used a bolt cutter to remove all the locks, yes. It's against policy to leave personal belongings on company property past closing, Aubrey. You know that."

"We weren't closed." I can barely speak through my rage. "I forgot to get my things."

"Like I said. Everything is in the box."

This seething jerk stole it. "*Give me my money.*"

Amit laughs. "Excuse me?"

"The white envelope full of cash!"

Amit rifles through papers on his desk as a crimson shade creeps up his throat. "I have no idea what you're talking about."

He does. He's practically wearing a red flag.

I could strangle him now, wrap my hands around him and squeeze, but I doubt I have the strength to pinch all that neck shut. "Don't pretend you didn't steal it, you fat fuck."

Amit drops the water bottle he pretends to be interested in, his face flushed with rage. "One more word and you're fired!"

Overworked and underpaid Amit saw my envelope stuffed with cash as a golden opportunity to rob me blind. I have no recourse if there really is a policy about lockers, and if I blow my top at him, all he has to do is fire me.

Win-win.

"Now if you are finished, I'd like to go home." Amit squeezes his bulk past me.

I grab his shoulder. "We're not done!"

"Miss De Rosa. I've told you many times to stop with the profanity. If you keep insisting on using foul language, I'll have to write you up."

"You think I care? This isn't high school, it's my life, and I had plans for that six hundred dollars. I'm not some kid you can rob—look at me!"

He blinks. "I see nothing but a troubled young woman who refuses to accept responsibility for her actions."

I could seize that crystal paperweight and go to town. His skull will resemble a crater by the time I'm finished.

Amit turns as I lunge for the glass ball.

"What are you doing?"

A vision of me smashing it into his face seizes my body.

He squares his shoulders. "Take another step toward me with that thing, and you're done."

"You think that scares me?"

"Let it go!" he shrieks. "That was a wedding gift!"

I toss it on the ground near his feet, and its weight cracks the floorboards. "Oops."

He yelps, jumping back. "Aubrey!"

I walk closer until I can count every blemish on his flat nose. "Give me my money, or I'll make a scene the district manager will never forget."

His nostrils flare. "That's it. You're done."

"Then I guess I will go straight to HR and tell them that you groped me in your office after closing."

A gritty tone filters through Amit's words. "Do that, and I'll report you to the police for your little oxy habit. Don't deny it. I found the pills in your pocket and looked up what they are. Such a shame. Never took you for a junkie."

"Fuck you."

He rolls his eyes. "You know, Aubrey, someday that mouth of yours will land you in a world of hurt. You should thank me for stopping you. That money would've been used to buy more, right? You were probably planning a bender on the weekend."

"I. Have. Cancer."

"Maybe. Or perhaps you're using it to cover up your drug habit." Amit grabs his jacket and heads for the door. "Let's go, Miss De Rosa."

————

MY TO-DO LIST keeps growing with a series of impossible bullet points.

1. Get money back

2. Kill Amit

3. Buy drugs

4. Kill Melissa

Getting rid of one person will be hard enough, but if it were a choice between him or Melissa, I'd pick Amit. The bastard deserves to die.

Slow down, Aubrey.

Customers roll into the parking lot of Ross Hardware store as I head in the direction of the gleaming purple Taco Bell sign. Patrick sits under a mauve umbrella, digging into fast food.

I sit across from him. "Hey."

Wiping sour cream from his lips, he nods at me. "What up, Hotness?"

My teeth grind. "I got robbed."

"Yeah, you told me. That sucks." He grabs another taco and shoves half of it into his gaping mouth.

A stab hits my gut, a deep searing pain I never experienced until I developed masses in my colon. The blood in my head pools to my feet.

It's hard to catch my breath. "Damn it."

Patrick straightens. "Whoa. You okay?"

"No. He didn't just steal my money. He took my goddamn oxy."

"Cold."

If I was looking for sympathy, I should've visited a pastor. "I want more."

He wipes his lips using the greasy wrapper. "And I need the next Battlefield."

"What the hell is that?"

"A sick game I'm missing out on because I went to the horse races with some chick. Anyway, long story short is I blew my rent money for the month, but it's cool 'cause I'm friends with my landlord's son."

"Patrick, I am not kidding. Painkillers get me through the day. Without them, working is impossible."

"You know how much it costs."

I gouge my nails into my arm until they break the skin and sweet relief floods into my body. "I can't afford them, but I can give you a hundred-dollar advance."

"Girl, there's nothing free in my world. And it's probably best you don't touch them for a while. They're addicting."

"Thank you for that fascinating insight. I know they're dangerous."

The dazed look disappears from his face as my voice carries across the pavement. "Chill. I'm not giving you more without payment. Sorry." He leans into his seat. "Why don't you ask your doctor?"

"They're not easy to get. Doctors are afraid to prescribe them." The pain in my stomach returns with an agonizing throb, eclipsing my nails gouging deep marks into my arm.

Patrick stares. "Maybe you should, like, invest in a stress ball?"

Choke on a dick. "Thanks for nothing."

"My pleasure," he drawls.

I stand from the bench and hobble toward my car. Agony shoots into my gut with every step. When I collapse into my Toyota's seat, a band of sweat streaks my forehead.

This is bad.

I can't work, and it's Amit's fault. Amit, that corporate-loving, micromanaging prick. He loves to lord what little power his manager position has. I knew he was a waste of space, but I never guessed he'd steal from a dying woman. Without that income, I can forget about replacing the six hundred dollars he stole.

He'll beg for my forgiveness before I'm done with him.

Watching the store, I wait for him to leave. Minutes later, a human beach ball rolls out the front doors, waving at customers as they walk in. His brown face shines with perspiration as he begins the arduous trek to his Mazda. He reclines the seat and throws his bag into the back.

If I'm right, and I know I am, this midlife crisis on two feet will head straight for his guilty pleasure before his wife comes home at six. Amit's a simple man with basic needs. He occasionally indulges in a beer at the local craft brewery. Every week, he attends a Warhammer 40k Meetup at the comic book store. When he's alone, he watches anal porn on his large flat-screen TV and doesn't bother closing the blinds. A bill for a subscription to a men's fitness magazine is mailed to his house each month, despite his lack of interest in exercise. I'm a magpie, hoarding bits of useless personal information as a plan swirls in my mind.

Amit starts his car. I turn the key, and my Toyota roars to life. Backing out, I watch Amit drive his tiny Mazda to the main road. I follow at a safe distance. Staying a block behind will prevent most people from realizing they're being followed.

Amit drives like the tedious jerk he is, stopping at yellow lights so that it takes twice as long to get to Target. When he strolls through the automatic red doors, he spends a good fifteen minutes rifling through the bargain bin DVDs at the front of the store. I follow him as he wanders to the Electronics department and points at something expensive under the glass. He reaches into his wallet and pulls out a fistful of cash. My vision blackens from the blood rushing to my head.

Is he buying a game console with my money?

I recognize the rectangular-shaped boxes with the red corners. They retail at roughly four hundred dollars.

Amit tucks the box under his arm and heads toward the exit. I turn around, seized by a vicious urge to grab a baseball bat from the sports display and chase Amit through the store.

The money's gone. Just like that. Amit couldn't care less. I'll spend the next month on my bed, twisting in my sheets as I writhe in pain so acute that stars burst in my head. He won't give a damn that I'll be too sick to work. If I'm not coming in anymore, the bastard will have a cast-iron excuse to fire me.

I imagine rear-ending Amit's Mazda as I follow him to his place in Daly City. Under the darkening sky, I watch him unbox his Nintendo and play video games for half an hour. Then he changes to porn and falls asleep with his hand halfway down his pants.

Watching him is torture. If I stay, I'll throw a brick through the window.

Giving up, I start the car and drive. My guts scream the whole way home, which is just as well because I have nothing to eat. I park and drag myself into my apartment, ignoring a text from Tom. Even he can't make this better.

I was counting on that money.

I could grit my teeth and push my plans back another month or two. Amit will feel superior for getting the best of me until the Nintendo loses its shine and he moves onto the next toy. I could let it go, but I won't.

Letting him get away with what he did can't happen. I have a moral imperative to bring him to justice. And more than that, I want to rub his nose raw against the dirt. A manager position at Ross Hardware Store does not make him God, and it's time he remembered that.

I consider my options. Buying a gun and storming the office would get me a life sentence without parole. Killing him anywhere else presents me with a similar complication: I have no idea how to remove a body, and I can't just Google it. The solution to my problem has to be nonviolent.

What do men like Amit have in common?

I collapse into the sofa and pull my laptop from the coffee table. I scan his Facebook for clues. No children. A wife through arranged marriage. Saanvi. She wears a pink sari I recognize from the few times she's attended company parties. He must bring her because everyone hates him and she's a sweetheart who makes amazing butter chicken.

What else is there?

I push the laptop away and check my cell. I swipe through the screen. Then it hits me—Tinder.

Yes.

I re-download the app and shove the phone aside while I search my computer for a stock image to catfish him. Assuming he's on Tinder, he's probably on other websites. A few clicks and I'm logged into OkCupid where I hunt for men thirty-five and older with below-average height. I scroll down, scanning pages until I find him.

Clicking his profile, I do a quick read-through. He lists his body type as normal. Lying scum. A list of favorite movies and books comprise his About Me section, along with two lines on his passion for customer service. Jesus, what a bore.

I skip to the "What I'm Looking For" paragraph and recite it with a laugh. "I'm searching for a partner in crime, someone who will be the co-captain of my ship." One of his photos has Saanvi cropped out. My stomach turns as I flip through them.

This won't be hard at all.

In five minutes I've found a stock image of an attractive Indian woman who isn't hot enough to raise suspicions but will catch his attention. I create a fake persona on Tinder and upload the photo, adding grainy filters over the picture. My username is HappyWanderer. That'll appease Amit's cheesy sentimentality. I've got the good girl vibe, but my profile makes it clear I'm looking for a fling. HappyWanderer loves long walks and is into anal.

He won't be able to resist.

Laughing, I narrow my search to a ten-mile radius and swipe left until I find him. Only takes a few passes before his goofy photo splashes on my phone. I swipe right. I've barely put my cell down before the app beams with a message.

Hungasaurus: Do you work on a chicken farm? Cuz you look like you can handle a cock. ;)

HappyWanderer: Haha. You have a way with words.

Hungasaurus: Bet ur tight. Send me pics.

HappyWanderer: Show me yours first.

He does. I close my eyes and try to erase the mental image of Amit's shriveled balls. When I've recovered, I take screenshots of the conversation and his dating profile, which I forward to my computer. Opening Photoshop, I enlarge the images and print them. The pages chug out sluggishly.

I make fifteen copies and arrange them in a stack on the coffee table, whistling as I work. Deleting the Tinder app from my phone is cathartic. For a moment the pain dulls to a distant roar as I crawl into bed. The bastard won't know what hit him. I grin in the darkness, thinking of Amit passed out on the couch.

It's the last good night's sleep he'll get in a long time.

12

MELISSA

"It's a surprise." As soon as I say the magic word, Stacy stops fussing with the car seat.

Her eyes go round. "Surprise?"

"Yes." I buckle her seatbelt, smoothing golden curls from her face. "We're going to see Daddy at work."

A frown wrinkles her forehead. No doubt she imagined something more exciting. A trip to the zoo or Mitchell's Ice Cream.

Too bad.

I shut the door to my Lexus and wave at the porch, where my neighbor stands with Grayson. He wanted to stay behind, and Barbara volunteered to babysit. I glower at the empty spot in my driveway. The Tesla is in the shop for repairs yet again. I'm regretting that ridiculous purchase, but it's not like I can suggest selling the car. Tom's in love with the damn thing, and after he told me the truth, I don't want the fight.

In the spirit of repairing things with my husband, I thought I'd surprise Tom with lunch. Pho was our go-to when we started dating, and God willing, Stacy will enjoy the savory broth and noodles. There's a hole-in-the-wall near his work we could try.

I tap my phone, thumb hovering over my email. Mission Digital is noise—I shouldn't let it affect me like this. There are more important things.

I hold my breath as I click, searching for a response from Emily. Nothing.

"Are we going now?" Stacy pipes up behind me.

The anxiety dims to a slow burn. "Yes."

Sighing, I put the phone away and start the car. I roll out of the driveway, wincing at the sight of my dead lawn, and head down the sloping hill. Stacy sings along to children's music booming from the stereo as I drive to South San Francisco, halfway to the mecca of tech in Silicon Valley.

Once there, I park in the giant lot next to his building, close to the sprawling biotech campuses. Remorse tugs at my heart as I step outside the car and take Stacy's hand. His work isn't the same as the dingy office I rented in Union Square for my company, but it's in the same world. Sometimes I long for the days of my crappy apartment in the East Bay, when it was just me and a laptop. I wasn't Tech Girl, founder of a startup that rocketed to success. There was no pressure to keep investors happy by releasing tedious updates and new features. All I'd wanted was to code my project in peace.

Stacy tugs at me, walking toward the building's revolving doors. "I wanna see Daddy!"

My spirits brighten at her wide smile. "Okay, let's go."

I grab the glass door marked with dozens of fingerprints and Stacy races inside. Once my sneakers hit the marble floor, the cool circulated air chills me to the bone. A blonde woman in a black polo and slacks looks up from reception and smiles at my daughter. "Hey," she says. "What are you doing here?"

Stacy lifts on her toes, not quite reaching the counter. "Wanna see Daddy."

I steady her as I slide my license across the white desk. "It's me again."

The receptionist's dark eyes gleam. "Here for lunch? That's great. You can go up."

Thanking her, I grab the visitor's pass and head toward security. A quick swipe of the card turns the stile green, and I walk through the gate. Stacy mashes her palm against the elevator button, jabbering away. The ride to his floor fills my daughter with transports of delight. "Let's do it again!"

Smiling, I stroke her curls. "Later, honey. Let's go see Daddy."

The doors hiss open, and I step into a bullpen maze, searching for my husband. A gasp drags my attention to a small Asian woman with wire-framed glasses who beckons at Stacy. "Look at you! Oh, you're so cute."

My daughter reaches for the bowl of golden sweets perched on her desk. "That's not yours," I chide.

With a dumbfounded expression, she releases the brightly wrapped candies. "Sorry."

"It's fine. Have some." The woman grabs peppermints and offers them to Stacy. "My name is Penny. What's yours?"

She doesn't waste a second diving her fingers into the bowl. "Stacy. I'm five."

"Nice to meet you," Penny says.

We really should get going. "I'm Melissa, Tom Daughtry's wife. Is he here?"

"Yeah, of course. He's there." She points in the distance. "You sent him those flowers, right? So adorable!"

"What?" The levity from meeting someone charmed with my daughter evaporates.

"They came in this morning," she says brightly. "A courier brought them in."

I ignore the pounding in my head, lips tightening. "Ah." I bury the frantic voice urging for calm. It can't be. I'm jumping to conclusions. "Can you watch her for a second? I'll be back."

"Sure." Penny stands and gives her seat to Stacy.

Relax. They could be from anyone.

With that in mind, I walk toward Tom's cubicle. I spot his golden mane as he pores over a laptop screen. A mousy-haired woman hangs on the wall, gesturing at the giant vase of stemmed red roses.

I stop. *Breathe, Melissa.*

He stands, frowning. Grabbing the heart-shaped card from the stems, he reads it and crumples the note in his fist. The coworker brightens when he hands the flowers to her. "Really?"

I read his lips: "Keep it."

Happily, she slides the glass onto her desk and arranges the roses while my husband tosses the shredded paper in the trash.

Tom's mother wouldn't send a bouquet of deep-red roses with a heart-shaped note. Too cheesy and sentimental—it's something a young woman might do.

A sharp pain hits my chest.

The way he foisted the gift onto his coworker proves his embarrassment. He doesn't want to be associated with them. He lied, and I bought it. Hook, line, sinker.

I turn away from my husband, nausea pitting my stomach.

The lie sinks into my skin, spreading through tissue like a parasitic growth. Who is she? Is she one of the women in this room?

I glance at Tom, ready to tear my throat raw at the sight of another woman sliding her arm around his waist, but he's alone.

I can't do this now.

Walking back to Penny, I hold Stacy's hand and lead her away from the cubicle. "We have to go." I wave off Penny's concern and march toward the elevators.

I can't fall apart.

Stacy looks behind her. "Mommy, where's Daddy?"

"He's too busy, honey." Throat thick with tears, I stab the elevator button. "I'll take you somewhere nice for lunch."

"McDonald's?"

"Sure." It's a mark of how upset I am that I'm willing to accept a fast food chain.

I fight the wave of grief. Losing control in front of my daughter isn't an option. I need to pull it together and bury the pain. Compartmentalize it, just like the cancer.

Stacy squeals with excitement as the bell chimes. Inside, she jumps with the descent of the elevator. I follow and push the lobby button with shaking hands. The metallic doors slide shut. I stare at my reflection, quietly judging the T-shirt and jeans. Did I let myself go? Is that why he's cheating on me?

"Mommy," Stacy says, suddenly quiet. "Are you crying?"

My cheeks are wet. I smile through a haze of mist. "It's okay, baby."

I don't know what to do. I wasn't looking for more evidence of an affair, but *flowers*? Someone sent them with a heart-fucking-shaped note. He tore it apart. Was it from a lover he spurned? Or was he angry they were sent to his work?

It doesn't matter. Our marriage is over.

The swell rises to my throat and blocks my air. My palm makes a wet streak on the wall as I brace myself. Sobs wrack through my chest.

I feel a gentle touch. Stacy's hand grasps mine. "Don't cry, Mommy."

Affection for my daughter drowns the roar of betrayal. I sink down, wrapping my arms around her small body. Her warmth pulses through my chest, softening the sharp edges of pain.

My children are all that matter. Through them, I'll find my strength. They're the reason I refuse to spend all day in bed. I can't tear their lives apart without all the facts. I owe my children the truth, and all I have is a piece of cardboard in the shape of a heart.

That's not enough.

13

AUBREY

HE DIDN'T EVEN *THANK* me. I sent the flowers and received nothing in return, not even a lousy text. It's been a whole week since I've heard his voice. I'm a patient woman, but my patience isn't without limits.

What's his excuse this time?

We'll have to talk seriously about this—soon. I am not a mind reader, and it'd be nice to receive a message once in a while reminding me how amazing I am. I know Tom loves me. He's capable of being romantic; I've experienced it firsthand. He needs to stop acting so comfortable around me.

The phone slips into my pocket as I greet the next customer. A pack of fertilizer rolls into my fingers. I scan the code as the speaker crackles.

"Attention Ross employees. Aubrey, please report to the office immediately." Amit's disembodied voice shakes with fury. "Aubrey De Rosa, please report to the office. Thank you."

From the next aisle, Zac looks at me, mouthing, *What did you do?*

I shrug and glance at the ceiling as though Amit is hovering above us like a malignant god.

He found them. Let the games begin.

A thrill runs through my chest as I flip the register's light to closed, grimacing at the queue of people. "Sorry, I have to go."

Amit must be frantic. I made sure to post our scintillating conversation all over the employee break room, complete with hi-res photos of his stubby chubby. I picture him shredding the evidence in his office while screaming a colorful stream of epithets. Strolling, I head toward the gardening aisle where the Employees Only door stands between racks of fertilizer. I force my lips to flatten in a neutral line. The security cameras can't catch me smirking.

My hand shakes as I slide my keycard. The lock clicks and I step inside.

The break room is empty. Everyone who clocked in this morning must have already seen the prints. I wish I could've been there to squeal in disgust and praise whoever did it with the others. A Hot Pocket wrapper lies crumpled on the table, probably Mike's. How the hell did he eat while staring at Amit's penis?

Bits of tape are stuck to the lockers, but the photos are gone. Their shredded remains are buried deep in the wastebasket. Amit stands in the middle of his office, his hands balled into fists. He steps into the light, thrusting his terror into sharp relief.

"Hey, Amit." I smile at him. "You needed something?"

"What the fuck did you do?" he hisses, throwing a wild look at the door.

A frown creases my forehead as my insides jump with glee.

"Wow. I don't appreciate the foul language. Isn't swearing against the code of conduct?"

The ground shakes with Amit's thunderous steps. "The photos! I know you had something to do with them."

"I have no idea—"

He slams his ham-like fist onto his desk, upsetting a pile of letters that slide to the floor. "Stop lying!"

Crossing my arms, I stare daggers at him. "I don't like your tone."

"You're fired," he snarls, inches from my face. "Finished!"

I brush the flecks of spit from my cheek. "You probably want to take a step back and reevaluate. I did nothing wrong."

Amit's mustache trembles with rage. "Are you kidding me? Look at these filthy photos—you did this!"

He grabs a picture that escaped the shredder and thrusts it into my hands. Laughing, I read the chat log. "Looks like you were the one saying disgusting things."

He utters a mad scream of frustration. "You did this!"

"How am I supposed to have done this? You know I'm a woman, right? I don't have a dick."

"You found me on Tinder—you pretended to be this person so you could steal my photos and ruin me! I can't have this in my life."

"Hold on. You think I'm the Happy Wanderer?" Chuckling, I toss the photo to the floor. "That's ridiculous, Amit. Why would I do that?"

His mustache billows. "You know why!"

"Are you referring to the cash you stole?"

He points at me. "I stole nothing!"

"And I didn't catfish you last night."

The desk trembles as he rests his sizable bulk against the edge, his face pale. "I can't breathe."

I watch him clutch his chest. "Your wife would appreciate a copy of those photos."

"No!"

"Why not?" He sputters and gasps. "She should know her husband's fooling around on Tinder. Whoever did this has a strong sense of justice. Just my guess."

Regaining some of his color, he shakes his finger in my face. "You do this, and I swear to God. I'll make you wish you've never been born."

"Do your worst." Doubt flickers in his eyes. "Fire me. Don't fire me. It doesn't matter. I won't be long for this world anyway. You, however, will have to live down this for the rest of your life. Think of the shame you'll bring your family when this gets emailed to your mother-in-law. Or the district manager. Amanda Underwood? She might not like one of her store managers sending filthy messages to women."

"What do you want?" he shrieks.

"My money back, for starters. Six hundred dollars plus interest for your unauthorized loan."

Trembling, he takes a seat at the table. "I'm not a thief, I swear."

"You stole from a dying woman."

"Who has a drug habit." Angry, he lifts his head. "Don't think I can't report you."

"Not before I ruin your life with those photos."

Moaning, he drops into his hands. "Promise you won't tell her."

"As long as you do everything I say, she'll never find out. You will continue sending me paychecks, but I'm not coming into work anymore. I decided you were right. Retail isn't the best fit for me."

He blinks. "K-keep you on the clock? I can't do that!"

"Then I hope you enjoy a bitter custody battle over your dog."

He drops to his slacks, clinging to my vest. "No, please! I swear to God—I'll do what you say!"

I wrench his hands off my clothes. "Good. Six hundred by the end of the day."

"You'll have it, I promise!"

"I better." My feet scrape the carpet as he stands. "And I want my goddamn oxy back."

"The bottle is in my desk." Amit grabs his white dress shirt and dabs at his eyes.

I open the drawers and find it, pocketing the pills. "What the hell are you crying for? You got off easy."

He mutters something indistinct as my skull pounds. The idiot does not understand what it's like to have his days numbered. If he had an inkling of the pain he's caused since he confiscated my meds, he'd beg for forgiveness.

Somehow angrier than I was coming in, I leave the room and head out the sliding doors. A storm rolled in late last night, sprinkling a fine mist that put an end to the dry spell.

My phone buzzes with a text from Mike: *Did you see the pics? LOL.*

Nothing from Tom.

I am an afterthought.

I am not even worth five minutes of time, and yet every week he puts his mouth on my tits.

He needs to learn a lesson too.

14

AUBREY

I STEP into the refrigerated cold of the grocery store. Bypassing the floral department, I head for the misted vegetables, where Melissa spends most of her money. She's a health nut and eats her weight in spinach every week. I pretend to browse the Washington apples as I peer at the shoppers, but I don't spot her anywhere.

This is reckless, but he leaves me no choice. Love isn't a switch I can turn on and off. I miss him. More than anything, I want Tom's arms wrapped around me. I can't stand the weeks of silence following days of nonstop texting. The way he treats me is unacceptable, and I let it slide for too long.

I am not his plaything.

Navigating the aisles, I walk past shelves of chocolate candy. My mouth waters at a bag of Almond Joy. I grab one.

Something runs into my legs with a shriek. A whirlwind of pink and blonde bounces from my body, landing on the floor. The girl in pigtails stares at me, blue eyes welling with tears.

Stacy?

I bite back her name, but I'd recognize those chubby cheeks anywhere. It's hard not to with Melissa posting photo shoots on Facebook every month.

If Stacy's here, Melissa can't be far behind.

"Are you okay?" I help her upright.

The little girl frowns. "I can do it myself!"

Damn. What a spitfire. "Sorry if I hurt you."

"I'm fine." Stacy fixes me with a stern eye so much like her father's.

Fascinating.

She's a pint-sized version of Tom, complete with the cowlick and head of golden hair, soft to the touch. Her grubby hands rip open the wrapper of a Mars bar.

"Stacy!" a hysterical voice calls from the other end of the aisle.

Melissa pushes a cart. A swell of jealousy curdles my stomach at how radiant she looks with her locks tied in a loose bun. White-blonde tendrils frame her elfin face. She wears a green, airy blouse with black polka dots.

Stacy bites into the chocolate bar. Melissa stops. "What did I tell you about running in the store?"

Stacy shrugs. "Don't do it?"

Sighing, Melissa points toward her side. "Get over here now." Stacy obeys, stomping her feet.

I move away. Melissa halts, suddenly recognizing me. "Oh, hey!"

I feign surprise. "Wow. How's it going?"

She lets out another sigh. "All right. Or it would be if someone would let me shop in peace." She brushes her daughter's head in an affectionate gesture that makes my heart clench. "Stacy, this is Mommy's friend, Aubrey."

Friend. She called me her friend. "Nice to meet you."

Stacy manages a shy smile before disappearing behind her mother's legs. "I wanted to thank you for the other day—inviting me to your house. I needed that."

"Anytime. You're always welcome—"

The sight of a blond man steals my breath. Tom peeks into the aisle with an armful of groceries, Grayson following close.

Oh God.

Melissa waves at him, and Tom approaches the cart dressed in khakis and a dark knit, depositing the goods. He frisks Grayson's wheat hair, his gaze sweeping over me like I'm a piece of furniture.

The indifference wrenches my heart. I stare at him, willing some sign of recognition.

Sensing nothing odd, Melissa smiles at him. "Tom, come meet my friend. This is Aubrey from the support group."

"Oh! Hi there," he says with a convincing amount of surprise.

"Nice to meet you, Tom." He doesn't blink at the emphasis on his name, even when he shakes my hand and I squeeze too hard.

"We were just getting things for dinner," Melissa says. "Actually, would you like to join us tonight?"

Tom turns his head too quickly. He makes a face and rubs his neck. "Er—is that a good idea, honey?"

"Of course it is!" Melissa's broad smile gives away nothing. "Please say you'll come. We'd love to have you."

I should decline.

I should tell her I'm not interested, but he glossed over me like a random item on the shelf.

I fucking *matter*.

"Sure."

"Great." She pulls her iPhone from her purse and we exchange phone numbers. She also tells me their address, which of course I already know. "Is seven okay?"

"Yeah."

Tom's unpleasant frown burns in my head the moment I turn my back. An angry stream of text messages pings my cell.

Tom: *Don't come.*

Me: *I'm coming.*

Tom: *You can't.*

Me: *I'm going. She invited me.*

Tom: *Why are you doing this?*

My thumb hovers on the screen, bile gathering at the base of my throat. The answer will always be the same.

Because I love you.

15

MELISSA

Tom's angry enough to kill. I pretend I don't notice the clench in his jaw. In stony silence, he drives us home with a white-knuckled grip on the steering wheel.

Having people over used to be a point of pride for Tom. When I was Tech Girl and my startup was the talk of Silicon Valley, he'd invite his friends, open a bottle of Opus One, and spend the night talking about my achievements as though he helped them become successes.

That changed when I got sick.

Tom was uncomfortable with guests firing question after question about the cancer. Even more embarrassing was our financial situation. How would we explain the state of the lawn to our rich friends? With family, the predicament was the same. Neither of us wanted to admit failure to our parents. The illness is yet another dirty secret. They know I'm sick, not that it's fatal.

Screw this.

If I have to tolerate flowers, movie tickets, and his late-night appearances, he'll sit through one dinner.

Once home, I start work in the kitchen. Tom spirits away to his man cave as I keep one eye on the kids and the other on my Bolognese sauce. It simmers on the stove as I watch the clock. At five minutes before seven, a chime hits the ceiling.

Tom's nowhere to be seen. "Grayson, can you get that?"

Grayson rises from the couch and strides to the door. Opening it, he stands back. "Hello. Welcome to our house."

"Thank you!" Aubrey's laughter fills the house. "You're so cute."

"May I take that?"

My heart bursts with pride as Grayson folds her wool jacket over his arms.

"Such a gentleman. And they say chivalry is dead." Aubrey steps through in an A-line black dress with a ribbon tied around her waist. "What's your name, sweetie?"

He hangs the coat in a closet. "Grayson."

"I'm Aubrey."

"I know," he says. "I saw you at the store."

"Good memory." Aubrey smiles at Grayson, who beams at the compliment. "I have flowers."

Aubrey's heels click as she wanders into the kitchen with an armful of a twelve-dollar bouquet they sell at Safeway.

"Oh, you shouldn't have. They're beautiful." I search for my husband, who finally stumbles into view. "Tom, look at what she brought us!"

Tom doesn't want to look at anything. I get a whiff of stale drink as he walks past me in a shirt half-tucked into his waist. He looks like he rolled out of bed. "Oh," he says with perfect indifference. "How nice."

Would it kill him to run a comb through his hair?

I take the wildflowers from Aubrey, grabbing a tall glass from the cupboard. With a pair of scissors, I snap the stems and drop the blossoms inside the vase, setting them next to the roses. I bought the same arrangement that Tom's mistress sent him. A few hours of Googling, and I found the florist. Sweet Buds sells cuttings from weddings at a reduced rate. It was worth it to see Tom's bewilderment when they arrived this morning by courier. He keeps glancing at them with a widened gaze that screams *guilty*.

Aubrey's gaze wanders the vast ceiling, the portraits on the wall, the furnishings. "Damn, you have an amazing home."

"Thanks." I gesture toward the plate of cheese sitting on the counter. "Help yourself."

Aubrey's bony hand seizes a cracker. She takes tiny bites, like a squirrel. Tom watches her eat with raised eyebrows. "So what do you do for a living?"

Aubrey finishes the biscuit, dusting her hands. "I'm a cashier at a hardware store."

"Oh," he says in a voice that makes me cringe. "Is it interesting?"

"It keeps me busy." She shrugs. "Anything that forces me to be active is good."

I agree. "That's why I'm at the gym all the time."

"Yeah, yoga's turned out to be amazing." A smile tugs at her lips. "I thought it was bullshit, but you do feel a difference after each class."

"Tell that to Tom!" I elbow his side, and he glares. "He's always going on about how I should stay home and sip more green shakes."

She shudders. "Listen, if I could eat I would. Whatever you're cooking smells incredible, though."

"Want anything to drink?" Tom shuffles toward the fridge. "Wine? Seltzer?"

"Whatever's fine," she says with a nervous giggle.

"Open the chardonnay, honey." I shut the burners off and ladle pasta onto plates. "My mom passed down this recipe. Every Sunday it was all about the gravy."

"Mine wasn't the greatest cook," Aubrey admits. "I ate a ton of tasteless ground beef boiled in the microwave, so anything from a stove is fancy."

"We still had boxed food." Shaking my head, I think about those countless cartons of Instant Mac. "Sometimes I wonder...if my diet had been a little better, would I have cancer?"

A loud pop interrupts Aubrey's response as Tom opens a bottle and pours two glasses. Having alcohol is strictly against my nutrition plan, but I pluck a glass and ignore Tom's narrowed gaze.

"I'll get the kids," he utters, carrying his wine with him.

"Great." I roll my eyes at his back.

Aubrey takes a sip of her drink, staining the rim pink. "Can I help you with anything?"

"Oh, god no. Everything's under control." I grab the last bowl. Thick Bolognese sauce pours over tagliatelle pasta. The roasted tomatoes and basil force images of our honeymoon in Florence into my mind.

A lump bulges in my throat, refusing to go down.

Tom and I used to be so happy.

Blinking rapidly, I take plates of food and set the table.

Aubrey helps me with the dishes, her face brightening when Tom reenters the room with the kids.

Amused, I watch as she toys with her hair, giving a strand a quick tug. A flush rises in her pale cheeks when she notices my stare. She's not the first friend who's had a crush on Tom, and she won't be the last.

Would Aubrey still glow at him if she knew my husband was a cheat?

Tom ushers the children to their seats. Stacy, dressed in overalls with a purple dinosaur, frowns at her bowl. "I'm not hungry."

Getting her to cooperate at mealtimes is a constant battle. "You need to eat, sweetie."

Her mouth quivers. "But my tummy hurts."

It worries me how often she complains about her stomach, but the pediatrician assured me they're just pleas for attention. "Finish half the plate."

Stacy's lip buds into a pout.

I take a sip of wine as Tom carries the bottle to the table. Aubrey tears her gaze from my husband to frown at my daughter, who is working herself to a cry. "Are you okay?"

Stacy screws up her face and rubs her stomach. "It hurts."

Exams at the doctor found nothing. "She does this all the time. Ever since the cancer, she's been acting out for attention."

Tom grabs the neck of the bottle, which rocks for a few seconds. "Oops."

"What did you say you did for a living?" Aubrey asks my husband.

"Software engineer," he grunts. "At Inicorp. I'm in the middle of a big project."

A sweet smile tiptoes across her thin face. "Right. Lots of late nights?"

He opens his mouth, but I speak first. "Tom finds all kinds of reasons to work into the night."

Aubrey spoons a mouthful of the tagliatelle. "Wow, this is good!"

At least someone appreciates it. Tom nudges the food as though it's cold porridge, opting instead for the wine. Grayson eats the pasta untouched with sauce. Stacy folds her arms in silent protest.

Guess I'm on my own as far as conversation goes. "Do you have a bucket list, Aubrey?"

Aubrey pauses. The fork hovering at her mouth trembles. "Yeah, um, sort of."

Tom shoots an unhappy look across the table. "Do we need to discuss this right now?"

"What?" The tomatoes singe my taste buds. It's been so long I've tasted anything this good.

He doesn't approve. "Depressing topic."

"Funny. You didn't say that on our night out." I turn away from Tom, watching Aubrey's face drain of color. "You know what I want to do? Climb Machu Picchu. Scaling those ruins has always been one of my dreams. I wanted to visit with Tom, but then we got pregnant."

Aubrey fingers the stem of her wineglass. "I guess I'd like to go to Rome."

"We've been there. It's beautiful. You should go."

She smiles wryly. "Maybe. Not really in my budget."

Tom stabs at the plate, uninterested in contributing beyond a few grunts.

Aubrey braves another attempt at conversation. "Do you enjoy your work?"

"No. I mean, it's not what I wanted to do." He glances at her like a sullen teenager, shrugging. "A job's a job."

My teeth grind at his response. I'd kill to be on my feet working instead of wondering what the hell my husband's up to.

"Oh, what did you want to do?" Aubrey asks.

"Well." He shoots me a furtive look. "It isn't practical."

The acidity of the sauce bites my gums. "Don't keep us hanging, Tom."

"Daddy wants to be a pilot," Grayson says. "He told me so himself."

Aubrey stares at my husband. "Really?"

Tom's ears burn as he faces his plate, looking like an overgrown boy. "I love air shows. Always have ever since I was a kid. My dad used to take me to Fleet Week every year to see the Blue Angels."

This is the first I've heard of it. "You didn't tell me that."

"Yeah, I did." He smiles, as though that can erase the edge in his voice. "It was a long time ago."

The wine scorches my throat. "Wow, that's news to me. You'd think a person would mention it more than once or twice if it were a passion."

A tic moves in Tom's jaw. "There never was a right moment to bring it up. It's an expensive hobby. You have to put in thousands of air miles to apply for a license."

I scourge my memory, and something floats to the surface— Tom mentioning flying lessons in passing. There was a Groupon for the first class. I can't remember if he bought it or not.

"The last obsession he had was 3-D printing." I stab the porcelain plate and twist the fork. "Expensive machine. And most companies don't accept refunds."

"I had a business opportunity," he says to Aubrey, face heating like a lamp.

Head swimming, I lean across the table. "We sold it on eBay after a week." My fingers bump into the empty wineglass. I grab the stem, steadying it, and pour more wine. "Aubrey, do you want more?"

Her smile flickers. "I'm good, thanks."

The golden liquid flows like oil. Thick. Pungent. My detox regime strictly forbids alcohol, but screw it. The holistic approach isn't working, and everyone knows it except my dear husband.

Furious, Tom works his jaw. "Melissa."

"Yes?"

He gazes at my wineglass, grimacing. "Honey, I think you've had enough to drink."

No, I haven't. My head's still careening with his betrayal.

Aubrey pulls the plate of greens toward her. "Who's your oncologist, by the way?"

Sweet of her to change the subject. "Dr. Stephen Greene."

"I've never heard of him." She mulls the name, shaking her head. "I thought I researched all the doctors in the city."

Darkness slides into my mind, poisoning the well. Aubrey can't remember him because Dr. Greene doesn't exist. Her confusion stirs an impulse to admit my lie.

Stacy's fork clatters against her plate. Tom sighs as sauce spatters her shirt. "Damn it. Can someone pass me a napkin?"

Leaping from her chair, Aubrey grabs one from the stack. He accepts it from her with a smile. "Thank you."

Blushing, Aubrey takes her seat after murmuring a response.

He dabs at Stacy's turtleneck. "Do you work at the Ross in Daly City?"

Aubrey startles at the question. "Yeah. How'd you know that?"

"I think I've seen you there." He balls the napkin in his fist. "Maybe a few weeks ago."

"Really?" Aubrey says.

I roll my eyes at the hope in her voice. Tom's not interested. He's just being polite.

I drain the last drop and reach for the bottle. My fingers bump into the glass. It topples over onto the dining table, but it's already empty.

"Oops." My face growing warm, I grab the bottle neck and head for the kitchen. Their voices murmur behind me, but I don't pay attention. I want my senses to die.

His voice is like a white-hot poker stabbing me in the gut. "Melissa, is that a good idea?"

I drop the bottle into the recycling bin and rummage through the wine fridge, picking a rosé. Tom bought this junk because it was on sale, but I'll open it. Aubrey won't mind; she drinks from a box for Christ's sake.

I turn my head in his direction, but a few seconds pass before I find him. "What?"

Suddenly I spot him, an amorphous khaki blob. "Babe, I've never seen you like this. What's wrong?"

"Nothing." I dig the sharp hook of the corkscrew into the bottle. Like everything else, it's a lot harder than it should be.

"Melissa." His soft voice flutters across my ear. "*Melissa*."

I stop. "Jesus—what?"

"You're drunk," he hisses. "And you're scaring the kids."

I smirk at the frown knitting his eyebrows. Behind him, Aubrey scrapes her chair and stands. "Um—I should go."

A brief moment of clarity wedges past the fog of alcohol. "No, don't!"

She hesitates. "You both need privacy."

I shove Tom aside and stumble toward Aubrey. "You barely touched your plate!"

"It's fine." She grabs her purse, clearly in a hurry to get the hell out. "I'll—um—see you at yoga?"

Deflated, I watch her shoulder the bag and head out. She waves at my kids. "Bye!"

They echo goodbye back to her as Tom snaps the door shut.

He faces me. "What the fuck was that was about?"

"Daddy!" Stacy yells. "That's a bad word!"

Wrath boils inside me the longer I meet his blues. I hate him for dividing us and forcing me to choose between my dignity and my comfort. And I loathe myself for being unable to bring up the flowers.

I stalk to the dinner table, Tom quick on my heels.

He grabs my elbow. "Don't walk away from me."

I shrug him off. "I had a drink. So what?"

"You embarrassed me, and you made a fool out of yourself." Tom shakes his head, seething. "I don't understand what's wrong with you."

The world spins in violent colors. "I didn't mean to get drunk. I just wanted—"

"What, Melissa?" he snaps. "What could've been worth what you did to yourself?"

I needed to forget you.

Taking my full plate, I walk toward the kitchen and sway in front of the sink. I release it too high. The dish shatters into three jagged pieces, scratching the stainless steel I fought to keep pristine.

Tom seizes my wrist, squeezing hard. "Jesus!"

"It was an *accident*."

"Melissa, you have to stop doing this to yourself." His voice cracks and he takes my hands. "I've had enough. You are sick. Take it seriously."

The desperation, the panic. He sounds convincing. The longer I listen, the more I doubt. I won't let him do that to me.

I stumble from his grasp, pain jarring through my steps as the alcohol gnaws at my stomach. God, I'm going to vomit. I leave Tom in the kitchen, banging off the walls in the hallway as my children's cries echo.

The bathroom is too far away. I grope the wall. Light flares through the room and everything spins. Round and round. My knees crash into the tiles as a violent force rises through my throat. Vile acid bursts from my lips, spraying the floor. My sickness soaks into my jeans. Saliva dangles and my vision clouds over. Sobs choke me as another wave of nausea strikes.

Strong hands lift me upright and smack the toilet seat. He threads my hair, brushing the strands from my mouth. Tom kneels in my vomit. He holds me as I purge the wine. My teeth ache with a familiar burn, and my stomach is hollow.

He keeps holding me. "You're okay, babe. You're okay."

16

AUBREY

A SECOND CONCERNED text from Mike flares across my screen.

Where R u?

I dismiss the notification with a quick flick of my thumb. I'll reply to him later. The kid needs to learn boundaries, but I should've expected my sudden departure from Ross Hardware would raise questions. I'll back whatever narrative Amit sells them as long as my checks arrive in the mail.

"Next one!" Lucy's bold voice echoes in the small studio. "Stretch your arms to the ceiling and tighten those glutes."

Distracted by Lucy's neon headband and pink tank top, I assume the following pose and lose my balance. So does Melissa.

There's something wrong with her.

Yesterday she spent only thirty minutes on the elliptical, and today she can barely get through yoga. The knot of her ponytail is frayed with brassy strands. Her face has lost its healthy glow, replaced by a thick foundation. The straps of her sports bra hang loosely around her shoulders. She's transitioning from lean to dangerously thin.

Melissa wavers for a few moments before giving up. She collapses on her mat, exhausted. Lucy continues the Moon Salutation, ignoring Melissa's slumped over figure. No one seems to notice her. Or care.

Class ends with a fifteen-minute exercise to "control our breathing," which really means "nap." My eyes shutter open when the music cuts and the lights flare on. Chatter spreads as women roll the mats and gather in pastel-colored groups, heading out the door to visit Starbucks.

Melissa watches them go, wiping her forehead with a thin arm. She picks herself off the floor, using the column for support.

Beside me, Emma frowns. "Not looking so good, is she?"

I'm worried. I shouldn't be. "No."

Emma lumbers to her feet, tying a pink sweatshirt around her massive waist. "Maybe you should find out what's up."

"Yeah, I will. Later."

Emma winks and heads out of the studio as I walk toward Melissa, who pretends not to see me. She rips the band from her ponytail. A startlingly thin wave of hair falls down her back. Melissa glances up from studying her chipped fingernails. She meets my gaze, unsmiling.

"Hey." I'm not sure what the hell to say. "You all right?"

"I'm fine." Melissa gouges her thumb, tearing away more teal. "Never been better."

Sarcasm drips from her tongue. She wants me to go away. I walk to the door until she calls for me.

"Wait," Melissa says in a thin voice. "Sorry."

On the floor, she blinks as though staying awake is a chore. I try not to stare. "For what?"

"Dinner the other night." She shakes her head, eyes glistening. "I was a jerk."

After that disaster, I spent the entire evening wondering if Melissa knows about us. I grin weakly. "We all have bad days."

Nodding, she wipes her face. "I'm embarrassed. Dragging you in the middle of our problems was messed up."

The part of me that I thought would be delighted is silent. "It's not a big deal."

Her smile is short-lived. "Thanks."

I need to get a drink in her hand. My stomach clenches. "Let's have a coffee at Starbucks or something."

"No," she says softly. "I can't—I have to go home. And I'm sure you have places to be."

"Honest to God, I don't." My voice drops to a hush. "Look, I know this is weird and uncomfortable, but you seem unhappy. You can talk to me. I'm going through the same things you are."

A tremor of her lips gives away her vulnerability. This pitiful, broken Melissa disturbs me on a visceral level. She's on her way out. Speeding the process should be easy, except poisoning her now feels worse than when she was in peak physical condition, like kicking a dog while it's down.

"Okay," she sighs. "Let's go."

Instead of Starbucks, Melissa suggests a Japanese crêperie a few doors away. Reading the menu, I gape at all the choices— buckwheat, gluten-free, organic. She orders a Nutella crepe topped with whipped cream, which is totally unlike her, and I order the cheapest one on the board. I offer to pay, but Melissa swipes her card.

I fill two plastic water cups and carry them to a glossy white table. Damn this place for being so brightly lit. I doubt I could spike her drink without being caught on camera. I eye the black domes in the ceiling as Melissa grabs our paper plates, sliding a mound of fresh strawberries and syrup in front of my nose.

She sits, her fork piercing a mountain of whipped cream. She hesitates before opening her lips. "I'm not supposed to have this. It'll make me sick."

"I tell myself that every time I pour another glass of boxed wine."

Melissa swipes the white foam across her tongue, shuddering at the taste. "Wow." She spears a slice of crepe and pops it in her mouth. "This is amazing."

I play with my strawberries, stomach turning at the sweetness. "So what's going on with you?"

Her shoulders tense. "Nothing—I haven't been sleeping much. Or eating." Cheerful music plays in the background as Melissa's eyes mist. "Everything's gone wrong."

I peel a napkin from the stack and offer it to her. "What do you mean?"

"Thanks." She dabs her cheeks, careful not to smudge her blush. "I'm just being hit with a thousand things at once, and I don't know what to do."

"Is this about Tom?"

Tears slip down her chin. "He's having an affair."

And she has no idea it's with me. "Did you show him the tickets? How did you find out?"

My lungs tighten as though an invisible hand reached through my ribs. The dull ache worsens with Melissa's quiet attempts to stifle her crying.

This wasn't supposed to happen. I can't sympathize with the woman I need to murder, but perhaps that option was stolen from me months ago. From day one, I worshipped Melissa's perfect life. Learned everything about her.

Now it's come full circle to bite me in the ass.

"Yeah, I talked to him about them. He said he went to see it—a romantic comedy of all things—with a friend, and like an idiot, I believed him. The kicker was when I saw a bouquet at his desk. They were from another woman."

Heat slowly rises up my face. "Did you read the note?"

"No. He didn't know I was there." She pokes at her crepe without enthusiasm. "Every day is a struggle, and now I have to deal with him cheating. I can't handle this on top of everything else I'm supposed to do. I don't want to talk to him about it."

"That's crazy. You have to."

"Do I?" She shrugs helplessly. "Let's say I gather evidence, divorce him, and win a custody battle. At the end of all that, I'm still going to die. It hurts so much that he doesn't respect me anymore. I mean, we built a life together. Two kids and he's out with some...some whore doing god knows what." She blots her face with the napkin, which is soaked through.

"The point is you pass away with dignity, surrounded by the people you love." I stab at my crepe, the brown sugar like sand in my teeth. "What are you going to do with him?"

The question seems to take her off guard. "The only thing I've committed to is writing him out of the will."

My plastic fork snaps into the paper. "What—why?"

Her nostrils flare. "He's not getting any of my money when I'm gone."

That could present a problem for us. "But—what about the kids?"

"They'll be fine. I'll put everything in a trust and name my mother as the benefactor. Once that's done, I don't know."

Wait. "You'll file for divorce, right?"

She shakes her head. "No."

I stare at her. What does she mean? "Why not?"

Miserable, she shrugs. "I'm sick."

"Yeah, but—"

"I barely have the strength to leave bed. And we have two children. I can't force a separation on them while their mother is dying."

Jesus. "Don't you think they will appreciate a less chaotic home?"

"That's exaggerating."

Be careful, Aubrey. "I just—I dunno. As someone who's lived through two parents fighting all the time, divorcing is easier on the kids."

"Not for mine. They've been through enough already."

A blender roars to life, the shrieking piercing my ear.

"Anyway," she says, shouting over the noise. "That's what I have planned so far."

My mind wrestles with guilt and pain. She plans to leave Tom destitute, and it's my fault. What Tom and I have is as real as the pulse through my head, the gnawing agony working to end my life, and now that she finally knows...she'll do nothing?

I don't get it. This isn't the Melissa I've followed for months. What happened to the assertive type A woman who couldn't let go of something she overheard?

Where's her outrage?

Melissa grimaces at the noise. "My appointment is in half an hour."

My jaw is clenched tight. "For what?"

"Oh, this holistic doctor I've been seeing. They call them vitamin B boosters. My energy levels are always better after them."

I must've heard wrong. "A naturopath?"

"Yeah. I go to him twice a week for infusions."

She sees a quack to treat her cancer.

Disbelief hardens to rage. All my pity for her vanishes. I thought she was different. She's not. Melissa is just like those rich idiots in yoga class, with their endless rotations of enemas and juice cleanses. It's bad enough when healthy people put their bodies through hell, but this is a personal insult. While the rest of us have to scrimp and save to afford our insurance premiums, Melissa spends her cash on nonsense.

Whatever, right? It's her money.

I can't accept that. She could've used that wealth to donate to research. You know, the actual institutions that help fight diseases like cancer. I thought I made my peace with the disease months ago, but the unfairness rails in my chest.

Melissa frowns. "Something wrong?"

A voice inside me screams to shut up. "I don't understand why someone like you would believe in that crap."

A moment of stunned silence passes.

"That crap?" Red patches of fury rise in her cheeks. "What's your problem?"

Back down and apologize. "If you looked in the mirror lately, you'd realize you were wasting your money."

Her chair smacks the floor as she stands abruptly. Furious, she seizes her purse, looking every bit as dangerous as she did when she told off Lucy. "You don't know me, Aubrey. Or my family."

If I ever want to be with Tom, I need to grovel. Now.

But I just can't do it. "You're a wealthy woman. You could do many things with that cash. Instead, you douse it with gasoline and light it on fire."

"I'm not rich." Tears darkened with mascara slip down her cheeks. "And it's none of your goddamn business what I do with my body."

Shut your mouth, Tom's voice growls. *You want her to hate you?*

No, I don't.

Shooting me one last withering glance, Melissa storms out of the café. Her hair fans like a gold banner as she walks past the glass windows, a tissue balled to her face.

17

MELISSA

Tom was out late last night. *Again.*

This time it was an after-work cocktail hour he couldn't get away from. His boss wanted to celebrate the launch of a new product, and as an engineer who worked on the project, he was required to go. Facebook seems to corroborate his story. Tom's coworkers posted selfies with festive backdrops and tagged my husband, whose cheesy grin I don't recognize. He looks like he belongs in a frat with that goofy smile and the red plastic cup in his hand. A young woman with a Roman nose clings to his arm.

Is that her?

The whiskey pours like water. It burns my lips and unsettles my stomach. I keep drinking anyway, as though I'll find the answer to my marital crisis written on the glass. At seven o'clock, I rifled through the pantry and found an old brand of Canadian booze tucked in the corner with a Christmas card still attached to the neck. It's not bad mixed with coffee, but it scorches a path down my throat.

In the bedroom, Tom gets ready for work. I listen to his passive-aggressive sighs and the gurgle of the iron as he attempts to make himself presentable. Every so often he shoots me an impatient look as he stands there, shirtless. The sight of him used flutter the butterflies in my stomach. I'd smooth my hands over the corded muscles rippling through his arms and trace the trail of dark hair leading straight down.

I study him and wonder where the bitch has touched him.

Tom stabs a button on the iron, shooting water onto the carpet. "Damn."

I smile at him over my phone's screen like the empty-headed wife I'm pretending to be. "Keep trying; you'll get it."

His eyes cut at me. Oops, did that sound too dry?

"Honey, I was wondering if you had any ideas for Stacy's birthday."

Shrugging, I drop the phone aside and cross my arms. "We'll have a cake and invite everyone for tacos."

He hesitates. "What kind?"

"Pulled pork and ground beef, I guess."

He winces. "I just—I don't know. Aren't tacos a bit pedestrian?"

I stare at him. "It's a party for a six-year-old."

"Right, but people who come to our parties are used to a little extra flair. We should attempt to be more exciting."

Where the hell are his priorities? "Our friends will find some way to enjoy themselves without a wait staff and an open bar."

"Melissa, hold on a second. I am not talking about hiring a bunch of help. I meant that we should make the event more upscale—Alaskan black cod and lobster instead of cheap meat."

He wants to maintain our illusion of wealth even though our friends have already noticed that I'm wearing last season's couture and we decline their invitations to go out because we can't afford one-star Michelin restaurants anymore. My fingernails are chipped. Our lawn is dying.

I'm not keeping up this charade.

"And who will pay for the lobster? You?" I laugh at the idea of children cramming fifteen-dollar tacos down their throats.

A crease forms on Tom's forehead. "You could show a little more interest in your daughter's birthday."

"What the hell is that supposed to mean?"

He rights the iron, sighing loudly. "You know what it means. Lately, everything's about you. Your battle with cancer. The kids want their mom's attention, but you're more into your damn phone than playing with Stacy for five minutes."

An explosion takes place in the pit of my stomach, one that sends fire racing through my blood. I rip the sheets from my legs and ignore the cold sting on my bare skin. "What would you know about being a stay-at-home mom?"

He flinches. "Mel—"

"All day I'm wrangling the kids to swimming classes and birthday parties! I make their lunches and break up fights while I swallow down nausea and try not to vomit on my shoes. I'm the one who goes to the PTA meetings. I listen to Stacy have a tantrum because she wants pizza. They depend on me, not you. And on top of all that, I have cancer."

Every word lands like a whip on Tom's skin. "I'm sorry."

That won't replace the stolen hours he spent with that woman. I slide from the bed and head toward the door. Tom moves to block me, and fire builds in my stomach. "Move."

A lump in his throat slides up and down. "I need to get this off my chest."

Finally.

Tom steps close enough for me to count the freckles on his nose. I brace myself for the sledgehammer of grief, waiting for the admission of guilt to fall from his lips.

"I'm sorry you have cancer," he says in a low voice. "You didn't deserve this. There's not a moment that goes by when I don't pray that some miracle drug will wipe this disease away. I know it's exhausting and you're constantly in pain, but you are not the only one affected by this. Do you think the kids like watching their mother get sicker by the day? The illness is all we talk about. It's consumed our lives. I just want to make Stacy's birthday special."

"And it will be, but I'm not paying for seafood she probably won't eat." I don't believe the softness in his voice. "You should be glad I'll be preparing food from cheap cuts of meat. It's the only thing she eats anymore."

"Jesus Christ, Melissa. If I knew giving the kids two pizzas would give me this much drama, I would've let them go to bed hungry."

"I'm not spending thousands on a kid's birthday party! Especially when it's money we do not have."

"Fine. I'll pay for the goddamn cod." He stalks to the board and grinds the iron, smoothing wrinkles but causing dozens more.

"Don't bother. On your salary, we can barely afford the mortgage." It's a low blow, but whatever. He deserves to have his balls ripped off, and by the crumpled look on his face I know I've hurt him.

Tom pauses, ignores the smoking iron as he glares at me. "What is your problem?"

My tongue rolls back as I bite the words. Now's not the time to confront him. "You should lift that up."

He follows my line of sight to the iron burning a hole in his shirt. "Shit!" He rights it. "You know, it'd be nice if you could do this for me."

"It would be, yeah." I scoop my spiked coffee from the nightstand and walk from the bedroom, slamming the door behind me. His screams of frustration die as I head down the hallway decorated with photos of our happy family. A large portrait of Tom embracing me in my wedding dress passes me. I want to seize it from the wall and shatter the glass over my knee.

Instead I slip into my office. I renovated it in shades of white and cool blue, with a wooden floorboard stained in warm tones. My feet slip on the plush, cobalt rug I bought from Pottery Barn, back when I had money to burn on five-hundred-dollar accessories. My fingers slide under the drawer to grab the two sheets I printed last night. Rows of numbers splay under my hands.

Somewhere on this list is Tom's whore, and I'm determined to find her.

I move my chipped nail down each line. Opening my laptop, I fire up Safari and search each number. It turns out all you need is a credit card to discover everything there is to know about a person. Most of the numbers belong to hospitals and clinics. This will take me all day, but I don't care.

Step one for revenge on cheating husband: Write him out of the will.

Check.

Step two: Find the bitch. Expose them both.

Step three: Divorce said cheating bastard.

Steps four and five: Succumb to cancer. Die alone.

There are no winners, no matter how I shift the steps around. If I don't leave Tom, I'll have to stomach his presence, knowing that the man I married is balls deep in another woman. Leave him, and I'm stuck dealing with this illness by myself.

She can't win.

My fingers move rapid fire over the keyboard, punching in ten numbers. I pore over endless rows of data that Google spits out. Then I go to Facebook and search for a number with the Mountain View area code. A woman pops on the screen. My insides curdle as I study her diving neckline, her collagen-injected cheeks—wait. That's Emily.

Emily Taylor. CEO of my startup. Why the hell was Tom calling her?

My fingers scrape the bottom of a drawer for a highlighter. I draw a thick yellow line over each conversation. Ten minutes. Twenty-seven minutes. There's one last week— sixteen minutes. Both incoming and outgoing to the same woman I chose to replace me.

My head buzzes with the strangeness of it. Emily is married, same as Tom. She came to the interview wearing flats and a black dress. She didn't pronounce her H's, and when I asked, she said she was from Switzerland. The chemistry was instant. By the end of the conversation, she invited me to her property in Basel.

As soon as she got the job, her emails became less personal and more professional, until they stopped altogether.

She took my company and ran it into the ground.

Did she steal my husband, too?

A horrible beat crashes against my ribs as I gaze at the late-night conversations. This must be the real reason for Tom's absences. Scooping the pages into a pile, I fold them and shove my chair aside. My heart swells to a size I can't keep behind my chest.

The room spins as I search it for evidence that my marriage was once happy and fulfilled. I seize the silver frame of Tom and me on my desk, judging the smile widening his face. Was he lying then? Did this start when the kids were born? When I was diagnosed and turned into a shell of myself?

The front door slams. He left without saying goodbye.

A rush of anger incinerates the heartbreak. I study my eyes reflected in the glass, and hate the weakness I see there. The picture frame drops, clattering on the desk as the folded pieces of paper tremble in my grip.

I want to fall apart.

I want to sink to my knees and scream. Shatter the family photos until my fists are bloody. Give in to every instinct of fury and just—lose it.

I rake fingers through my long, frayed hair that desperately needs a touch-up. God, how could this happen to me? How did I become the woman who gets cheated on?

My phone vibrates. I seize it from my pocket. Another stock alert? Please show me good news.

I glance at the screen.

MISSION DIGITAL SOLD FOR $2.4 MILLION

It's gone.

The air is thin.

I clutch my cell and the pages, stumbling into the hallway.

Thousands of black dots rise up the walls, swallowing the world.

A child's voice pulls me from the void. "You okay, Mom?"

Tiny hands touch me. My son's face is shrouded in darkness. His tone rises in alarm. "Mom?"

Will they remember me?

My heart lunges forward like an unhinged racehorse. Too fast.

I bend to embrace the only drop of color left in my vision, and the world pitches to the side. A scream pierces the silence. Blackness consumes me.

18

AUBREY

I'M GOING to the Bahamas! Tom booked an all-inclusive resort, which means unlimited drinks. I haven't stopped grinning since he forwarded the airline tickets. They were a total surprise. I had to rush-order a passport, but it's our first-ever weekend getaway. A relaxing, drama-free vacation is exactly what we need. Lately, we've been too wrapped up in our lives. We have to unplug. Get away for a while.

His wife thinks he's going to Chicago on a business trip, but he'll be with me for four nights. Four uninterrupted nights.

I can't wait.

My suitcase bursts at the seams with clothes. Some of the resort's restaurants have a dress code, so I shoved heels and summer dresses inside. My shades, sunscreen, razors, and all the accessories I'll need for a beach vacation are crammed into my carry-on. The floor is vacuumed. My kitchen is clean. I took out the trash. Swept the entry. I bought a new pair of shorts to replace the ragged ones from high school and splurged on a coral lipstick from Sephora. It was thirty bucks, but worth the hum in my body.

I can't wait anymore.

It's too early to leave, but I call an Uber anyway. Outside my apartment, I stand in thigh-length jeans and imagine a balmy breeze instead of cold fog. Teeth chattering, I smile as the gray Cadillac pulls up to the curb.

The driver greets me with a cheeky grin. He takes my suitcase and lifts it into the truck with hardly a grunt. "Where you headed?"

I duck into the passenger seat. "The Bahamas. Just for a few days. My boyfriend's meeting me at the airport."

"Nice," he says. "What airline you taking?"

"Virgin, I think." I recheck my email. "Yeah."

Warm air blasts my feet as we drive to SFO, which I've only been to a handful of times, only for dropping off friends. The farthest I've ever been was Yosemite during a high school trip. Hell, flying in a commercial jet will be an experience.

The glow of SFO's rainbow lights fans into the murky darkness. I clutch the armrest, waiting to throw open the door. The car halts next to the curb, and I step into the night stung with cold. It's freezing in my shorts, but at least I won't have to change once I'm in eighty percent humidity.

Victor rolls my luggage to the sidewalk. "Have a great trip."

I grab the handle. "Thank you!"

I walk through the revolving doors, struck by the high ceilings and the cacophony of overhead speakers and distant shouts of employees. Pain throbs between my temples, but even a migraine can't dull my excitement. Four days with Tom.

He's nowhere to be found, but that's not surprising. After a few minutes of relaxing in a seat and watching people zip to their gates, I open my phone and scroll through a book I bought for this trip. I read a few sentences before exiting the app, mind blazing with the image of Tom. Any second now, he will stride through those doors in a jacket, broad-shouldered and gorgeous. He'll sweep me into his arms, and for the next few days, nothing will separate us.

Time ticks past with agonizing slowness. Eight minutes until we're supposed to meet. Five. I train my eyes on the door, teeth grinding hard from grinning. Tom's cutting it close. Any second—

My phone vibrates with a chime. It's Tom, probably calling to tell me he'll be late. He's never been very punctual.

I accept the call, smiling through my massive headache. "Tom! Are you here?"

He sighs. "Babe."

When I hear his despondent tone, my good mood evaporates. "What?"

"I'm so sorry, Aubrey." Another loud sigh blows across the speaker. "Christ, this is awful. I hope I can make this up to you."

"I don't understand." A roar builds in my ears.

"Babe, I'm not coming."

My hand slips down the handle of my suitcase. "What are you talking about? You have to go. You wouldn't book two nonrefundable tickets if—"

"Melissa's really sick. I can't."

My romantic life is whatever moments Tom and Melissa will let me have. "You can't do this to me. Not again."

His tenderness fills me with rage. "I know it's awful, but

my wife is ill."

A scream builds in my throat. "Of course she's sick! She has fucking cancer. That's never going to change!" My voice carries to the clerks standing behind the desks, but no one glances my way. "I can't believe this."

Tom continues in anguished whispers. "I'll make it up to you. I swear to God. Let—let me at least call an Uber for you."

I grip my phone so hard I'm sure the screen will sustain yet another crack. I could strangle him, but I refuse to utter another word.

"Babe. Babe, you there?"

His whimper echoes in my head when I end the call. *Please forgive me. I'm sorry. Don't be mad.*

How many times have I heard it before?

I hail a taxi outside, and the driver makes a few failed starts at conversation before giving up. I don't want to talk about my nonexistent trip or how I was stood up—no— shoved aside for another woman, yet again. Once again, he proves his loyalty to Melissa, not me.

I stagger toward my apartment as the throbbing, hammer-like pain reaches a fever pitch. My hands somehow find the keys. I stab the lock repeatedly. The driver helps me haul my suitcase into the foyer. With a cheerful goodbye, he leaves.

The door shuts, and I scream. My throat tears with the agony. I shake with the fury of this disease and being cast aside, again and again. I'm not good enough for him.

I grab the vase June gave me as a housewarming present and hurl it at the wall-to-wall mirror. It explodes with a loud crash. Jagged pieces snap as I walk over the carpet. One of them snags my ankle and draws a thin, bloody line. The pain barely registers.

All I can think about is that I'll never have him. As long as his wife is still alive, he won't choose me. That's what just gets me. I've set my schedule aside countless times for him. Tom couldn't care less. The therapist warned this would happen—did I listen? No.

Seizing the champagne I stowed under the sink, I smash it against the granite counter, knocking a chunk away. The shock jars through my arms when the bottle breaks. Shattered dark green glass rains down. I feel like the pieces under my feet.

Jagged. Broken. *Useless.*

I drag a chair into the kitchen. My heart pounds as it sways over my head. I let it fall, aiming for the table. It bounces off harmlessly. A stack of clean dishes sits on the counter. I slide one off and hurl it against the fridge. The dish smacks the floor, refusing to break. I lift my foot and jam the heel home until the ceramic cracks. The plate splinters into three pieces.

A loud series of thumps shakes the ceiling. My neighbors must want me to pipe down. With all the noise I've made, I'm lucky nobody called the police.

What am I supposed to do?

My feet crunch bits of broken glass and porcelain, chest heaving. Stabbing my phone, I check the time. Nine fifty-eight. Melissa will be in bed by now, curled up in my lover's arms.

I can't do this anymore.

Breathing deep, I slide my purse off the counter and head for the door. He'll be furious when I show up at his house, but I've put his feelings above mine for too long. Nothing matters except the woman in my way.

Salted air whips through my jacket, chilling me to the

bone. I wrap it around me, ducking as a beam of light sweeps my feet. Headlights flash from the car parked out front. Someone opens the door, stumbling from the driver's seat. The heavyset man braces himself on the hood, hand clutching his chest.

I step from the porch as the streetlights illuminate his round face. "Amit, what the hell are you doing here?"

He struggles to straighten himself, teeth gnashing in pain. The steel buckles with his weight until he pushes himself off, staggering toward me. "You—fucking—bitch."

I freeze.

Something's wrong.

The Ross Hardware vest dangles on his shoulders, and his front two buttons are undone. An unhealthy, pale sheen covers Amit's skin. "You told my wife."

"About the pictures? Of course I didn't." Why would I ruin our sweet deal?

"You're a bitch." He climbs onto the sidewalk, the effort winding him. "You shoved those photos in my mailbox! Saanvi found them. Now she wants a divorce!"

Goddamn it. "Why would I do that? This inconveniences you as much as me."

"Incon—inconvenience?" His words come out in staccato bursts. "I—lost—my—job! The district manager saw them in an email."

"Damn." That puts a wrench in my plans. "Well, I didn't do it."

Someone must've grabbed a photo before Amit found them. The person who did it was most likely an employee with an ax to grind against their boss, like Michael. Jesus, kid. Way to screw things up for me.

Amit regains his composure, stabbing my chest with a thick finger. "You will not get away with this. I'm taking you to the police station."

He's in no shape to haul my ass to jail. "How will you do that?" I watch as Amit takes a step and stumbles. "How many drinks did you have?"

He swells like a bullfrog. "I don't drink!"

Right. "If you go to them in your state, they'll throw you in a cell. Before I hit you with kidnapping charges."

Heaving for breath, he clutches his chest. "I was supposed to get a bonus. Now I have no job, no wife, and no home."

"You want to lose your freedom too? You stole from me first, asshole. It's not my fault all this happened."

"Fucking bitch."

I laugh when he sinks to his knees. "You think you have it bad? I'd trade all your drama for my cancer in an instant. Stop blubbering. There are thousands more shitty retail jobs to work your way up to customer service manager. You'll be fine."

"I h-hope you get tumors in your asshole." White-faced with fury, he bellows out nonsense. "Shit—fuck!"

Sighing, I shake my head. "I know English is your second language, but shitfuck isn't a swear word."

"No," he gasps. "Think I'm—heart attack."

Grinning, I watch him clutch his arm. "What are you talking about?"

Amit collapses. I jump away as he rolls on his back, air rattling through his lungs. A guttural sound prompts me to kneel beside him. I sink my fingers into his thick neck. A wild beat throbs into my skin.

I study Amit's fluttering eyes. "Hey, you all right?"

The left side of his face sags as though paralyzed. I pinch

his wrist, but he doesn't respond. Amit isn't dramatic; he's having a goddamn stroke. The blue tingeing his lips can't be a good sign.

Damn. He won't have much longer. I should call an ambulance.

Why?

The question fires through my brain, halting my trembling fingers. My thumb hovers over the phone's glowing screen, which illuminates Amit's twitching face.

With Amit fired, there's nothing more he can do for me except die. The asshole threatened to go to the police. What if he does? I'm not spending my last months in jail.

He's running out of time. I need to decide.

I grit my teeth. "Goddamn it."

Shaking, I dial the numbers. I'll hate myself for doing this.

"Nine-one-one, What's your emergency?"

"I need an ambulance, now. My boss is having a stroke. His face is all lopsided." I give the operator my address as I stare hopelessly at Amit's shuddering chest. "He's breathing, but I don't know how much longer."

Wildly, I look around for someone. "Help me!"

My voice carries across the lonely street. Amit's rattling breaths grow desperate. Rolling back his eyelids, I stare into his bloodshot, steady gaze. "Amit, can you hear me? You need to stay awake."

Bitch, I imagine him saying. *Burn in hell, bitch.*

He's still. Trembling, I sink my fingers into his neck and search for a pulse.

One feeble beat. And another.

Then a sigh groans from Amit's mouth, and he lies motionless, no longer fighting.

19

MELISSA

I SNAP awake to a world of pastels. Soft pinks and blues obscure my vision, dissolving into sharp edges when I blink. My eyelids feel like sandpaper. The swirling shapes of pink and blue combine to form a pattern that belongs to a woman's shirt.

"Melissa." She repeats my name. "Melissa. Can you hear me? You had a fall, but you're safe."

I move my head, and a wave of nausea creeps up my throat. Forcing my lips shut, I breathe through my nose, inhaling the smell of bleach. A throbbing, icy pain snakes through my veins. Plastic tubing runs from a bandage on my hand to a bag of saline hanging above.

Panic shooting into my chest, I gaze at the four curtained walls brushing my bed.

I'm not in my house. "What's happening? How did I get here?"

The woman in scrubs moves back, her tanned face swim-

ming into view. "I'm Jackie, your nurse. You fell and passed
out. You're in the hospital."

"But—how?" I remember nothing except my frantic
search for Tom's affair, searching through his phone records.

Phone.

The word shoves an image to the forefront of my brain, a
screen with glowing words: MISSION DIGITAL SOLD FOR
$2.4 MILLION.

A horrible thrill shoots into my chest as I struggle upright.
"I need to leave."

"Absolutely not." She fusses with my sheets, tucking them
around my arms as though I'm a frightened child. "The doctor
will want to admit you."

I'm in a hospital. "What? I don't understand."

"Your boy called the ambulance when you fainted."

I stare into her dark eyes. "Grayson? Where—"

"He's at home. Your neighbor's watching the kids," she
says, stroking my shoulder.

I need to get out of here. "Oh, God. They must be
terrified."

She squeezes my arm. "Don't worry. Your husband's
coming."

My body tenses as his distraught voice filters through the
curtains. As though on cue, Tom strides through in his work
clothes. He bends to plant a rough kiss on my cheek. "You're
all right."

Buried in Tom's neck, I smell floral notes. My lips burn
with everything unsaid—his affair, the calls to Emily, the
flowers.

He pulls back, stroking my hair. "What happened?"

All I can recall is sinking to my knees in the middle of the hall, Grayson clutching my shirt and screaming. "I don't know —I fainted. Grayson must've called nine-one-one."

"Jesus." He rubs his forehead. "We need to get home. They left the kids with Barbara."

We agree on that count, at least. I peel the sheets as the nurse listens to my heart.

Yanking the stethoscope from her ears, she pushes my shoulder. "Melissa, you have to stay in bed."

Besides the ache in my head, I feel fine. "I think I'm okay."

"Even so, the doctor will have questions."

"He can't do anything for me. None of you can." I spit back what they told me months ago. "The heat made me light-headed. We don't have air conditioning."

"We're dealing with pancreatic cancer," Tom explains to her slowly. "The doctors said—"

"Who's her oncologist?" The nurse grabs my chart from the foot of the bed and scans for a name.

A chill tiptoes down my spine as Tom gives me a nervous look. I refuse to be subjected to endless rounds of tests.

They don't understand my pain better than I do. "I want to leave."

Jackie balances the board on her hip, penning my vitals. "I can't do that. Your electrolytes were dangerously low when you came in."

"Well, I haven't eaten in a while. I wanted to, but the nausea's bad. Drinking water can be a struggle with this disease." I glare at Jackie, who continues to write. "Let me go."

"You're not fine," she says to the clipboard. "I'm concerned about your erythrocyte sedimentation rate."

I know I'm dying.

Explaining my prognosis is draining. I'm tired of watching horror and pity unfold on people's faces when I tell them about the cancer. I'm sick of the countless treks to and from doctors whose sole purpose is to badger me about how ill I am. God, I'm done with it all. Aubrey's comments at the crêperie were cruel, but one hundred percent correct.

This isn't getting better. Every day it's worse.

"Tom, let's go home." I will not be their lab rat. "Can you get release papers for me?"

Jackie rips the Velcro cuff from my bicep. "If you leave, it'll be against medical advice. Are you sure you want to do this?"

Do I have to say it again? "Yes."

She appeals to my husband. "Your wife is very ill. She needs to be admitted."

"I'm aware of that." He sighs. "She's made her decision."

I offer her my forearm. "Take this thing out of me."

Shaking her head, she flattens my arm and picks at the piece of tape. "I strongly advise you to stay for the night."

"Noted."

The IV slides out, and I rub the injection site. Tom supports me as I swing my legs over the bed. My toes hit the cold floor. I brace myself for dizziness, but I'm fine.

"Easy," Tom whispers.

The sight of his face knitted with concern makes me want to scream. I shake him off and grab the bundle of clothing sitting on the chair. My blouse is wrinkled—great.

"I'll get your release forms," the nurse says, quietly leaving.

Tom helps me untie the hospital gown. The same fingers that touched another woman graze my skin. A shudder of disgust runs through my body, and I rip myself from his grasp. Under his gaze, I dress as quickly as possible.

"I was so worried about you." Tom watches me through hooded eyes. "When Grayson called, I thought you were dead."

"Tell the kids whatever you want, but I don't want to see you for the rest of the day."

His mouth opens. "What?"

I button my blouse, my heart making the paper-thin fabric flutter. "The announcement went through that my company was sold."

"Seriously?" he says, angry. "Is this the time? You fainted while watching our kids."

I shove my legs into the jeans. "Maybe I felt overwhelmed because my husband has been sneaking around behind my back."

A red flush burns his cheeks. "You think I had something to do with it?"

"I know you did! All those late-night calls with Emily. What did you talk about?"

"You went through my goddamn phone records?"

The temperature between us drops to sub-zero.

Tom stares at me as though he doesn't recognize me. "I thought we were better than this."

"Me too." I shoulder my purse, heading for the door.

He blocks my way. "Where the hell are you going?"

Away from you. "What did you talk to your whore about?"

"Jesus Christ, Melissa. I am not having an affair!" He matches my movements, keeping me from walking forward. "Those phone calls were just conversations between two concerned friends. Do you want to know what we talked about? You."

My finger digs into the shoulder strap as he rakes his hair. "She wanted updates on how you were doing, and I'm sorry. I don't like lying. So I explained everything."

"You told her I was *sick*?" She was the one person I begged him not to tell. This betrayal hurts worse than anything I could've imagined. My pulse gallops ahead, and the room spins. I balance myself on the bed, trembling.

He continues in a soft voice, "I needed someone to vent to."

Laughter forces from my chest. "And you didn't think to confide in your wife? I was right here."

"Babe, I can't talk to you about everything. I wish I could."

"Like what? What the fuck could you possibly have to say to the CEO of my startup that's so goddamn important?"

"I asked for a break from this shit. You were losing your mind checking your phone all day. I wanted her to exclude you from discussions about the company's future, and she did. It was the right thing to do."

It's his fault. "How dare you?"

"Melissa, it was going to happen anyway. You wouldn't have been able to stop it! The investors demanded their money back."

He treated me with kid gloves even though he swore not to, and now I've lost the chance to save the company I slaved over because Tom thought I couldn't handle bad news. It's like I'm in grad school, listening to men tell me what I should do with my career. No matter what his intentions, it was wrong. Unforgivable. And this wasn't his only indiscretion.

Tom's lip trembles in a convincing display of remorse. "I'm sorry."

That's all he can do these days; bleat his apologies and expect me to forgive him. "Get out of my way."

"Wait. Where are you going?"

I don't answer.

For weeks he kept me in suspense about his activities. It's time I do the same to him.

20

AUBREY

The pig is dying on my lawn. Amit's glassy eyes reflect the clouded skies as paramedics pump his stiff chest and squeeze air through his mouth. It doesn't look good. The shock of losing his job and his wife, the damned photos—it must've been too much.

This is your fault.

No, it's not. I didn't fill him with butter and salt for years. That's on him.

Flashing red lights illuminate a handful of people standing outside their apartments in pajamas. A woman jogs to my lawn barefoot. "You okay, hon?"

"I'm fine." *He's not.*

Rubbing sleep from her eyes, June walks to my side. "What happened?"

"My boss—uh—collapsed. I think it's a heart attack." I scratch deep red lines in my forearm as she gapes at me.

"Your *boss*—" The doors to the ambulance close and an

179

earsplitting shriek cuts off June's sentence. "What was he doing here?"

"Jesus, I don't know." *Too defensive.*

"Aubrey, enough with the J word. I was just curious."

I shrug, refusing to meet her gaze. "He takes his job too seriously. I probably screwed up closing a register and he came here to tell me off."

"Well, I'm sorry this happened." She crosses her arms against the cold and gives my bare legs an odd look. "You sure you're all right?"

I forgot about the damn trip. "It's been a long night. I think I'll turn in."

She squeezes my shoulder. "Try to get sleep."

How the hell will I do that?

I wave at June before returning to my porch. An hour earlier I walked out, convinced I was headed for a weekend getaway. Numb, I push open the front door and walk inside.

My apartment is in shambles.

I ignore the destruction and head for the kitchen, groping for the handle of a drawer. I seize a bottle, shaking out three pills. My headache is like a hammer jarring against steel. I swallow the oxy and wash them down with water, waiting for the medicated calm to coat my troubled brain. Pacing the apartment, I glimpse my whitened face through the jagged piece hanging on the wall. I could bash my skull against the mirror.

No job. No future. No *money.*

Amit dying wasn't part of the *plan.* There was only supposed to be one death weighing on my conscience. The idiot shouldn't have worked himself up. He should have gone to the damn doctor instead of bullying me.

Sure, he was an asshole. But I never wanted him *dead*.

Now my meal ticket's gone.

Someone pounds at the door. I moan at the state of my apartment. They're bound to ask questions.

The knocks are relentless. I head for the foyer. "Hold on!"

I twist the doorknob and open, eyes widening at my visitor. "What are you doing here?"

21

MELISSA

Aubrey's gone. She must be.

The ambulance pulls away from her curb with an earsplitting shriek, barreling toward the hospital. I didn't see her body, but why else would the ambulance be called to her apartment?

My fingers gouge my chest as the siren fades in the distance. The crowd gathered on the lawn slowly drifts away like ghosts.

I need to be sure.

Frantic, I march to her porch and pound her door. I don't stop until I hear the slide of a lock.

The door opens, revealing a woman in thigh-high shorts and flip-flops. Fear pinches Aubrey's features. She casts me a terrified look. "It's you."

Relief floods my veins. "Oh my God. I thought—I thought something happened to you."

"No, it was my boss. He had a stroke."

My pulse gallops ahead. "That's awful. I'm sorry about the

hour." I tuck my keys into my purse. "I'm not here to start a fight, swear to God."

"Oh, I-I didn't think you were."

I bite my lip. "Can I come in?"

She stands aside, blinking slowly. "Don't mind the mess."

I step through the threshold and gape at the scene. The mirror wall to the left is gone. Shards of glass and porcelain litter the carpet and linoleum.

Oh my God. "Did you have a break-in?"

"No, just a tantrum." Aubrey offers me a bleak smile that I don't return. She gestures toward the couch, one of the few surfaces untouched by the mess.

"You mean—you did this?" I gape at her, and she nods. "Why?"

She doesn't look away. "Because life sucks."

I try to visualize her rage. She must've blown through like a tornado, hell-bent on destroying everything. A cracked vase lies in splinters at my feet.

I understand the impulse. When I discovered I had cancer, Tom took the kids for ice cream while I locked myself in the bathroom and screamed.

I sink into the couch. "You were right. The treatments are a waste of my money and time."

A blush fills Aubrey's cheeks. "Sorry I was an asshole about it."

"No, it's fine. Honestly, I needed to hear that."

She shakes her head. "I shouldn't judge what makes you feel better. I've been sensitive to holistic therapies ever since my aunt told me I should touch the bones of some saint in Montreal. Like that'll fucking do anything."

"Tom seems to think they help." I flush at Aubrey's wry

smile. "I know he's just being supportive. It's obvious I'm not doing well."

"Sometimes they do sort of work. It's called the placebo effect." Aubrey hunches over her knees, looking so small and thoroughly exhausted.

"Sorry, this was a terrible idea." I bend, grabbing my purse. "I shouldn't have come."

"Stop. It's fine." Aubrey shrugs. "You're here. Tell me what's up."

"I just—I don't know. You're the only one who understands what I'm going through, and I don't have many people to talk to. I guess I'm feeling lost."

She peers at me. "This about Tom?"

A car's headlights stream across the blinds. The roar fades before I answer Aubrey. "I need to know who the hell it is."

"Maybe the marriage is done. Relationships survive on trust."

"We've been together ten years." Perhaps I've become one of those women I despise. I cradle my head, massaging my throbbing temples. "We built a life together. I need all the facts before I confront him. He's seeing someone. I want to know who and why."

She throws me a look filled with pity. "It will not make you feel any better."

"That doesn't matter."

"Okay, fine." She slaps her thighs, resigned. "And I'm supposed to help you with that?"

"My daughter's birthday party is this weekend. She's turning six. I'd like you to come. It's this Saturday."

Silence fills the space between us, broken only by Aubrey's restless foot tapping the floor. "Of course."

"I know this is crazy, but I'd appreciate it if you could keep an eye on the guests. I'm not positive, but he might be having an affair with someone from my old job. Her name's Emily Taylor."

Aubrey heaves a sigh. "Melissa, I don't think I'll hear anything. It's not like she'll brag about fucking your husband."

"I'm aware it's a long shot. Just—please—watch her for me."

"Whatever," she laughs. "Sure. Nothing will happen, but I'll be glad to stalk her for you."

I squeeze Aubrey's bony shoulder. "You're amazing."

A part of me knows she's right. Tom won't make eyes with his lover at our six-year-old's birthday, but I have to try. I owe it to our kids to find the bitch who ruined our family.

22

AUBREY

I WALK TO THE DAUGHTRYS' front door, and it's the strangest sensation. My instincts scream to hide, to watch them through the bay windows like I have for weeks. Even though I'm invited, I definitely shouldn't be here.

Flanked by two McMansions, Tom's much smaller house looks like a pink and purple toddler. A giant cardboard portrait of Stacy is attached above the garage door. I follow her beaming face into the driveway packed with Priuses and head for the entrance, which is surrounded by colorful streamers. I squeeze inside the roar of conversation, scanning the crowd. The guests are a mixture of Pacific Heights super rich and flannel-wearing tech bros.

Pink and purple banners hang from the ceiling—Happy Birthday, Stacy! A fuchsia dinosaur with a cheesy grin beams on every plate, cup, and balloon. A three-tiered cake sits on the kitchen counter, well above the reach of grubby hands. Children run into my knees as they race the gargantuan property while the adults quietly get plastered. I slip past a coterie of rosé-drinkers and gape at the mountain of gifts piled on a console table. I tuck my present behind a much larger one, fingering the card attached to the ribbon. Tom won't ignore me after he reads my message.

Today's the day.

I decided when I woke up that I'd abandon the attempt on Melissa's life, which blows because I wasted money on more nitro before I made the decision. Killing her is an unnecessary risk when a wedge between them already exists. All I have to do is drive it deeper. The note will force Tom to tell her the truth.

Outside, dazzling sunshine filters through tall magnolias that double as a privacy fence. Children jump in the massive inflatable castle with a pink dinosaur's head bobbing with the movement. People sit in lounge chairs from Pottery Barn next to a covered, kidney-shaped pool, loading their plates with food from heated aluminum trays on the banquet table. I search for Melissa and spot her in a group near the bouncing house. She looks as though she's eaten a couple of square meals since last I saw her, but she's still not herself. Her appearance lacks her usual polish

I grab a red cup filled with punch and sip, disappointed with its lack of booze. I'll need the alcohol if I will pretend to scout for Tom's filthy mistress all day.

A woman with shriveled, tanned arms and an alarmingly taut face steps in my path, giving my dress an approving nod. "I love your outfit, hon! Name's Barbara."

I approach her, extending my hand. "Thank you. I'm Aubrey."

Her gaze flicks up and down my body. "Pleased to meet you."

I wait for the inevitable pause as she tries to work out what illness I have. Her handshake is limp as hell. "Great party, isn't it?"

"It's wonderful." A boy shrieks with excitement and Barbara cringes at the noise. "Wonderful."

I take another sip of the vile punch, trying not to wince at the sugar. "How do you know the Daughtrys?"

"We live next door." She gestures toward the McMansion rising above the hedges.

I stare into the windows and imagine what she does with all those guest rooms. She strikes me as a person who hosts lavish Black & White themed parties and weekly book clubs in which the entire meeting is spent discussing which actors should play the characters in the event of a film adaptation.

I pretend to be awed. "What a beautiful home."

Hers is a smile made with collagen. "Thank you."

Flattery is all she expects from someone like me. "My place isn't nearly as nice. I live in Daly City."

"I've heard they're developing that area. Eric and I have been thinking of investing. How long have you lived there?"

"Four years." I scan the crowd above Barbara's head, searching for Melissa. She's nowhere in sight. Damn.

Barbara nods. "So you bought before the real estate boom? Fantastic."

Good Lord. This woman thinks I'm an investment banker or a tech employee raking in a mid-six-figure salary. What gave it away—the designer dress Tom gifted me months ago?

Best way to get rid of her would be to tell her the truth, that I have less than five thousand dollars to my name. "Oh, I don't own. I'm still renting. Probably will be for the rest of my life unless I can find a sugar daddy. Parties like this are good for that, right?"

"Oh." Barbara's face falls. "Um—"

"Perfect." I spot Tom's golden head next to the pink hydrangea bushes. "Excuse me. I think I see one there. Catch you later!"

She stammers a goodbye as I walk around her. A trio of children run across my path as I stroll toward a brightly colored arch of balloons. Underneath them, a man with face paint and striped pants makes a dog for a pig-tailed girl.

Stacy approaches the clown, bouncing on her feet. "I want a bicycle."

The clown's white face sags. "Wouldn't you rather have a nice giraffe?"

"No!" she shouts.

Tom palms her upper back. "Sweetie, you already have one. Remember?"

A frown creases Stacy's forehead as she thinks it over and shakes her head. Then a commotion at the door draws her attention. Melissa stands near the sliding glass, cupping her mouth. "Kids! It's time for the cake!"

A dozen young voices scream in ecstasy. The clown forgotten, Stacy leads the stampede of children inside. Everyone squeezes into the kitchen, where a three-tiered monstrosity with six glowing pink candles rises from the counter.

Stacy claps with a happy squeal as Tom records his daughter with his iPhone. We break into song as Melissa heaves Stacy in her arms, propping her on a stool. Her cute curls bounce on her head as she leans forward and blows with more spittle than air. No wonder adults never eat the cake at a child's party.

Wedges of dark chocolate are passed on paper plates, followed by flutes of champagne as Stacy digs into her piece. The children grow louder, energized by sugar and birthday bliss. I attempt to penetrate the thick crowd surrounding Melissa, who's hell-bent on making sure every single person enjoys themselves.

The sides of my cup buckle as a high-pitched shriek hits my ears. I grit my teeth as the nail-grating sounds stab my brain like an ice pick, and poke in my bag for the pillbox. Finding the bottle, I pop open the lid and pour out an oxy, breaking the capsule into my drink without looking. I raise the glass to my lips.

A tear rips through the air, followed by excited squeals. I follow the noise into the foyer with the mountain of gifts, where Stacy kneels on sheets of wrapping paper.

No one watches her, not even her parents.

A ripple of anger runs through me. If I had kids, I'd want to experience every moment. The laughter and the tears.

Joy blossoms over her cute face as she unwraps a Lite-Brite. "Wow."

I hunch at her side. "That's cool. Can I play with it sometime?"

Stacy hugs it to her chest, giving me a slow nod. "Maybe."

At least she's honest. "Want to open the one I got you?" Her eyes light up as I grab the box from the middle of the pile. "Here."

Ripping the card off the ribbon, she tears the paper in a frenzy and gapes at the Polly Pocket. "Ooh."

"See the little pieces?" I point at the small figurines. "They're like teeny tiny worlds. I used to collect them when I was your age."

"Thank you." Stacy beams for a second until her smile becomes a pout. "I have a stomachache."

Poor thing. "Did you eat too much cake?"

Tears bead in her eyes. "I dunno. It hurts."

"Okay." I stand. "Let's go find your mommy and tell her."

Stacy grabs my hand before I reach out. An impulse to pick her up and carry her from the party strikes me. I've never felt an attachment to anyone's kids before now. Maybe because she'll be my stepdaughter someday. Who knows, she might forget all about Melissa and call me Mom.

I tighten around Stacy's clammy fingers. She squeezes as we search for Melissa, who stands near the banquet table with a plastic cup of punch. Beside her, Tom refills a guest's glass with a pitcher of the bright red juice. He sets it down and takes a sip of the drink, eyes scanning his backyard.

I meet his gaze, angry enough to scream until his face broadens with a look. Our look.

"Hey," he mouths.

A wave of calm drowns the flames. I just want him to watch me like that for the rest of our lives. Maybe I was too quick to judge him. Tom's always made me feel—

"Daddy!" Stacy releases my hand the moment she spots her father and runs into his knees.

Tom gives his daughter a bearlike hug, beaming with a tender glow I thought was for me. I follow the little girl and stop a foot from Tom. My throat is raw, as though I've been screaming.

Look at me. Acknowledge me, you bastard.

Tom's eyes glaze over me. Indifferent. Uncaring.

I'm the other woman, after all. The wife comes first. It's

always my wife, my wife, my fucking wife. Without taking a sip of my drink, I set it on the table.

Melissa smiles at Stacy, who wraps her arms around her thighs. "Are you having fun, baby girl?"

Stacy shakes her head. "Stomachache."

An edge creeps into Melissa's voice as she addresses Tom. "You shouldn't have let her have that second slice."

"Give me a break, Melissa." He takes a quick swig of punch. "It's her birthday."

"That doesn't mean she gets to eat herself sick—Oh!" Melissa drops the acidic tone as I approach. "Hey, Aubrey! Sorry I haven't said hello. It's been hectic."

"No problem." I force my lips to curve. "I was opening presents with the birthday girl. She told me she didn't feel well."

"Stacy, you were supposed to wait for Daddy to open gifts." Melissa sets her plastic cup inches from mine.

"My stomach hurts," Stacy wails.

"Too many sweets will do that, my dear." Sighing, Melissa turns away. "Tom, go get the Tums."

I face Melissa, whose hand reaches for her drink. Before Melissa takes a sip, Stacy tugs her shirt. "I'm thirsty."

Melissa pauses.

I'm distracted by the way the sunlight dances on Tom's gentle waves. Shades of white gold and yellow, brassy tones pour down his neck. Absentminded, I reach into my purse to send a text, moving aside the bottle of nitro.

What?

My heart stops as I gaze inside the bottle's contents, counting one pill missing. A freezing sensation snakes through my limbs. I thought I was spiking my drink with oxy, but instead I dosed it with nitro.

I could've *killed* myself. Good Lord. This is what I get for having my head in the clouds. Better find the drink fast and dump it.

A sharp blow hits my chest as I glance at the table where I left it, finding one halfway filled with punch. That's not mine.

So where the hell is it?

I look around me. Panicking, I watch as Melissa stoops and offers a glass to Stacy. The six-year-old girl wraps her hands around the red plastic.

"Wait!" A scream builds in my throat. "Don't!"

The liquid touches Stacy's lips. She swallows the heart-stopping drug. It's too late to stop what never should've started. The bottom drops out of my stomach.

I killed her.

Perplexed, Melissa gapes at me. "What's the matter?"

Tears spring to my eyes. "She—she drank—"

Juice spills all over Stacy's overalls as she drops the punch. "Stacy!" Melissa admonishes. "Why did you—Stacy?"

The blood leeches from Stacy's face. "Stomach...ache."

Melissa retrieves the cup, frowning. "Sweetie, you okay?"

Slowly, she shakes her head. "Mom, I don't feel good."

Melissa feels her daughter's forehead, which has turned a nasty shade of gray. The six-year-old parts her lips, taking deep, shuddering breaths. Melissa grabs Stacy's wrist, checking her pulse. "Stacy?"

The girl collapses.

23

MELISSA

It's a scene ripped from my nightmares. My daughter lies motionless under a team of paramedics as they move her onto a stretcher. Pink streamers and balloons float near the ambulance in a parody of a birthday party. My husband's screams drown my thoughts, and a circle of horrified guests closes around me.

White-faced, Aubrey approaches Tom. "I'm so sorry."

This isn't real. One minute she's breathless from chasing other children in a game of Duck Duck Goose, the next she's on the ground. The sight of my baby's golden curls tangled in blades of grass breaks me.

I sink to my knees with a choked sob. "Stacy!" I shake her motionless shoulder. "Stacy, wake up!"

The paramedics work quickly, inserting an IV into her forearm.

"Is she dying?" None of them will tell me anything. "What's happening to my baby?"

My demands for information are swallowed by utter

195

silence, broken occasionally by my husband's yells. They wheel her toward the gate leading to the front yard. I race with them to the ambulance, hands clenching her tiny fists.

"It's okay, Stacy." Tears blind my vision. "You're safe. Mommy loves you!"

Her body jolts as the stretcher bounces off the curb. They open the back doors of the van and lift my baby girl inside. I follow them, hesitating when a voice calls behind me.

"Melissa, wait!" Tom sprints toward me, vaulting up the steps in a single leap.

I push him away. "No, you can't! Grayson—"

"Your mother's watching him," he blurts. "Let's go!"

With a metallic slam, the ambulance lurches forward, alarms blazing.

He slides next to me, thigh pressing against mine. "Is she okay?"

"Christ, Tom. She's here. Of course not!"

"She's conscious," says a paramedic with a pixie haircut. "But her heart rate is a little fast."

"Oh my God." I grasp Stacy's bare ankle as they slice through her clothing with a blunt-tipped pair of scissors and attach nodes to her pink chest.

Tom crushes my hand in his grip. "She's awake. Thank God. Baby, can you hear us? You'll be okay."

Seconds later, the van grinds to a halt, and the doors burst. Two women in soft blue scrubs grab the stretcher as soon as it touches the ground. My daughter's head flails with the movement, oxygen strapped to her face. Her eyes flare open, wide and fearful.

I sprint with the doctors into the hospital and down corridors, until the paramedic who rode with us pulls me aside. "This is where you'll have to wait."

Tom gapes at her as though he's forgotten the meaning of the word.

"Someone will give you more information shortly." She squeezes my arm. "Please try to remain calm."

My daughter disappears behind two wide doors after collapsing from something horrible. I failed to protect her— my little girl. The light of my life.

A scream finally rips from my throat.

––––––––

ENDLESS QUESTIONS CHASE each other in my head, all of them pointing back to what happened. What made my six-year-old drop to the floor as though a lightning bolt struck her heart?

I don't know.

Tom and I bounce theories, poring over our family histories to find out if there was something we missed. The only notable illnesses were multiple sclerosis from my aunt, and strokes on Tom's paternal side. He caresses my hand as I imagine a clot forming in my daughter's brain, choking her oxygen.

I stand, unsticking myself from Tom. "I can't take this."

A sprawl of uncomfortable chairs line the waiting lobby, which is filled with the soft cries of children. My gaze sweeps over a boy tugging his mother's sleeve. Her vacant expression strikes a cord inside me. Was I like that with Stacy?

Tom's low baritone urges me to stay calm. "Stacy needs her parents. Panicking won't help her."

"You're right." I inhale a shrill breath as a man in a white coat enters the room.

The doctor makes a beeline for us. Streaks of gray run through his brown mane. A tremor runs through my body at his solemn expression.

"Hello, I'm Dr. Trotter. Are you Mr. and Mrs. Daughtry?" he says in a quiet voice.

"Yes." Tom shakily slides his arm around my shoulders. "Is she okay?"

He nods in a measured way. "Stacy is breathing on her own. We're running a tox screen. Until the blood work comes in, we won't have any more information, but she's in stable condition for now."

My vision blurs in a kaleidoscope of color. "Can we see her?"

"Yes," Dr. Trotter says. "Come with me."

Breaking into a swift walk, I follow the doctor to the pediatric wing. My stomach turns at the soft purples and pinks decorating the walls.

He gestures to the numbered door near the nurse's station. "She's sleeping, but you may sit with her. I'll be back with updates."

"Okay." Tom gives me a worried look before walking inside.

My heart slams against my ribs as I follow him without breathing. I swipe the curtains aside. It's not quite the terrifying scene I imagined. Stacy lies on a bed too big for her small body, a tube running oxygen to her nose. Her golden curls are crushed against the pillow. Relief floods my veins when I notice her skin has returned to its healthy, pink glow. I sit in the chair by her side and stroke her cheek.

Tom grasps Stacy's feet. "I don't understand." He breaks the silence in a whisper. "She was fine—right?"

I shake my head, blinded with tears. "She said she had a stomachache and collapsed."

"Stacy's been saying that for weeks," he says.

I blink away the mist. "Yes. I took her to the pediatrician. He told me she was doing it for attention."

Anguish transforms his face. "Jesus. We didn't take it seriously."

"I don't know. She was running around all day. I knew it was a bad idea to have all that candy on display." My hands shake as I tease out the tangles in her curls.

"Melissa, she did not faint because she had too many sweets." He releases a rough sigh. "It's no good torturing ourselves before the labs come in."

"I can't help but wonder." All the deadly traps in our home cycle through my mind: the Drano hiding under the sink, my pills in the nightstand, the goddamn cocktail of cleaning supplies. "Oh God. Do you think she got into my medication?"

Frowning, he shakes his head. "No."

I tuck in the sheets around her body, wiping my eyes. Nothing will dislodge the horror. I didn't listen to her. I'm supposed to be the one in the hospital, not my daughter, never my children. Cancer is nothing compared to watching her suffer.

Seeing her wrapped in paper-thin rags makes me tremble with rage. All those times I ignored her cries for help run through me. My baby was sick, and I brushed her pain aside.

The guilt sticks like a lump refusing to go down my throat. Head throbbing, I glance at a pile of folded laundry sitting on the chair. Stacy's overalls ripple in my hands, a jagged line running through the chest.

I lose it.

The silence breaks with my sobs. I'm aware of Tom's presence, his soothing voice. It's not your fault. She'll be okay. They roll over my back because they sound like the worthless platitudes people used to tell me. You'll be fine. Things will turn around.

What if they don't?

I force my mouth shut to keep the noise from waking her and swallow the pain I want to scream to the world. This wasn't supposed to happen to my child. I would fill my body with a dozen more cancerous tumors to take away her torment.

My cries shake free as her ruined clothes drop and with it a fluttering piece of cardboard with bold red ink. The small rectangle lands on the fabric. Tape attached twine to the card. I flip it over and read.

Your wife will never keep us apart - A

I pick it up from the floor. The bottom of my stomach drops. Your wife—

This is a message to Tom.

My husband's *whore* put this on my daughter's birthday present!

Oblivious, Tom straightens from the bed after kissing Stacy's forehead. He wipes his face. "I'm going to get water, want some?" He pauses before heading out the door. "What's that?"

Trembling, I offer it to him. "A note from your slut."

"What?" He reads it, eyes widening.

"Stop lying and admit it. You brought your whore to our child's birthday party."

He dares to look confused. "What are you talking about?"

I slam his broad chest. "She—was—here! Rubbing your affair in my face!"

Rereading it, Tom frowns. "I don't know who the hell this is and I'm tired of having this conversation. I'm not cheating."

"You're seriously going to deny you're fucking another woman? Again?" My voice rises to a yell. "The evidence is right there!"

"I'm not having an affair! Jesus Christ, Melissa. How many times do I have to say it? This was meant for someone else!"

The walls are closing in. Stacy is in a hospital bed. I have end-stage cancer. Every time I think it can't possibly get any worse, the knife in my side twists. "The note was attached to a gift for your daughter! Do me a favor, Tom, and stop lying. Right now!"

The last ringing notes of my scream fade as Tom watches me, hands clenched into fists. He slams the card on the table. "I'm telling you the truth."

My fingers dig into the roots of my hair. I'll rip out every strand if he doesn't leave. This is a nightmare.

"I saw the flowers!"

With gut-wrenching satisfaction, I watch as two angry patches rise to his cheeks.

"They were on your desk, a bouquet of red roses," I say. "Who sent them? Was it Ashley?" Looking outraged, Tom shakes his head in tight jerks. "Who is it?"

"I don't know," Tom says. He grabs my shoulders, face softening.

I lurch away from him. "Don't touch me!"

"You need to listen. I've been receiving flowers in my office, that's true, but I have no idea who they're from. A stranger keeps sending me these notes, but I swear to God, I'd rather die than be unfaithful to you!"

A humorless laugh shakes my chest. "That is the most pathetic lie I have ever heard."

"It's the truth!" Blood rushes to his tanned face. "Damn it, why won't you believe me?"

"Because having cancer didn't turn me into a moron! I know you're up to something. I've known for months." My confession dangles from the tip of my tongue, but I bite it back. "Get out of this room."

He gestures toward the bed. "Our daughter is sick."

"And I'm perfectly capable of taking care of her without you."

Crossing his arms, he doesn't move a muscle. "I am not going anywhere."

"*Tom.*"

"No, you can't force me to leave."

It's the sight of him standing there, as though he belongs here, that lights a fuse to the bomb swelling in my chest. My hands make fists. They crash into his body—his shoulders, wherever I can reach.

"Get out!"

Tom grabs my wrists. "I'm not leaving her."

A nurse bursts into the room, staring wide-eyed at the scene. "Mrs. Daughtry, I'm surprised at you. Your daughter needs rest!"

"He h-has to go."

"Both of you must leave," she snaps. "Now."

The door opens again, this time admitting an older woman

who looks at me as though she's never seen anything so disgusting. "What's going on?"

I follow her gaze to my little girl, who sits bolt upright in bed, fully awake and alert.

Shame buries the rage in sickening nausea.

II.

Dear Tom,

I'll keep this short.

I am deeply sorry for what I've done. I never meant to hurt your baby girl. It was an accident. I swear to God it was, but that's no excuse. That doesn't erase the fact that I poisoned a six-year-old.

I'm sorry.

I'm sorry.

I'm so *fucking* sorry.

I haven't stopped crying since I saw her fall. It keeps replaying over and over in my head. There must've been something I could have done to stop it.

Yes, I'm disgusted with myself.

I harmed an innocent girl.

If I were brave, I'd admit it to you both right now. Tell you how sorry I am. How my love for you twisted my brain and turned me into a selfish bitch. Instead I'm writing this massive text that'll be sent moments after my death.

The drug she ingested is called nitroglycerin. It's for patients with heart conditions. In high enough dosages, the drug can cause heart attack, stroke, coma, and even death. I don't know how much your daughter took, but I'm terrified it was enough to make her heart stop beating.

You might loathe me. I don't blame you. I doubt you can hate me more than I hate myself. You changed my life—gave me a reason to wake up in the morning. Tortured me with stolen moments from your wife and children, but gave me the greatest bliss I'll ever experience. And how did I repay you? By killing your daughter.

I am wretched with grief over this. I assume she's gone by now. Please know that I spent my last moments hoping for your family's health and happiness.

From the bottom of my heart, I'm sorry and goodbye.

I won't hurt anyone ever again.

24

AUBREY

My fingers are frozen stiff. It's way too cold to eat ice cream, but I jam the It's-It sandwich into my mouth and bite through the freeze. Mint-chocolate and oatmeal cookie singe my taste buds.

But even murderers of little girls deserve a last meal. Let's face it; the world will be better off without me. This is the second person I've killed in less than forty-eight hours. Amit was a mercy killing. He was a judgmental, thieving asshole who had no qualms about stealing from the terminally ill. But Stacy...

She was innocent. Her death was an accident, but that doesn't mean I shouldn't be punished.

And it's the end as far as Tom and I are concerned. There's nothing left for me here. Wind from the Golden Gate tears at my face and clothes. I walk and try not to think of the even deeper chill below my feet. Chances are I won't feel the water freezing my bones. I'll be dead upon impact. Jumping from this height might as well be like slamming into concrete. My body will explode into bits of shark bait.

Walking close to the rust-colored railings, I gaze at the Bay. The waves look cold. White peaks crash against the rocky shore and crawl back. Fog drifts over the water, and I imagine it as the ghost of a jumper forced to watch traffic for all eternity.

I lick the last crumbs from the package and tuck the garbage into my jeans, somehow more unsatisfied than I was before the ice cream. My teeth chatter as I wrap the jacket around my chest and keep walking. I'll jump from the center of the bridge, where the water's the deepest.

I grasp the edge of the rail and gaze into the freezing water. The cold stings my cheeks. I sigh, but the wind steals it away.

Will Tom miss me?

Will anyone?

I imagine my aunt will go to the morgue to identify my body, but chances are no one but the landlord will notice I'm gone. They might never recover my remains. Tom wouldn't think to file a missing person's report. Most likely, he'd guess that I moved on. Once he reads the message I prepared for him, he won't give a damn about what happened to me.

Who can blame him?

I clench the phone in my pocket, withdrawing it with shaky hands. So fucking cold. Thumbing the screen, I open messages and click on Tom's name.

My breath catches in my chest as I hover over the button. The letter I wrote condemning myself is already pre-written into the box. All I have to do is tap once, and it'll be done. The love of my life will want nothing to do with me after this, and it's my fault.

I tuck the phone in my pocket without sending the message. I'll do it before long, but I need to be dead before his vitriol reaches me.

My foot hooks on the concrete block of the railing. Beyond the rail is a suicide net I'll have to clear. That'll mean taking a flying leap off the Golden Gate or crawling over the steel. Either would be terrifying.

Cars zipping past might think to call 911. I can't let them. This is what I deserve and I will not back down because I'm scared of heights. Death was coming for me anyway, and I made my last months about killing another man's wife to take her place.

I hoist myself, straddling the bar as I slide over the edge. Good God, this is high.

The height is around two hundred feet. I know because I looked it up before I started the trek. How many seconds of pure terror will I experience before crashing headfirst into the water?

I look at the turbulent bay, which is a mistake. Fear kicks me like a hoof to the chest. My fingers whiten as I cling to the bridge, my breaths billowing in panicked gasps. There's still the safety net to jump over.

But I have to do it, right? There's nothing to look forward to now. The police will know what I've done. I'd live my days in a shoebox knowing I killed a little girl. Making amends isn't an option for me. I don't believe in God, so prayer circles are out. There is no running from this.

I need to jump. Really, really far.

My legs bend as I cling to the bar desperately. I force my hands to let go, swells of panic stabbing my chest when my balance wavers.

Goodbye, Tom.

Shaking, I prepare to spring. My mind doesn't want to leap, but my body does, so I manage a pathetic hop off the bridge. A scream rips from my throat as I fall. I lunge for the rail, fingers scraping metal, and then I swing violently.

My shoulder crashes into solid steel, the blow jarring my head. Tears leak from my eyes as I moan, rocking back and forth. I get to my knees, trembling. Somehow, my phone survived the impact. It lies face-up, a new crack running down the screen.

I won't need it anymore.

Several feet ahead, the net ends. All I have to do is crawl toward the edge and ignore the panic freezing my limbs. I creep over the steel mesh and cringe against the biting cold. A few seconds of terror, and I'll be gone. I look down, waves of dizziness crashing into my head.

This is it. One nudge, and it's done.

My body refuses to cooperate. I move my leg an inch before sheer panic overwhelms me. It's so high and death— death is so final.

I don't want to do this, but I have to.

In the distant shore, white foam crashes against rocks. I imagine my body impaled by a buoy. Laughter shakes from my chest as my teeth chatter from the cold. My fingers curl over the edge.

A vibration near my feet distracts me. I glance at my blinking phone and seize it, grateful. Tom's name glows on the screen.

He called.

I need to listen to his voice one more time. "T-Tom?"

"Aubrey?" He sounds breathless. "Where are you? It's really loud."

A violent wind lashes my hair. "I'm—I'm on the bridge."

"The bridge? What are you talking about?"

"Tom, I'm jumping." Tears fly from my cheeks. "This is something I have to do."

"No," he growls. "Aubrey, don't you dare!"

"I don't want to do this anymore." Gasping, I clutch the rungs of the mesh. "Your daughter—"

"Do what?" His frustration grows with my silence. "Stacy is—"

"I hurt her, Tom."

"What are you talking about? She's fine, Aubrey."

That's not possible. "But—"

"Stacy is okay."

My lips are numb. "I don't understand."

"She's *fine*," he says again.

Joy soars in my chest. I laugh into the phone, tears blurring the endless crashing waves. "I'm so happy."

"Why would you do this to me?" His voice cracks. "This is so fucked up. I don't know where to start."

"I'm sorry. I'm so sorry."

"Stop crying. I hate it when you—you know how that makes me feel. I had no idea how upset you were. If I did, I would've done things differently."

My lips tremble. "Are we—" I clear my throat. "Are we over?"

"No." His sigh hisses into my ear. "I must be out of my mind, but no. Babe, I'm in love with you. I can't live without you." He breaks into sobs, and I clutch the glass to my face as though it's a lifeline. "I promise I'll be there for you. Just don't —please don't hurt yourself."

I lift the phone away.

It's all I wanted to hear.

25

MELISSA

I CAN'T FALL to pieces. Stacy needs me.

She sits upright, propped up by three pillows. Occasionally her gaze drifts from the television screen blaring a Disney movie to the tube attached to her forearm and the bag feeding her with saline. A pink shine has returned to her cheeks, but her breathing is shallow.

"It's cold," she complains, rubbing her arm.

"Here." I grab the heavy fleece blanket Tom brought from the house and lift it to her neck, tucking in the sheet. "Better?"

She nods, blinking slowly. "Where's Grayson?"

I stroke her hair. "He's with Grandma, sweetie. Your brother will visit later. Does that sound good?"

Stacy's head jerks backward with a sudden spasm. Her eyes shut, mouth twisting with a pained grimace. A low moan bursts from her lips, rising into a shriek.

I grasp her hand. "What is it?"

Tears slide down her cheeks. "Stomach."

Jesus.

"Nurse!" I glance over the bed surrounded by her favorite stuffed animals. "My daughter needs help!"

A woman wearing dramatic eyeliner and rose-colored scrubs rushes into the room and approaches Stacy. "What's wrong? Where does it hurt?"

Stacy points to her abdomen, gritting her teeth.

Banita glances at the heart rate monitor, flicking through the settings before taking Stacy's blood pressure. Grabbing the chart, she makes a note of the number. "Everything's stable."

Exasperated, I smooth the blankets over Stacy's legs. "Can't you give her something for the pain?"

She shakes her head. "The doctor will have to make that call. Do you want more ice chips, hon?"

A loud wail fills the hospital room.

Fuck's sake. "Where the hell is he?"

"He should be making his rounds. Let me see if he's available." The nurse squeezes my daughter's arm. "Won't be much longer."

Then she backs out.

Stacy's wails grate against the frozen block in my head, and when she realizes Banita is gone, her cries become shrill.

This is my fault—both our faults—but mostly mine. I was the stay-at-home parent who ignored the signs, and the doctors don't have a clue what it is or how many weeks it's been wreaking havoc inside her.

Minutes later, the door blows open to admit Dr. Trotter. "Hello, Mrs. Daughtry." He strides into the room and grabs my daughter's chart.

"How long does my daughter have to scream to get medical attention?"

"I apologize, Mrs. Daughtry." The courteous smile evaporates from his face. "But I have news. I looked at her labs, and we didn't find any toxins in her system."

Why does he look so grave? "That's good, right?"

He grabs a seat next to the bed, speaking in hushed tones. "She has a low white blood cell count and sedimentation rate."

"Wait—what does that mean?"

"It could indicate many things. I'm concerned she's fighting an infection in her small intestine. I want an MRI to get a better look at what's going on in her abdominal region."

Nodding, I glance at Stacy, whose sobs cut into my heart. "Why haven't we done one already?"

"Your daughter's adrenal levels aren't great. I'm worried the iodine for the test will make them crash, but we can't proceed any further without images."

Oh my God. "Her kidneys are failing?"

"It seems to be an acute case of kidney disease. Mrs. Daughtry," he begins in a softer voice. "The important thing to remember is that we're doing everything possible."

My hands tremble like autumn leaves. My daughter's organs are shutting down because I didn't listen to her. "This can't be happening."

"I need your consent for the test," he says.

Is he serious? "There has to be something else."

"Your daughter's weight is in the seventieth percentile." Grabbing the chart, he shows me a graph. "This is an average six-year-old's body mass index. See the line? That's the mean. Your daughter is over here." He points at a dot far from the curve.

"There's nothing wrong with how much she weighs." Stacy's small, but she's always been that way. I was the same as a child. I would never starve my children. Who makes sure they eat homemade? I do. Who feeds them fresh, organic produce and heart-healthy meat? Who doesn't let her leave the table until she finishes her plate? I do.

"She's under average," he says firmly. "And her blood work concerns me, Mrs. Daughtry. Stacy is stable for now, but with no idea of what this is, I can't treat her."

My throat thickens, and I raise a stained tissue to my eyes. "D-do the test."

"Sign here."

He shoves a pen and paper into my hands, and I read the disclaimer with ever-increasing dread that I might be making the worst mistake of my life.

What choice do I have?

"Good," he says as if we're discussing the weather. "I'll get her prepped for the procedure and—"

"I need—I need some air."

Dr. Trotter stands, nodding in his complacent way. "Of course. Take a few minutes to collect yourself."

I smooth my daughter's curls and kiss her forehead. "Stacy, honey, I'll be right back."

I can't hold it together for another moment, and I don't want her to see me cry. Flying from the room, I stride down the bright hall and crash into a body.

"S-sorry." I glance up his solid chest into a pair of soft blues. "Tom."

He grabs my waist. "What happened?"

I pull from his grip and walk away. "They're doing an MRI. The doctor thinks it'll give him a better idea of what's going on."

"They still don't know?" His voice echoes after me. "Melissa."

I want to claw at the parts where he touched me. "Stay with her. I'm heading to the café."

Angry, he follows me. "Can't you put aside our drama for one second? We have to be there for her. Goddamn it, look at me."

"Our drama?" I whirl at him. "You fucked another woman. I will tolerate you until Stacy's better, and then you need to leave the house."

He gapes at me. "Did you not listen to anything I said?"

"I don't have to," I snarl. "It's all lies."

"Melissa, I swear to God I have no idea where the gifts are coming from!"

"Sorry, but I don't buy that. I think the only reason you're still with me is because you're waiting for the sale to go through."

Sputtering, he moves backward. "That's—that's insane."

"No, the crazy part is I was willing to stick with you for the kids. Not anymore." I look at him, and my mouth fills with bile. "You are not getting a penny when I die. I changed my will—everything goes to our children."

"You think I care about the money?" Red-faced, he points at Stacy's room. "While our daughter was sick, you were protecting your estate."

"I didn't know she was ill. Don't you dare put this on me!"

"Who else is to blame?" Veins stand out on Tom's neck. "You were the one at the fucking house. If you paid attention to her for five minutes instead of obsessing over your company, this wouldn't have happened."

He's right.

Shaking, I head toward the stairwell.

He grabs my shoulder, voice softening. "Melissa, I'm—"

I shake him off and wrench open the door, hurtling down the steps. The flights of stairs disappear under my feet when I reach the bottom. Panting, I exit to the main lobby. I walk the polished floor, mind buzzing with fatigue. The tiles shift as I stand still.

Get it together. Just breathe.

I pass the receptionist, who leans across the counter to slide a piece of paper to a woman with shoulder-length black hair. A cherry-red grin staggers over her pale face. Our eyes meet for a fraction of a second. "Melissa?"

Do I know her?

The pretty girl grabs a bouquet and approaches me with a timid smile. God, it's Aubrey. She's wearing makeup. A faint dusting of eye shadow, some blush, and I don't recognize her. "What are you doing here?"

"Visiting your daughter." Her eyebrows knit together. "I mean if that's okay. How is she?"

I open my mouth to repeat that she's fine. Instead I choke. "It's been awful."

She touches my back. "Tell me what happened. Hold on, let's talk here." Stricken, Aubrey pulls me into the lobby with dozens of chairs and guides me into a seat.

"I can't deal with this." I collapse into the cushions. "This is beyond—"

Aubrey lets the flowers splay over her lap. Her expression is frozen. "I thought she was fine."

I shake my head, which feels as though it'll crack from stress. "The doctors don't know what's wrong with her. They're doing tests right now, but she's very sick."

Aubrey's hand flies to her hair. "How come?"

"No idea!"

"That can't be," she whispers. "Is Tom with her?"

"Fuck him," I grind out, meeting Aubrey's shocked stare. "I never want to see him again."

"Can—can I ask why?"

Wiping my face, I glare at her. "He brought his *whore* to Stacy's birthday party."

She parts her bright lips. "His—you mean the woman he's having an affair with?"

"Yeah, she left me a fucking note."

I dig into my pocket and recover the rectangular piece of cardboard, unfolding it to the thick, angry letters signed by A. Was it Ashley from HR? "He says he has no idea who sent it—what a load of crap. Ten years I've known this man, and it all falls apart because of one stupid bitch. Whoever it is cost me my marriage. Sorry for unloading, I'm just so furious."

"I understand," she says in a measured voice. "Here—um —these are for you. I know they're not much, but I had to do something."

Yellow cellophane crinkles into my lap as Aubrey passes the bouquet of mixed roses. "Thank you. That's really thoughtful."

She bites her lip. "Least I could do."

The soft petals roll between my fingers. "Tom used to get me flowers all the time. When we were first dating. Some-where along the line, he stopped. The small, loving gestures disappeared, and he became complacent. I didn't notice until now."

"You'll come out of this stronger." Aubrey takes my hand, squeezing. "This doesn't mean you have to give up on love."

"I don't care about that anymore." Though the tears

running down my cheeks suggest otherwise. "He will pay for this. I'll take the kids away from him."

She releases me with a gasp. "You can't do that!"

"Why not? Have you any idea the destruction he caused my family?" I wrap my fingers around the rigid stems. "Instead of paying attention to my children, I was going crazy trying to figure out who he was fucking."

"That doesn't give you the right to take them away, Melissa. He's not a bad father."

She's awfully defensive. "You don't know him."

"He was attentive at Stacy's birthday," she says.

My hollow laughter resounds through the room. "You mean the hours he spent drinking punch or when he recorded my daughter for a couple minutes?"

Aubrey rolls her eyes at me. What the hell is her problem?

I shift the flowers in my lap. A familiar bold, red ink strains the card sticking from the bouquet.

Get Well Soon! - A.

She didn't have the decency to make it subtle.

Aubrey? He's seeing *Aubrey*?

Shockwaves roll through my body. No, it can't be. Tom wouldn't be interested in a stick-thin replacement unless he fucks her out of some kind of deranged wish-fulfillment fantasy. Aubrey's hardly the younger, hotter version of me I envisioned. She's the sick girl. He's the hero who gets to heal her.

I'm beyond saving.

I smile through my contempt. "Everyone thinks he's an amazing husband. They don't see the stacks of dishes he leaves everywhere and the passive-aggressive hints that I should iron his clothes. They haven't a clue how bad he is with money. He hates giving oral, but I guess you know all about that."

Wide-eyed, she stares at me as I shove the flowers into her chest. "I'm sorry." She breaks from my gaze and gazes at her feet. "I love him."

I believe her. "You poor, stupid girl."

The rage will not come. It's buried under a mountain of stress and fatigue. Right now I don't give a shit about my husband's slut.

My daughter needs me. "You can have him."

A ghost of a smile lights up Aubrey's face.

I won't forget this.

26

AUBREY

She knows. We can finally be together.

My body hums, pulses, and glows with a joy I can't describe. I'm one of those, a person without a care in the world. I'm Phoebe in *Friends*, a happy-go-lucky idiot. I bounce in my seat and count the minutes until I'll have a normal life. Foamy lattes, yoga, play dates, strolls on the beach, fucking in a king-sized bed, hell, lounging on a sofa in sweatpants and not feeling guilty about it.

I can't wait.

The steering wheel slides under my wet palms. I watch their house from my car, picturing the moment when Tom greets me at the door. Rereading his text sends waves of giddiness throughout me.

Come over, baby. The place is ours.

At long last, he's mine. We won't be officially together until they divorce, but still. This has been coming for a while, and I won't apologize for being happy, though it wasn't fun watching how badly I hurt Melissa. In time, she'll understand that Tom and I are a better pair than they ever were.

The sun beats down as I leave the Toyota with the flowers I brought to the hospital. My beaten-up car is hilariously at odds with this neighborhood, but Tom can decide what to do with it when I move in. Maybe he'll buy me another one—or we could just split that Tesla of his. Of course, I'll need a transport of my own to take Grayson to soccer practice.

The kids will love me.

I'll be their new mom, a great mom who always puts them first. I'll be the loudest one at sports functions—the helicopter parent that gets banned from PTA meetings.

I'll be there for them, *forever*.

A door opens. I look up from the ground. A woman descends the steps of her McMansion. Clad in pastels, Barbara makes a half-hearted wave as she picks up the newspaper at her doorstep. With a frigid glare, she disappears behind the door, and it slams shut.

Well, that wasn't very neighborly, but I can't expect them to warm up to me after news of Tom's infidelity spreads to the gossip circles. They'll turn around. It might take several seasons of potlucks and community cookouts, but they will love me. Just as Tom loves me.

Nerves jangling, I stroll the sidewalk to his house. I cluck at the browned lawn and the decaying bushes, which look awful next to the pristine lawns on either side. No matter, I'll get to work on landscaping the yard. The people here will appreciate someone who gives a damn about appearances.

Melissa's Lexus is gone from the driveway. Good. I walk up the concrete steps, bypassing the pile of yellowed newspapers, and knock.

Biting my lip, I wait for my lover to throw open the door. He'll scoop me into his arms with a wide grin. I'll gasp when he throws me over his shoulder and marches off to bed. We'll tear each other's clothes off and fuck until our legs stop working and we're too exhausted to do anything but sprawl on the sheets. Afterward, he'll take me to the kitchen where the breakfast he made is stone cold, but I'll eat it anyway and pretend it's the best eggs and bacon I've ever tasted.

Tom's heavy footfalls pound the floor until the lock clicks open and the door swings. It reveals a disheveled man dressed in a button-up shirt that looks like it was slept in. A three-day strawberry-blond beard grows on his handsome face, which is frozen in polite surprise. I want to leap into his arms, but the look in his eyes is forbidding.

Something must've happened to his daughter. "Hey."

"Aubrey?" Confusion furrows his brow. "What are—Oh, thank you."

He takes the bouquet, apparently at a loss for words. This must be as nerve-wracking for him as it is for me.

"Can I come in?"

Sighing, he backs from the doorway and leaves it ajar. "Sure. I guess."

Not the warmest welcome, but I'll take it.

I push the heavy door to squeeze through as Tom shuffles to the kitchen. He lays the flowers on the counter without finding a vase. The house feels like a tomb. It's dark, and the curtains are drawn. Tom's lonely voice echoes in the cavernous space.

He grips the marble, eyes shining. "She's very sick. I'm worried."

It breaks my heart to see him like this. Listless. Lost. "Where's Grayson?"

"Gone. He's staying with Melissa's mother for now...until we figure things out."

My gaze wanders the ceiling, the spotless furniture devoid of knickknacks, and the utterly empty kitchen. Even the family photos hung on the walls are like faded memories of the American dream. Everyone wants a perfect Facebook timeline, but nobody ever admits how hard it is to maintain the illusion.

The pursuit of perfection was how she lost Tom. "How are you doing?"

He shrugs, lips curling into a bitter smile. "Dealing, I guess. I've never been away from my kids this long."

"It must be awful."

"You have no idea," he says.

No, I don't.

With Stacy in the hospital, Tom's not in the mood to celebrate. I get it. If they were my children, I'd curl up into a ball and scream. He doesn't look like he's on the verge of having a meltdown, but he's devastated.

I take his hand. "Everything will be okay. You'll see."

My pulse jumps when he squeezes me. Tom slides from the stool, releasing a sigh balled in his lungs. He lets go, pacing the kitchen in a tragic way that reminds me of an animal searching for its cubs. I could be a piece of furniture.

Doesn't my presence count for anything?

A jagged slice of hurt tears at my heart. He won't even look at me. It's as though he blames me for what happened. "You'll get them back, Tom. She can't keep you away from your children."

Tom scowls at the empty coffeepot and yanks the cone, dumping the grounds in the trash. "Want some?"

"Sure."

I bury my smile as Tom spoons coffee into the filter. This is a preview of the rest of our lives. He'll make cappuccinos. I'll cook breakfast. He'll grill the steaks. I'll clean the dishes. Brushing past him, I open the cupboard where the cups are kept and take out two.

Tom watches me slide the mugs next to the machine, arms crossed. "So—ah—what are you doing here? Melissa's gone."

Damn, Tom has a lousy memory. "I'm here to check on you."

The frown creasing his forehead deepens. "So...you came here to see me?"

I stare at him. "Of course."

He gives me another weird look. "Thanks for the flowers, but I'd rather be alone right now."

What? "You just asked if I wanted coffee."

"I'll make you a cup to go."

My joy shrivels like newspaper to fire. "I don't understand."

"What's there to understand?" he asks, bewildered. "My daughter is in the hospital. Melissa won't even speak to me. I don't know when I'll see my boy."

Translation: You're the last thing on my mind.

Fuck him.

For months I was the better person. His needs always came first, never mine. He says he'll be there for me—and he ditches me. I tell him I'm committing suicide—he begs me to stop.

What does he want with me?

Is he a sadist? Does he enjoy my pain?

He keeps stabbing me in the chest over and over.

"Sorry, I know I'm being rude." His tone implies otherwise. "Melissa's always been better at this. I appreciate the flowers, Aubrey. Thank you, but I'd like you to leave."

He's a robot. "Leave?"

The discomfort in his gaze grows. "Yes, please."

Everything's wrong, and I don't understand why. He told me to come. Now he wants me to go. I'm sick to death of this.

My eyes burning, I abandon the cups at the counter and approach him. He doesn't make a move to touch me.

I walk into his chest and throw my arms around his waist, clutching him tight.

Slowly, he returns the embrace and pats my shoulder. "Stacy's a tough girl. She'll be okay."

He thinks I'm emotional about his daughter—how sweet of him to think the best of me. The truth is I'm a selfish bitch. I want him to love me as fiercely as I love him.

My head tips, Tom's blond stubble visible through the pearly lens. I blink away tears and stand on my tiptoes, leaning into his chest. My knuckles graze his chin. My fingers dive into his hair. I taste his breath.

He jerks from my touch. "What the fuck?"

Shocked, my eyes fly open to a portrait of rage. Tom grabs my neck and pushes me. "What are you doing?"

His scandalized tones fill me with confusion as I stagger from him. "You shoved me. What is the matter with you?"

"You tried to kiss me."

"So? I need permission to do that now?" A ripple of anger runs through me. "My God, Tom, it's like you don't want me here. You're the one who said to come. The second I walk in, you tell me to leave. The hell is your problem?"

Silence fills the kitchen as Tom works his mouth, apparently at a loss for words. "I didn't ask you to come over."

Okay. *What?* "Are you gaslighting me?"

He laughs. "No."

"You texted me this morning! Told me to hurry. I asked if you needed space, and you said no."

The amusement fades from his eyes. "Someone's playing a prank on you."

"The text came from you, Tom. I'm not an idiot."

"I don't have your number," he bellows. "You're Melissa's friend, or at least, I thought you were. Why would I call you?"

This is a sick joke or Tom's gone insane with guilt and decided to deny my existence. "You have been calling me for months! Ever since I saw you at the—at the farmer's market. You gave me your card! I called the number and—why are you looking at me like that?"

He's not laughing anymore. "I never met you until that day at Safeway, when Melissa invited you for dinner. Who do you think I am?"

"I—you're my boyfriend." My heart beats quickly. "Sure, we haven't met in a public place, but that doesn't mean we—"

"We're not in a relationship," he bellows. "I don't know you!"

Now he's pretending he never called me his girlfriend. "Tom, whatever joke or con you're trying to pull—it's not working. I'm not falling for it."

This is bullshit.

Tom's openmouthed horror stabs at my head. I dive into my purse, rummaging for my phone. "I have no idea why we're playing these stupid games, but here. There's months worth of messages."

With shaking fingers, I open the app and click on Tom's name—except it's not there anymore.

He moves to my side and glances at the screen. "I don't see anything."

Neither do I.

This isn't happening. "Wait—they definitely were here! What the hell?"

He had just texted me. Not an hour ago.

The only messages are to a phone number with no name. The app opens with a long list of blue bubbles—every message I sent Tom. They're all there, but his responses aren't. I thumb up, and read tiny errors under my texts: Could not be delivered.

What does it mean?

Tom refuses to meet my eyes as he walks to the counter with the flowers, yanking the card out of the bouquet and reading the note. "Jesus," he says, scanning the letter. "It was you all this time."

I can't breathe. "Tom, I d-don't understand. Quit lying, okay? This is not—I'm not a game!"

He gestures at me. "You're the crazy bitch who's been sending me gifts all year!"

My stomach clenches. "Don't talk to me like that."

"Melissa thinks we're having an affair because of you."

Why is he still playing dumb? "I told her the truth!"

"Get out." Outraged, he hurls the flowers on the floor. "You are insane, and I want you out of my fucking house!"

He's a liar, and I won't let him get away with it. "We've been together every weekend and you—you made plans to go with me to the Bahamas and chickened out at the last minute because that's what you do. This is you trying to screw with me because you don't have the balls to tell me you're not interested!"

"I'm not interested," he seethes. "Leave."

I will not. "You're a lying piece of shit!"

He seizes me, his thumbs gouging my shoulders as he steers me toward the door. "This is all your fault. My marriage is on the line because of you."

It's so typical of him to blame me. "Don't you fucking dare. I didn't give you that rose. I didn't put a business card in your hand."

"Aubrey, you're sick in the head."

Pain stabs between my temples. "I'm not going anywhere until you admit what we have."

He shoves me. I catch myself on the doorframe. His fist smashes into the wood, inches from my face. I leap away with a scream. A sharp ache shoots into my flesh as he yanks me.

He speaks through shaking, white lips. "If you don't leave, I'm calling the police."

It's as though I'm a stranger—a crazy bitch who burst into his house—when I've spent months pining for him. There's zero remorse on his face—only fury.

What did I do?

He wrenches the door open to the brilliant sunshine. "Get the fuck out."

Tears spill down my cheeks. "Tom, please."

He shoves me over the threshold. "Don't come back."

27

MELISSA

Stacy is dying.

My little girl is fading like an old photograph before my eyes. Color drains from her cheeks and hands, transforming her rosebud mouth into a beige that blends in with her skin.

"It'll be okay," Mom says, gripping my hand. "She'll pull through."

I've lost count of how many times I've heard that. She adjusts the sheets on Stacy's bed for the hundredth time because there's nothing else to do but wait for the doctor. Blowing into her hands fiercely, she rubs them together. "It's so damn cold in here. Don't they know we have a sick child?"

The scene displayed in front of me doesn't feel real. It's a vivid nightmare; so absurd I can't sense anything but a dull horror beating in my chest. The iodine in the MRI test gave Stacy a seizure while she was in the bathroom. Tom was supposed to be watching her. Now there's a thick bandage wrapped around her head. Occasionally she stirs enough to moan through her pale lips. I want to seize one of the many vases surrounding her and bash in my husband's face.

Not content with sitting, Mom paces the room and fires question after question. My mother is pragmatic to a fault. Most of the time I'm grateful for her can-do attitude, but I don't feel up to an interrogation. I answer her in monosyllables, and her frustration with me grows with every response. "Did Stacy have allergies?" "No." "Did you get her tested?" "Yes."

"Where the hell is Tom?" I stay silent. She stamps her foot. "Melissa, wake up! Where is Stacy's father?"

My gaze tears from my motionless daughter to the pantsuit blur of my mother. "I sent him out."

"What?"

I haven't told her about the affair because I know how she'll react—with loud, noisy sobs. Grief for my failed marriage is more than I can bear right now. "Tom and I are having issues."

"Whatever they are, they can wait."

"Drop it." She doesn't understand the hell I've been through, and I don't want to dive into it.

Mom's stare bores into me. "Melissa, you can't keep him away from his daughter."

"You need to stay out of it."

"He's her father."

"Don't, Mom." I stand from the chair. "I'm not in the mood."

She crosses her arms. "Is this about the cancer?"

It always comes back to the illness. I squeeze past the bed, my foot slamming into the side table. "Damn it." Mom's unrelenting stare needles me. "No, it's not. Can we move on?"

Her brows furrow. "Stacy's not the only one I'm worried about. You're too thin."

All my life I was "too fat." The moment I lose a few pounds, everyone loses their minds. "I'm fine, Mom."

"Melissa."

"Stop talking to me with that patronizing tone." It brings me back to uncomfortable memories of my mother hovering over my seat at the dinner table, insisting I finish the plate. "You know I hate it."

"I'm worried about you. We all are." She fixes me with a penetrating stare filled with more scorn than concern.

"What is that supposed to mean?"

An impatient sigh blows from her mouth. "I spoke to your father, and he says that you haven't invited him over in weeks. That you told him he wasn't welcome at your house anymore."

Trust her to speak to Dad after they've ignored each other for God knows how many years. "Dad was causing too much friction in my home. He kept undermining me to the kids. Every time he babysat, I'd come back to a mess I'd have to clean up, and he'd feed them junk."

"That's not what he said." Mom's lips curve into a half-smirk that I loathe. "He told me he made a comment about your illness and you banned him from the house."

It was more like an insult. "I won't have negativity around me."

"I understand that, but he's your father. He's just trying to help."

"Telling me to eat a *cheeseburger* isn't helping." I force my voice to stay even. "My weight is a work in progress. It's not ideal, but I'll be okay."

"You believe that, don't you?" Wordless, she continues to

gape at me. "Honey, lose any more pounds, and you'll disappear."

A series of soft knocks hit the door, and it swings wide without waiting for a response. The team of doctors sweeps into the room. My heart turns to stone as I study all the new faces.

I find Dr. Trotter. "What is it?"

"I have the results of your daughter's MRI." A deep frown knits his eyebrows together. "Stacy has an abscess in her small intestine. It's a pocket of infected fluid caused by a bacterial infection. We need to drain it as soon as possible."

He pushes a consent form in my hands, and I suck in my breath. "Surgery?"

"Unfortunately, reaching the abscess with a catheter would be too challenging. This is a common, routine procedure. There's nothing to worry about, Mrs. Daughtry. My colleague, Dr. Bernard, will be taking on Stacy's case from here on out. He's a pediatric gastroenterologist."

I shake the dry hand of a man in his sixties. "What's wrong with my daughter?"

"I suspect a form of inflammatory bowel disease," he says. "Have you ever heard of Crohn's disease? It's a chronic condition that affects the lining of the digestive tract."

"No, I haven't." As far as I know, no one in our families has that illness. "She's been sick for a long time, hasn't she?"

His eyes soften. "It's not an easy illness to spot with her symptoms, especially in children. This isn't your fault."

That's where he's wrong. I ignored her complaints for weeks because I thought she was being rebellious. All she wanted was her mother to believe her, and I utterly failed her.

His hand grasps my shoulder. "Mrs. Daughtry, are you all right?"

My signature sprawls across the line, and my heart races as I stare at it as though it's a death certificate. "I need to step outside for a moment."

"Of course," he says, stepping aside.

Mom brushes my arm. "You okay, honey?"

"I'll be fine. Stay with her."

Mom purses her lips ever so slightly as she nods in agreement, and I leave the hospital room, breathing in the abrasive scent of antiseptic. The smell brings a vision of my mother, bent over a bathtub to scrub bleach into a nonexistent spot. She'd lock herself in the bathroom and clean, the astringent cloud perfuming the air for hours. When I was old enough, I joined her obsessive cleaning rituals that I realize now were coping mechanisms for my dad's cheating. We all make sacrifices for our partner's flaws, but I will not be her. I can't stay with a man who doesn't respect me, who breaks his vows with a woman in my cancer Meetup group and lies about it.

Hospital employees bustle down the halls, and I stagger toward a fountain. The cold water stings my throat, but I drink as though it'll give me clarity. I splash my face, rubbing my raw eyes. Blinking through the drops, I glimpse a sign across the hall: CHAPEL.

God knows I could use a prayer.

I open the door to a wedge-shaped room with minimal lighting and multicolored plexiglass. Two sets of pews sit on either side of a concrete altar with nothing but a brass cross. A man sits in the first row, his face buried in his hands. Blue and red light splashes over his head. Guilt pits my stomach for intruding. I stopped believing when I was thirteen, and I have no business here. All I wanted was a quiet area to gather my thoughts. I slide into a pew and close my eyes.

I wait for a feeling other than the terror rattling my ribcage, something to make me feel better about the fact that I okayed a form to cut open my daughter. My teeth grind, the pain gnawing through my jaw.

Please save her. She's just a child.

The scrape of a shoe interrupts my plea. My eyelids crack as the man shuffles toward the door.

He stops at my row. "Melissa, we need to talk."

The grief knotting my chest bursts. "You can call my fucking lawyer."

He doesn't move. "You gotta listen—"

This is the man who slept with Aubrey, a person I was starting to think of as a friend. "You're in my way."

He grabs my arm as I shove past. "That psycho came to our house."

"Who?"

"Aubrey. The girl you invited for dinner." He runs a shaking hand through his tousled hair. "She showed up with flowers and said they were for me. She's the one who's been sending me the gifts. Melissa, she thinks we're in a relationship."

"Maybe you should've explained that you only wanted to fuck her." My head reels with the strangeness of my husband calling the woman he slept with "the girl," as if he doesn't know her.

"No," he thunders. "You don't understand."

"Give it up already. She told me everything."

"I never touched her! Her number isn't on my phone. Melissa, this girl is insane."

"You expect me to believe she imagined something between you?" Clearly, he does. "You're unbelievable."

I won't endure any more of this. Shoving him aside, I walk down the aisle. Leaving my daughter's side was a mistake.

He grabs my arm, forcing me to face him. "On my mother's head, I'm telling the truth!"

"Your daughter lies in a hospital bed, and you have the balls to lie to me about betraying our family?"

He threads his fingers through his hair. "I'm not—"

"I'll never understand why you picked her." I dig into my palms to stop the tremble in my voice. "What the hell does she have that I don't have already?"

"Nothing," he says desperately. "Nothing."

"Maybe you're into vulnerable women who'll do whatever you want. Whatever. Get out of my life."

He digs into his coat and brandishes a medicine bottle. "Until you come to your senses, you need to take your pills. It's been five days since you've had them."

He's like an infection spreading through dermis, poisoning my blood. I don't want to believe the last ten years were a lie. "She said she loved you. Do you love her?"

"How could I when she's a stranger?" He thrusts the bottle into my face. "Melissa, take it."

Ignoring him, I walk into the hall filled with hospital personnel.

Tom dogs my footsteps. "Do you want to get sick? Because that's what'll happen if you keep skipping your meds."

"Like you give a damn." I round on him, and he flinches violently. "I've told you a thousand times; those pills make me vomit."

He rolls his shoulders with a full body sigh. "That's a

temporary side effect. It's completely normal, and it will pass. Don't take this out on yourself because you're angry with me."

"Why did you stay with me?" I want to know why he didn't cut and run the moment he started his affair. "Seriously, what's in it for you?"

"Melissa, Aubrey is lying. She's not right in the head." He groans in frustration. "You're not even listening to me anymore."

He doesn't get to play the victim card when I'm the one he's wronged. I picked this man. Part of the blame is mine. It's agonizing to know a quarter of my life has been meaningless.

Tom sighs in defeat. "You won't give me the benefit of the doubt."

"I trust my brain more than my heart, but this time they're both saying the same thing. You're a cheating bastard."

"No, I'm not! Melissa, stop. You need to take these."

He shoves the bottle into my hands, and I slap it away. It bursts open, scattering the pills over the gleaming floor. Hundreds of dollars' worth of guava extract. Funny how unremarkable they are—the drugs that are supposed to save my life.

With a howl of rage, Tom stoops to the ground. "What are you doing? Do you know how expensive these are?" He desperately scoops them into the bottle. Passersby give us strange looks as the pills clunk into the plastic.

The oncologist's last words repeat in my head:

Melissa, there's nothing I can do for you.

No, there's nothing anyone can do.

28

AUBREY

THE SPRINKLERS SEND an arc of water across my knees. Soaking, I stand in the middle of Tom and Melissa's lawn with my hand in my purse. I finger my keys, but my impulses scream for me to beat Tom's door.

What just happened?

I can't make sense of Tom's whiplash behavior. He was cruel. He denied our very existence as a couple, something I know is real.

Almost every week, he finds a day to book a hotel room. Sometimes he comes over. Friday was the last night we were together. He dragged his tongue on my tits and fucked me until I couldn't speak. My body was sore for days. Maybe the reason for his rude behavior was because his wife has a nanny cam and he had to put on an act. It would explain his attitude, but not why he invited me in the first place.

The blank screen on the Messages app sends a dagger of fear through my heart.

This makes no sense.

A second cold blast slices across my abdomen as the jet of water swings back. I grimace and take a few staggering steps toward my car, not before I throw an ugly look at his house. On top of everything, he's watering his lawn during the worst drought in Californian history. What a piece of shit.

I should march to that door and force him to listen, but what's the point? He doesn't want me. If he did, he would've welcomed me with open arms. He wouldn't have pulled away from my kiss. Tom's done with me.

Story of my life. I meet an amazing guy who's incredible in bed, sweet, attentive, and loving. Then it goes downhill. First with the lying and emotional abuse, and then I'm kicked to the curb. Literally. He threw me out of his house.

It's over.

My stomach caves in as though from a blow. The hurt reverberates into my chest with every footfall as I stagger past mansions the size of small hills. There's nothing left to do but go home, so I slide into my Toyota and shut the door.

And then I scream.

I pound the wheel until my fists are bruised, and when my bones start to ache I cry. I don't understand. Why did he talk me from jumping off that bridge? He promised to be there for me and ended things at the first opportunity.

Wiping my face, I grope for my keys and find them in the cup holder. I stab the ignition. The floor roars beneath my feet. I drive almost blind. Tom's house is a blur. Sobbing, I turn the wheel toward my apartment in Daly City. Somehow I make it to my place through a haze of tears and stop my car, mind pounding. The pain is like a hammer against steel, vibrating in my head.

I drag myself across the lawn, stepping on the grass where

Amit died. A fresh wave of remorse hits me, not for Amit, but for all the things I did for Tom. He never saw a future for us. He wasn't willing to bleed for me, and apparently, he doesn't think we had a relationship.

Why would he say that?

Heart beating fast, I walk past the threshold. A sharp pain stabs my temples as I run to my bedroom in a state of panic. I can tell myself it was cowardice, but there's no good reason for Tom's behavior. I have no explanation for the missing texts except a sinking feeling, but what if—

No.

I didn't spend half this year chasing a ghost. He took me on dates. I remember every detail: the food, the sauce on my plate, the bottle of wine he bought. With perfect clarity, I can recall the tang of the mango salsa served with the fresh cod at the Spanish tapas restaurant. I can feel the curve of his lips against mine, his fingers gently nudging toward the seam on my panties. That wasn't imagination.

It was real.

I walk to the shelves and seize the heavy tome of English literature. The book sits on my knees as I thumb pages, searching for the rose. Leaves of paper fall in a cascade, and I find the John Milton poem where I last saw the flattened flower.

It's not there.

My heart beats unnaturally fast.

Going backward, I flip through. Nothing. I tilt it upside down and shake violently. Any second, the flower will drop like a card, and the world will right itself.

Nothing.

Slamming the volume on its spine, I grab fistfuls and tear.

It must be in here somewhere. I scatter paper everywhere, scanning for a hint of green and red. The bedroom becomes a flurry of white as I rip huge chunks until it lies there like a carcass picked clean of its flesh.

Slipping on the discarded pages, I yank open my closet and seize the plastic bin of mementos. I saved every receipt and tissue—every chocolate wrapper and movie ticket. Tearing the blue lid off, I gaze at the empty bottom. A livid scream tears from my throat as I toss it aside and crash through the kitchen, ripping through cabinets to search for the champagne bottle.

Gone.

I seize my phone, searching for any evidence of Tom. My contacts list is bare. All the heartwarming messages he sent me—vanished. The emails. Photographs. Love poems.

Everything. Is. Gone.

He never existed.

And if he didn't, that means I invented this. I created a fantasy of a boyfriend who doted on me with champagne, showered me with affection, and made me feel loved. For the first time in my life, someone gave a damn. A gorgeous, intelligent, thoughtful man chased me through a crowd, pressed that rose into my hand, and I went home with his business card that didn't even exist and called the number that was fake.

I had a two-hour conversation with him—who the hell was I talking to?

No one. None of it was real.

A wave of grief knocks me to my knees. Sobs wrack through my chest as I hunch over the carpet. This agony is different. I haven't loved and lost because there wasn't anything to love. The best time of my life was a fantasy. I planned a murder around a fictional relationship. I'm a delusional, brain-damaged idiot who wasted her final months obsessing over a ghost.

My fingers gouge my chest. I want to tear the pain out. There was never anyone. I'm alone, and I'll die alone. Sitting up, I yank the kitchen drawer near the sink and scrape the false bottom, grabbing the bottle filled with nitroglycerin.

I won't live like this.

Five pills remain. Should be more than enough to stop my heart. I shake four into my palm. One by one, I drop them in my mouth and swallow. I hope it'll be quick. Patrick said it would, but I wouldn't put it past him to sell me half-strength bullshit. I wipe my brow and wait for my pulse to race.

I gaze at my destroyed apartment. Slowly, I walk to the sofa and sink into the cushions. My fingers stab the power button on the remote, and I pick a random show from Netflix. Something friendly.

A camera pans over rolling green hills and sheep pastures. I ignore the English accent booming through the speakers.

Any minute now.

Violins swell as the voice continues to narrate. "If you fancy rustic, old-world architecture, you'll love today's program. The Cotswolds was designated an Area of Outstanding Natural Beauty for the limestone grassland habitats."

My eyes flare open to a vivid image of a stone cottage against a pastoral backdrop. I stare at the screen, waiting for a violent squeeze in my chest or my pulse to race. Run-of-the-mill anxiety rushes through my veins. My hands twitch, but otherwise, I feel...fine.

There's no change. It's been ten minutes.

Maybe it's a delayed reaction?

But I'm not any different. No pain. It's as though I swallowed a placebo.

I charge through the living room and seize the bottle of pills, opening it. The last pill rolls onto the granite. I break it open with a butter knife.

Large white crystals explode from the capsule. I wet my finger, dab it in the powder, and taste. It's sweet. The granules grind my teeth, exactly like sugar. I grab my bowl to compare them to the dust on my counter. They're the same.

It isn't nitro.

I never poisoned Stacy.

I never came close to murdering Melissa.

Patrick conned me.

———

I'VE HAVEN'T BEEN in the Walgreens where Patrick works. He always stressed how important it was that I keep a distance. You know, because of the huge risks he took for me.

Like selling me fake nitroglycerin.

I search for Patrick's moon face as I walk aisle to aisle. My shoulder bashes into an end cap, knocking down the display of peanut butter cups. I don't stop to pick it up. Such is my rage. Instead I power to the glowing pharmacy sign and join the queue for prescription pickup. There he is, the little bastard.

Patrick slides into view behind the plastic barrier, wearing a short white coat over an asinine T-shirt of a giant space cat. He fills prescriptions, bobbing his head to the music. I can only imagine the garbage he listens to—probably house because it makes him feel like he's in a club. I can't believe I let this asshole get the better of me.

I will kill him.

The line shortens with agonizing slowness, and then it's my turn. A pimple-faced teenager gapes at me as I toss a packet of Tums on the counter. "Picking up a prescription?"

"Nope. I had questions for your pharmacist about this drug." Also, I need to remove his spleen. "Could I talk to him for a minute?"

He glances at the package. "They're just Tums, dude."

Mouth breather. "Right, but I have cancer, and I'm taking other medications. I want to make sure there are no inter-actions."

"Oh, okay." He turns, calling over his shoulder. "Patrick! We need a consult."

Behind the clerk, Patrick grunts in approval. The teenager gestures to the side. "He'll be with you in a second."

"Good." I slide down the counter, watching Patrick rip the earphones out and stuff them in his pockets. My skin heats as his round face widens with a smug grin.

He takes in my fury with a shrug. "Sup, Aubrey?"

"We need to fucking talk."

"Whoa. What's with the language?"

I grind so hard my teeth crack. "Meet me outside, or I'll leap over this and choke you."

"You should take a chill pill." He points in the distance. "They're in aisle five next to the hemorrhoid cream. You're welcome."

"You sold me fake drugs, you piece of shit!" I hiss under my breath as Patrick rolls his eyes. "I'll make a big scene if you don't follow me."

"And then what?" He grins. "You'll beat me up? Aubrey, I don't have time for this. I'm working."

Lunging across the counter, I grab the microphone for the store and stab the button. The loudspeakers boom with my frenzied voice. "Attention all shoppers! Walgreens is offering free cough syrup. Not Tylenol, the good stuff. Just head to the pharmacy for a limited tim—"

Wide-eyed, he rips the mike out of my hands. The speakers shriek as he cuts off the power. "Are you insane? You'll get me fired."

"There's a tragedy," I snarl. "Deadbeat drug dealer loses his job."

He glances over his back nervously. "Fine. I'll be at the front."

"Five minutes. Or I call the police." I leave Patrick looking dumbfounded and walk past a line of dazed customers.

A man with a Walgreen vest races to the pharmacy. "Who said that?"

Outside, I stare at the bleak clouds as a cold drop hits my forehead. Sighing, I watch the automatic doors. Patrick charges out a moment later, searching for me. He marches to the parking lot, face flushed. "Aubrey, what the hell?"

"You sold me sugar pills for six hundred dollars."

He rakes his shoulder-length hair. "Yeah, I did. So what?"

"I want my money. Now."

I bristle when he grimaces. "Can't. It's gone."

I hammer his chest. "You son of a bitch!"

He absorbs the blow with barely a whimper and snatches my hand. "Whatever, babe. I did you a favor."

Even this brainless jock must realize what he did was unethical. "You stole from me."

"I knew what you would do," he says with a smirk. "You were going to off that guy's wife."

My lips move soundlessly. How did he know?

"The way you talked about her, it was obvious what your plan was. I'm not a moron, Aubrey. You wanted to kill that woman so you could have him for yourself." Patrick gives me a sad little smile and releases my hand. "I guess I felt sorry for you. I didn't want to see you inside a prison cell, so I gave you those sugar pills."

His head whips back as my fist crashes into his face. "Ow!" He gingerly touches his jaw. "What is wrong with you?"

"You conned me!" I could gouge his eyes. "Why didn't you just say no?"

He hisses through the pain. "Because you were a goner and I needed the money. Seriously, you have no right to judge me. You're the one who wanted to kill some random chick because you were jealous." A smirk tiptoes across his face at my shock. "You deserved it."

Stunned, I gape at him, unable to hurl an insult. His shoulder bumps into mine as he heads back inside Walgreens. Gradually, life stirs in my limbs. He's not getting away with this.

I grab my phone and hunt for an anonymous line to the local police. Calling the number, I talk into the speaker the moment it connects. "Yeah, I'm standing outside the Walgreens next to Ross Hardware where an employee just offered to sell me narcotics. His name is Patrick Mulligan."

I hang up and search for the FBI online tip service, submitting his name for good measure. After I've burned Patrick on all fronts, I take a deep, shuddering breath.

Now what?

What is there left to do besides waste away to cancer?

Melissa. She still thinks her husband cheated on her because I confessed.

The enormity of my delusion crashes over me once again. All those nights with Tom were fragments of my soul. I was desperate for love, and he felt real. I'll die alone, but I don't have to destroy any more lives.

My fingers whiten around the phone as I scroll through my contacts list and find Melissa's name.

I send her a text: *Call me now. We need to talk.*

29
———

MELISSA

Aubrey can't take a hint. This is the third call I've ignored, but she keeps begging me to listen to her rambling voice messages. I am listening. I'm not sure who or what to believe. Aubrey's story of being hoodwinked by a delusion in her brain and my husband's eager acceptance plague me with doubt.

I don't know what to think.

Dismissing the notification with a stab of my thumb, I put the phone aside, face down. I wipe a drop of water on my neck and study myself in the mirror. My hair looks thinner than ever, especially when it's wet. Pink shines through the rows of meticulously combed brassy yellow. I need to schedule an appointment, but beauty took a seat on the back burner with everything that was going on.

"You look great, babe." Tom wears a red baseball shirt that reminds me of our first dates. He's not that different from when he was twenty-five. If anything, he's grown more handsome with his cheeks hollowing and streaks of gray running through his wheat hair.

As he stands behind me, the contrast couldn't be more obvious. He's the picture of health, and I'm very sick. The hollows under my eyes have deepened into the thousand-yard stare I see at my cancer Meetups, which I stopped going to. I haven't had the energy or the motivation. I've finally reached the point of being horrified by my reflection. My hipbones jut out, but Tom runs his hands over me as though I still have curves.

It makes my skin crawl.

I step away, grabbing the pink robe that doesn't do my figure any favors. Silk isn't forgiving for less than perfect bodies, and mine is closer to skeletal every day.

Not according to Tom. "Seriously, you look better. The new treatment is working."

I glare at Tom. His fake cheer wears on me. "Drop it."

Hurt blossoms over his face. "What?"

"You don't have to lie all the time." My bottom lip trembles. "Everyone and their mother knows I'm worse than ever."

"It's been a rough couple of months, but you'll bounce back. Just wait." Tom's reassuring smile fails to inspire hope. He's been saying the same thing for ages, and I know he's trying his damnedest to keep a positive attitude. The never-ceasing encouragement shouldn't make me angry, but it does.

"I should weigh myself." I scan beneath the bathroom sink, but we got rid of scales years ago. After I turned thirty, I didn't want constant reminders how I was letting myself go.

Tom makes a face. "Is that the best idea?"

"Probably not," I say as Tom's body warms mine. I bite the

urge to tell him my need for space, and then he grabs my arms. Gooseflesh rises in rows across my skin. "Tom."

His smile falters. "How much proof do you want?"

I don't know. Aubrey sent me texts after I refused to contact her. It was hard not to respond and find out what exactly she imagined between them. The whole thing could be a lie to get him off the hook.

After Aubrey texted me, Tom came home armed with printouts of bank statements to prove he never purchased a second cell phone. It didn't matter that my heart refused to trust him. The evidence was there. I couldn't tell him to leave when he did nothing bad.

Aubrey was the one in the wrong. She believed she was in love. She sent those unwanted gifts and flowers. She came into my house and stuck that deranged note on my daughter's present.

Aubrey is sick.

I should be glad that my marriage isn't in pieces. My family is still whole. Stacy was discharged from the hospital. The surgery went well, and she'll be on a regimen of anti-inflammatories for the rest of her life, but she's not dying. Within a week, she was flying around the house as though nothing happened.

Everything's fine. Except it's not.

Tom is not fucking another woman, but those liquor bottles didn't drink themselves. Plenty of nights, he comes home late without an explanation. Something is eating his mind. He says it's stress. I wish I could believe him.

Tom frowns. "You look upset."

This is crazy. He's done nothing but support me. "These

last couple weeks have been insane. I'm trying to forget what happened, but it's hard."

"I get that." The tension in his jaw tells me he doesn't. "Melissa, we should see that lawyer."

"Which?" I know who he's talking about and I can't explain my reluctance.

"The will, Melissa." He swallows, his Adam's apple moving up and down. "I need to get on the will. We're both in our mid-thirties. If something should happen to one of us, the kids must be taken care of."

There's no good reason for me to hang on to this suspicion. "Yeah, you're right. We'll change it on Monday." Explaining to my lawyer everything that happened will be painful, but it needs to be done.

I snatch my comb and fight a wave of dizziness. Standing upright takes a lot out of me these days. I barely have the strength to groom myself.

Tom beams at me. "Okay. That sounds awesome."

Black dots creep over my vision. I inhale deeply, willing my heart to slow down. "Maybe I should get a blood test."

"Suit yourself. You know how it always goes, sweetie. They never believe you even though the results are staring at them."

Sometimes it feels like the whole world is mad. "I don't understand why. I'm sick."

For a moment, pain blooms over Tom's face. "I know."

A mass of blonde curls sticks to my comb. Shaking, I slide my fingers through what used to be a thick mane. Now it's so thin, like the rest of me. Another large clump falls into my hand. "Oh my God."

Tom glances over my shoulder. "Yeah, um, one of the side effects of this new treatment is temporary hair loss."

I gape at him. "You didn't think to mention that to me?"

"It's just hair, babe." He rubs me. "It'll grow in."

"That's not the point, Tom. I'm falling apart." Wringing my hands, I charge into the bedroom and remove the silk robe wrapped around my waist. He doesn't understand how many hours I've spent dedicated to my appearance—the Botox, the tanning, the makeup, the endless salon appointments, the manicures. Yes, my life's back together. My husband isn't cheating. The children are safe. All is right in the world— except I'm still stuck in crisis mode.

Tom follows me, his voice stricken. "I hate to see you like this. How about I—ah—visit the kids for the afternoon and you can go to the day spa?"

"Sure." Just what I need. More time alone with my thoughts.

I can't be angry with Tom. He's trying so hard to be there for me after I threw him out of the house. It must be over- whelming. I don't know what to say to make it better. More than anything, I wish I could talk to someone, but the women in my cancer Meetup won't return my calls. I hate to admit it, but I need Aubrey. She's the only one who understands.

Tom kisses me on both cheeks, rubbing my arms. "Okay. We'll get pizza and maybe visit the mini-golf course."

"Not pizza," I say quickly. "Stacy should be avoiding greasy food."

"Yeah, you're right." He leans in to give me another peck. "Love you."

Tears skate down the moment he turns. Distantly, I hear him phoning the kids and the door slamming. I sink to my knees. I'm so tired; thinking is a struggle. After fifteen minutes of sitting, I convince myself to walk to the kitchen.

Hunger pangs claw at my insides. I grab the bowl of grapes, peeling the skin off each and wincing at the intense sugary taste. I swallow a handful before my stomach grumbles in protest. This god-awful nausea makes it impossible to keep food down. My gaze passes over the line of bottles mounted on the kitchen table. Vitamins. Natural remedies. Herbs. Tom's dedicated to trying every holistic treatment there is. I always thought it sweet, that he cared so much he was willing to try anything.

Why can't I shake this awful feeling?

Sliding from the stool, I wander the empty house as pain wracks my chest. I wish I could call Aubrey and scream at her for fantasizing about my husband, but I can't muster any outrage for her. I was so convinced he was lying, and then Aubrey changed her story.

It's too convenient.

I burst into Tom's study and my nose wrinkles at the stale air. Tom's office is the brightest room in the house. He insisted on it for his work, saying the word as though creating pivot tables was akin to painting the Sistine Chapel.

I yank open the drawer of Tom's Cocobolo desk and rifle through its contents, scattering pens and Post-it notes aside. I scrape the bottom, finding nothing, and jerk the next so violently it almost falls out of its runners. What the hell am I looking for? A note with a woman's name and number— would Tom be that stupid?

I find old receipts and office supplies. Sighing, I search the keyboard tray and spot a business card. I flip it over.

Patricia C. Garrison
Probate Attorney

My blood runs cold as I scan the rest of it: Estates, trusts, and wills.

He contacted a lawyer. What the hell was his plan?

Tossing it aside, I head for the living room. His laptop sits on a small desk next to the leather lounge chair. Going through it would be a violation of trust, but I need to know. I won't be able to sleep otherwise.

Grabbing the computer, I open the lid. I click on Safari, checking his recent search history. A boring list of recipes and news websites pops up, and then I find his Google searches. Probate lawyer. Will lawyers. Horrified, I read the dates. When our daughter was in the hospital, he was searching for probate lawyers. What I said must've sent him in a flurry of panic, because he searched at least twenty times that day.

I follow the breadcrumbs to his personal email, which is mercifully blank. My heartbeat slams into my chest. He over-reacted. Looking for representation isn't a crime. I should stop this horrible invasion of privacy and rebuild our trust.

I log out and click on the username that corresponds to his private work email. Autofill generates the password for me, and a stream of job-related emails fills the screen.

See? You're paranoid.

Typing in the bar, I enter "lawyer." A deleted chain pops up in the search with a damning subject line: Need to Contest a Will.

Shaking, I click on the first one.

Hello, Patricia,

I'm seeking advice on how to contest a will due to lack of capacity. My wife was diagnosed with a psychiatric disorder earlier this year. Recently, her mental health has taken a turn for the worst, and she met with lawyers to have me written out of her

life insurance policy and estate. I have a paper trail from her
doctors, proving that her mental faculties were disabled when she
made changes. Please advise.

Regards,
Thomas Daughtry

I reread the sentences, his betrayal refusing to sink in.
Psychiatric disorder?

My hands tremble over the keyboard as I click the next
email, reading the lawyer's suggestion that they meet, them
agreeing on a time, and a chain of attachments. He gave them
my medical history, a copy of a prescription for Xanax that I
never filled, pamphlets from another doctor who insisted I go
to a mental rehab facility. I remember that leaflet—I threw it
in the trash. He must've dug it out and kept it somewhere safe
so he could use it against me. He lied about my health to
make a stronger case to his lawyer.

The room spins in violent circles as a pressure squeezes
my skull.

I don't want to read any more.

I won't accept this.

30

AUBREY

I COULD BE IMAGINING THIS. For six months straight I hallucinated orgasms and planned someone's murder based on a fantasy. But I have to trust what I see. Otherwise it's all pointless.

Tom slides from his Tesla in a sky-blue T-shirt and thigh-length shorts, wearing a slightly longer beard than he did when I last saw him. Beams of sunlight throw the wrinkles into sharp relief. His disheveled appearance raises alarm bells. With the stubble and his frumpy outfit, he's a typical hipster, nothing like the clean-shaven doctor who sleeps in my bed.

Something's wrong.

Tom doesn't do casual unless he lounges in the house. He rarely leaves home in sneakers, and when he does, it's for his weekly five-kilometer run. During exercise, he's a brand whore, always decked head to toe in Nike. Today he's sporting Skechers that look like backup shoes for gardening.

I close my eyes and rub them hard as though the vigorous

movement will clean visions from my brain. The scan made it clear I'm a lost cause. Cancerous growths dotted the MRI in milky-white spots, explaining the terrible headaches and my six-month vision quest through existential despair. It was a lot to take in, so I settled back into old habits. Namely, stalking.

It's not my fault.

Melissa won't answer my phone calls. She stopped coming to yoga and flaked on the cancer Meetups she RSVP'd yes to. I don't know whether she's dodging me, or if something horrible happened. Staking out her house isn't an option. She'd recognize my car and call police in an instant, but I've lurked near her usual haunts, and she's never there.

I can't trust my eyes, but navigating the world with them shut is impossible, so I follow the man who inhabits my thoughts and hope I'm not stalking an apparition. Tom heads straight for the organic produce section, piling bags of green beans, bell peppers, spinach, and carrots into his shopping cart. I pretend to study the Concord grapes as he loads with more vegetables than physically possible to consume in a week. He ignores the meat and frozen dessert aisles, turning into a row of bottles. Scanning them, he grabs a few from the shelves and tosses them into the cart. A small white bottle falls, and he picks it up, grabbing six more.

Watching Tom buy kale extract won't help me find Melissa, but I don't know what else to do. I'm not welcome at their house, and it looks like she's holed up inside. I could let them go and fade into the background, but I can't while Tom sneaks into my bedroom every night. This strange hobo version of Tom might be a construct of my mind.

But *she's* real.

In the last few weeks, I watched Melissa's skin turn white

with neglect. I was there when she stumbled through the Sun Salutation for the first time, and I pretended to shop for groceries when Melissa collapsed in the middle of Safeway. She roused herself enough to refuse medical treatment, and then she piled herself into the car and drove off. On a whim, I looked up her doctor and couldn't find him. There's no website or Yelp page associated with a Stephen Greene. The closest one lives in Utah, and he's an internist.

She lied to me, and I won't rest until I know why.

Tom wheels the shopping cart in my direction, and I duck into the next aisle, heart pounding fast. He rolls the cart into the checkout lane, exhaustion pinching his features. His pale gaze sweeps over me as I approach.

My lungs freeze into place. "Hey."

Tom looks more tired than angry. "What the hell do you want?"

I flinch at his tone, but I suppose I deserve nothing but hostility from him. "Melissa hasn't been at her classes or the Meetups. I just want to know if she's okay."

"She's fine." Tom guards his shopping cart as though I might suddenly run and attack. "Please leave us alone."

"I would if I believed that. She collapsed a week ago."

His eyes narrow in suspicion. "Are you following her?"

I think I'm still in love with him. "Yes."

Tom sucks in a breath, swelling his chest. "You need to back off."

"I'm worried about her." That horrible moment in the grocery store replays in my head. I didn't run to her side because I was afraid she'd recognize me. "If Melissa called me, I'd breathe easier."

"She wants nothing to do with you," he sneers.

"Funny, you'd think she'd block my number." I cross my arms as Tom's grip whitens over the cart. "My texts are going through, but I don't know why she's not responding."

"You're nobody to her."

That might be true. "I want to see Melissa."

"That will not happen." Tom moves into the checkout lane, glaring at me. "If you come near us again, I'll ask my lawyer to file a restraining order."

A piece of paper can't stop me from pressing my face against their bay windows, but it's still a threat. One I'm not too eager to challenge with my recent brush with the law.

I leave the store, returning to my Toyota to watch him wheel outside, looking for me as though I might be lurking behind a parked car. He loads the bags into his Tesla and sits in the driver's seat for a good fifteen minutes. I can't quite make out what he's doing, but I glimpse him rifling through the bag. Seconds later, he leaves and stuffs something into the garbage. He walks stiff-legged into the car and fires the engine, driving away.

I fling open my door, walking into the parking space to pull out what Tom tossed into the trash. It's a bag, and it makes a curious sound, like thousands of beads hitting cardboard. I look inside and see a rainbow of pills and bottles.

What the hell?

I seize one of them, reading its label: Need For Speed Caffeine supplements. At least six different varieties, all empty. I grasp a small red tube. Synephrine. Bitter orange. The tag says it's a banned substance in sporting events.

Why is he buying this shit?

Head reeling, I take everything to the car and inspect the

multicolored capsules. Sifting through them, I find the receipt and glance down the long list. The bitter orange and caffeine are on here, and six different vitamins and supplements. The bag's heavy with pills.

I don't understand what I'm looking at.

It doesn't make sense why he'd load up on caffeine. Melissa can't be taking them. In her condition, it'd be downright dangerous to ingest stimulants. Especially the synephrine. A quick Google search on my phone tells me healthy people have been sent to the hospital for irregular heartbeats for ingesting bitter orange. Either Tom's more of a meathead than I thought, or something weird is going on.

A blue gel capsule rolls in my hand. I read the tiny black print and swallow a tide of vomit.

Holy shit.

———

I can't get there fast enough.

Driving is a nightmare. The tumor must be pressing on my optic nerve because the streetlights are doubled with huge star-bursts. I don't know what is real—if the bag sitting in the passenger's seat is really there, or if this is some warped revenge fantasy.

It's not true.

Stopping at the light, I wipe a clammy streak of sweat from my forehead. I need to pause for a second and think this through, but I'm scared to death I'll wait too long.

No, I have to talk to her now.

The skies flare with double green orbs. I press the gas,

driving in between the splitting roads. Please God, let me climb this fucking hill without crashing. I drive to Tom and Melissa's street and park next to the mammoth-like home. A nail seems to ram into my skull. Staggering from the car, I walk on the sidewalk. The bay windows offer me a clear view of their house, which is dark.

Maybe she's not here.

My mind plays tricks on me. Flickers of color burst into brilliant flames. I have no business driving, let alone walking, but I have to see Melissa. I owe her.

With the bag in my arms, I raise my fist and knock, hitting stone. My hand moves to the right and finds the smooth wood. "Melissa? It's Aubrey. We need to talk."

No answer.

I turn away, crashing through the bushes. Rose thorns slice me as I fight toward the bay windows, collapsing against them. The back of a cream white leather sofa looms in front of me. I squeeze into the narrow passage to the garbage and open the gate—they really should have locks—and slip into the back-yard. A kidney-shaped pool quietly hums with the motor, its turquoise waters trembling.

My gaze sweeps the lawn and expensive patio furniture. Movement near the doors catches my eye. A pink-robed figure stands next to the kitchen table.

Must be her.

Swallowing hard, I climb the steps and approach the glass. She will call the police, and this will be worthless. Fear pulses in my neck as I rap the window.

A skeletal face turns toward me.

The air breaks with my scream. She reaches out, claw-like, to open the door. The effort seems immense. It's as though someone scooped the fat in her cheeks, leaving them hollow. Dark bruises cover her arms, which are so thin. Paper-white skin covers what flesh is left on her bones.

"Oh my God." I step forward, grabbing her arm. "What has he done to you?"

31

MELISSA

THE SUN BLEEDS in orange with swift brushstrokes, staining the navy blue sky. Gold scatters over hedges and the rippling pool. Sunbeams at her back, Aubrey stands in a halo of light. It would be beautiful if the sight of her didn't bring me dread. The insistent knocks must've been her. Answering the door is low on my list of priorities, as well as dealing with whatever Aubrey wants. She trespasses into my backyard as though she's earned the right to barge into my life.

I don't have time for this. "What are you doing here?"

Aubrey doesn't move, speak, or do anything to indicate she heard me. She gapes at me with the same openmouthed rudeness as the assholes at the grocery store.

I snap my fingers. "Hey."

"Sorry." She squints at me, clutching a paper bag close to her chest. "What happened to your arms?"

I rub the ghastly purple marks covering my skin feverishly. The bruises won't disappear. "It's the cancer."

Aubrey swallows hard, her gaze finally meeting my eyes. "You look like you've been beaten within an inch of your life."

The clerk at the store probably had the same thought but didn't have the nerve to voice it out loud. Kudos for Aubrey. "Tom has never laid a hand on me. Are you here to make me feel like crap or is there something else?"

"Sorry, I didn't mean to upset you. I'm just shocked." Her fingers tighten over the bag. "Can I come in?"

The balls on this girl.

I laugh at her silhouette. "Why would I let you do that?"

Her nostrils flare. "Because we need to talk."

"You've said that a thousand times in your voicemails. I don't care about anything you have to say."

"I followed Tom!"

The door digs into my palm. "*What?*"

"I didn't have a choice, Melissa. You refused to talk to me. I hadn't seen you in weeks. I was worried, so I waited outside your house until Tom left."

My jaw drops at her confession. How many hours did she sit in her car, waiting for Tom to leave? "You need to learn boundaries, Aubrey."

"My therapist says the same thing."

I'm not surprised. "Maybe you should listen."

"Let me inside." She peeks around me. "Is Tom here?"

"No."

"Good. Let me in." Aubrey doesn't give me a choice as she grabs the sliding glass door and yanks it wide. I consider slamming it shut on her fingers, but I don't have the strength or the energy.

Sighing, I step back and allow her inside. Aubrey walks into the dining room, clutching a brown grocery bag. She blinks from the light until I yank the shutters closed and bathe us in darkness.

"Let's make one thing crystal clear," I say to her figure. "We are not friends. I'll let you get whatever it is off your chest, and then you have to leave."

Shrugging, Aubrey walks to the wall and hits a switch. The sudden blast of light forces my eyes shut. Through my eyelashes, I watch her slide the bag over the dining room table.

She avoids my gaze. "I found something about Tom."

"I bet you did," I say. "We're not exactly in the best place right now. I need to call my lawyer."

Aubrey squints at the numbers glowing on the microwave. "It's six-thirty."

Damn. "Then I'll draft an email."

"Can it wait ten minutes?"

"No, it can't." My footsteps echo as I march toward the living room where Tom's laptop glows in a bright blue square. "You asked me what he did to me. Here's your answer."

She hesitates before picking it up. The soft glow lights up Aubrey's wasted face as she scans the screen. "Wait, what is this?"

I grip the leather chair. "He sent this email to a probate lawyer when our daughter was sick in the hospital. He was going to lie about my condition."

Her back zips straight. "There's a prescription for an anti-anxiety medication here."

"So?" I don't like the pity blooming on her face.

"In the email, he doesn't mention the cancer. He says you're mentally ill." She tears her gaze away from the computer, frowning. "Don't you think that's odd?"

"No, not really." This conversation is heading in a direction I don't like. "He's obviously lying."

"But his claim would fall through the moment you gave evidence about your diagnosis." She closes the lid. "You were diagnosed, right?"

I bite my lip. "Of course I was."

"Then I don't see what's so urgent about this. Legally, he doesn't have a leg to stand on." Aubrey adjusts herself on the couch, giving me her full attention.

Dread fills my stomach with lead. "I don't have a paper trail."

Her brows furrow. "What do you mean?"

"I've never been treated by an oncologist," I say in a small voice. "The doctors never believed me."

Aubrey's jaw drops as she stares at me, unblinking. "Are you serious?"

Two burning patches rise in my cheeks. "*Yes.*"

"So you *think* you have cancer." She stands, still wearing that frightened expression. "*Why?*"

Tom looked like that whenever I confided in him about my fears.

I was worried about this. Why would she believe me when no one else has? "Aubrey, I'm sick. Look at me. Look at my hair. My arms."

"I hear you. You're ill, but you don't have cancer."

"Yes, I do! I feel it, Aubrey."

Uncomprehending, she shakes her head. "But how can you know—"

"The tumors press into my side and send aches throughout my body. It started six months ago. I knew something was wrong, but my blood work came back fine. All they wanted to do was give me referrals to psychiatrists. Do you know what that's like?"

Clearly, she doesn't. None of them understand the nightmare I went through.

Pity fills her gaze. "But if you had cancer, the labs would've had signs."

She's using the same pleading tone Tom would use on me. "There are no tests that can confirm a diagnosis without a biopsy. Every doctor I saw refused me."

"Then why do you still—"

"Why don't you believe me?"

"Because you're not making any sense!" she shouts.

"I have proof!"

"Okay." Sighing, she runs a hand through her hair. "Show me."

My muscles tense. "Tom will be home any second."

She approaches as though she's afraid I'll bolt. "I'm on your side, but I need more than just your opinion."

"*Fine.*"

I move through the house, flipping light switches as we enter Tom's study. The filing cabinet stands in a column of black metal. I yank the bottom drawer and leaf through the files. Finding my medical folder, I pull it out, Aubrey helping me. The MRI of my abdomen slides onto the wooden floor.

Aubrey traces the circled gray tumors, shaking her head. "How do you know what you're looking at?"

"Because Tom got the results. He picked them up the next day, and the radiologist interpreted it to him."

"They can't do that, Melissa." Her forehead darkens. "Tom told you that you had cancer?"

"Yes." I point at the spots. "It's right there."

Shrugging, she glances at the gray blob. "There are dozens of shapes. I don't know what the hell I'm looking at."

"You don't need to believe me. I know what's happening in my body." I grab the MRI copy and stow it away. "You should leave."

Undeterred, Aubrey follows me into the kitchen. "If you have cancer, why is Tom switching out your supplements with caffeine pills?"

"What are you talking about?" My iPhone chimes and I dig it out of my pocket, glancing at the notification reminding me to drink water with lemon. Tom's latest diet involves citrus infusions. Lately, I haven't been able to keep anything down.

"I saw him at the grocery store." She follows me like an annoying shadow as I pull a glass from the cabinet and fill it with filtered water. "He bought a ton of bottles and sat in his car for a while. I couldn't see what he was doing, but then he went outside and stuffed this bag into the garbage."

Aubrey grabs the bag and opens it, reaching inside to grab fistfuls of pills.

I stare at the gel capsules, dumbfounded. "I've never seen these before."

"That's because you haven't taken them." They drop in a colorful cascade as Aubrey tips her hand. She grabs an empty white bottle, showing me the label. "You've been taking these instead."

"Caffeine?" I shake my head. "Absolutely not."

She bites her lip. "Does Tom take them?"

"No." I slam the half-filled glass on the counter. "What are you getting at?"

Her eyes bore into mine. "He's been switching out your

medication, Melissa. That's why he changed the containers in his car and dumped all the supplements in the trash."

My nails pierce my flesh. "Why would he do that?"

"Look," she says, grabbing the receipt. "That's his name. He bought all this caffeine and synephrine."

I don't believe what she's saying—she's out of her mind. "Tom wouldn't—"

"Your story about the MRI doesn't make sense. A tech can't diagnose cancer. A doctor wouldn't discount those test results."

"I don't know what you want me to tell you!" I watch as Aubrey backs away from the sound of my voice. "Jesus —*fucking*—Christ!"

"All right. Calm down!"

I'm not crazy. "I brought the MRI to the last oncologist I saw. He *said* there was nothing he could do for me! That's why I've been doing these stupid treatments."

Aubrey gives me a sharp look. "Why are you taking supplements that don't work?"

Frustrated, I let out a deep sigh. "Because Tom wants me to try them." Her eyes grow wide as saucers. "I know what you're implying, but he's not—Tom wouldn't do that."

"So he's the only one who heard the tech's diagnosis, which they're not allowed to do. Only a doctor can confirm the presence of tumors. Tom lied about that, and then he convinced you to take pills that would make you worse."

Slowly, I digest the absurdity of her words. "Are you—are you saying he *wanted* me to get sick?"

"No. He wants you to die."

I laugh at the suggestion. Tom, the sweetheart I met in a dive bar who walked me home after dates, father of my two children and light of my life, is trying to kill me? "You have an overactive imagination."

Growing impatient, Aubrey slams the empty bottles on the counter. "Melissa, look at the facts. *He* enabled your sickness. *He* switched out the pills."

It comes down to whether or not I believe Aubrey saw him do this. And I don't. "How do you know this isn't another fantasy?"

For a moment she looks confused. "His name's on the receipt."

It is. "That doesn't prove anything."

Frustrated, Aubrey stabs at the piece of paper. "Just look at it, Melissa."

"I did. Your theory's ridiculous. I've never heard of anyone dying from caffeine."

"It happens all the time—kids overdose on caffeine pills and energy drinks. A cup of coffee won't do that, but you're taking unsafe amounts. You're dying because you're starving, Melissa. And you're starving because you're nauseated from the caffeine you've been ingesting. Right? When was the last time you ate?"

"I eat tons of vegetables!"

"He's forced you onto a low-calorie diet claiming it'll heal the cancer, but you're just getting sick. You're throwing it all up. He can't outright kill you, but he can make you waste away. And everyone sees it. Everyone knows you're losing weight. He's waiting for you to starve yourself to death!"

Tom noticed the change. In tears, he begged me to take more pills as a last-ditch effort to save my life. I did it only to placate him.

"He probably increased the dosage gradually so you

thought you were getting worse." Horrified, her mouth drops open. "He's getting ready to finish you off."

I stare at her. "That's crazy."

"You look like you're wasting away from cancer, but you're not."

"Yes, I am." This is getting really old. "It's a fascinating theory, but it's wrong."

She grasps my shoulders. "I'm telling you the truth!"

"I don't believe you! Why would the doctor tell me there was nothing he could do?"

"Probably because he's an oncologist, and you don't have cancer!"

No, that's *not* what happened. I remember the room we were in, the spot on the doctor's tie, how the world dropped away when he said those words. The fight inside me was extinguished. All I could do was hold Tom's hand.

"Tom wouldn't do that." I shake my head. "You're insane."

"Really?" She gestures toward the laptop. "He laid out his plan right there in that email."

His plan. It's laughably Machiavellian. *Ridiculous.*

Aubrey frowns as I chuckle at her stupid theory. That's what it is—a wild story Aubrey cooked up because she loves drama and my husband being a money-grubbing asshole wasn't enough.

Aubrey takes my hand and leads me toward the door. "What are you doing?"

"Taking you the hell out of here."

I slide out of her grip. "I'm not going anywhere."

"Damn it, Melissa." She whirls, snarling. "We have to leave before Tom gets back."

The whites show around her eyes as she presses her shaking lips together. Aubrey's scared. She believes Tom's dangerous.

My smile evaporates. "Aubrey, Tom isn't *after* me. I've known the man for ten years."

"How much more proof do you need?" Her voice hits the ceiling. "Don't you understand? He wants you dead. He's poisoning you."

"There's nothing you could say that would make me believe you. Stop it, Aubrey!" I yank my arm from her grip. "You almost destroyed my marriage. You thought you were fucking my husband. You put that disgusting note on my daughter's present. I don't care if it was a figment of your imagination. You're a selfish, *sick* girl, Aubrey. I don't want you around me."

She flinches as though my words are physical blows. "I'm really sorry. I put you through a lot of pain. You're right about everything, but I am trying to do better. I want to be a good person."

"Then leave my family alone."

She purses her lips. "I can't do that."

"It's time for you to go." My head pounds with my frantic heartbeat. "I'm not kidding."

"Neither am I." Aubrey seizes my hand, pulling me toward the entrance. She grinds to a halt, throwing a terrified look at me.

On the other side of the door, a key scrapes the lock. The sound of a man's cough sends a thrill into my heart. The deadbolt clicks, and the door yawns open. Aubrey pauses, squeezing my fingers until they whiten. Tom steps through with a shopping bag.

He freezes as his gaze sweeps over Aubrey. A bright red

flush crawls up his neck, burning the tips of his ears. Without breaking his line of sight, he slams the door shut, his fury shaking the floor.

Tom tears his gaze away to glare at me. "What the fuck is she doing here?"

I could laugh at the terror on Aubrey's face. "Relax, Tom. She came here to apologize."

"Good," he booms, facing Aubrey. "Now you can leave."

Aubrey squares her shoulders, balling her hands into fists. "I think I'll stay."

A very ugly look darkens Tom's features. "Get out!"

"Tom, lower your voice," I say.

Furious, he turns toward me. "You're going to take her side?"

"Melissa, remember what I told you," she says quickly. "Just look at the evidence."

"I have and I don't buy it. Sorry." Walking closer, I take her shoulder and guide her toward the door. "Just go."

She digs in her heels. "I swear to Christ, I'm not lying."

Maybe she's not. Maybe it's another delusion that she wants to save me from. It doesn't matter.

"What is she talking about?" Tom demands. "*Melissa.*"

"I don't—"

"I know what you're doing to her." Aubrey cuts across me. "You're a fucking monster."

He seizes her arm, wrenching her forward, and Aubrey's head snaps back with a force that alarms me. I've never seen him like this. Aubrey's eyes plead with me as he pushes her through the open door. Her heel catches on the threshold and she trips. Tom slams the door as she lets out a painful yelp, and he faces me, chest heaving. The sight of Aubrey crumpled on my doorstep disappears from view, but her twisted grimace burns in my mind. I try to match that image with the man I married.

"When did she get here?" he says, still glowering at the door.

Heart beating fast, I clutch my chest. "Not—not that long ago. She was in the backyard. Should we call the police?"

Tom lets out a shuddering sigh and runs a palm down his face. "No. I think she got the message."

Muttering, he dumps the bag of groceries on the island. He methodically puts the vegetables away, slamming a row of supplements on the counter, and then he spots the empty containers Aubrey left behind. He stops.

"What the hell is *that*?" Tom grabs the receipt, his lips shaking with a white fury. "What is this, Melissa?"

Why is he so angry? "Aubrey brought it over."

The paper crumples in his fist. "What did she say?"

"She thinks—well—it doesn't matter." I stare at him as he tosses the balled up receipt under the sink. "She's a lunatic."

"Right," he says finally.

Then why did he destroy the receipt?

A chill spider-crawls down my spine as he seizes the empty containers, the brown paper bag, and stuffs them into the garbage with the air of making them disappear as quickly as possible.

I'm as delusional as Aubrey if I put *any* stock into her claims. Tom doesn't hate me. My husband has flaws like any human being. He played a nasty trick with that lawyer, but he's not a killer. Sometimes people do hurtful things out of love. Eventually, I'll forgive him. He forgave me for believing he was cheating.

It's only fair.

I will *not* let her ruin us.

Tom opens each vitamin bottle that he bought from his trip to the store. The protective seals are already punctured through. Another horrible chill runs through me as he makes a show out of tearing off the paper and removing the cotton inside. Then he slams several pills on the counter. My evening meds.

Tom pools them in his hand and offers them to me. "Here."

"What's this blue one?" I count four new pills I've never seen before.

"Something new I picked up," he mutters. "It's Vitamin B-Complex. You haven't been eating a lot of carbs, so I thought it'd be a good idea."

A warning from Aubrey screams in my head. *He's finishing you off, idiot.*

I want to believe she's wrong.

I need to believe.

Tom's pale eyes glaze over as he fills a glass with water, pushing it into my hands. "Go ahead."

I don't take them. A smile tiptoes across his handsome face. Once it would've disarmed me.

"You don't believe her, do you?"

It can't be true. Everything she says is a lie.

He sighs, frustrated. "*Melissa.*"

I know it's crazy, but I can't get her voice out of my head.

The voice that says my husband is trying to kill me.

32

AUBREY

He's killing her. Behind those doors, Tom's convincing Melissa to take a cocktail of drugs that'll send her into cardiac arrest. In her weakened condition, the synephrine will be enough to stop her heart. I'm sure of it.

I pace the perimeter of their house, heart slamming into my chest. I have to do *something*. Melissa's not right in her mind. I don't know if I got through to her.

I search my pockets for my phone, but it's not on me. In my hurry to get here, I must've left it behind. Damn it. What else could I use? I look through their bay windows, watching the long shadows of Tom and Melissa tremble until they split into two. I shake my head until they shrink back into their spots.

My feet stumble over a hard surface. In the dark, I grope for an object to hurl through the windows. Thorns stab my fingers as I pat the earth, touching a rock—*yes*. I heft it with both hands, pulse jumping in my throat.

I need to make her see the real Tom.

Holding the rock over my head, I hurl it at the windows. It smashes through, raining glass over the bushes. The angry tones of a deep male voice boom through the shattered hole. A light flickers on, illuminating Tom's strong silhouette.

The door swings open, and Melissa steps outside, gaping at me. "What did you do?"

I hurry to her side and grasp her hand. "We need to *go*!"

"*No*." She pulls away from me, retreating inside the house.

"Melissa!" I follow her inside, making a grab for her arm.

Tom blocks me from reaching her. He smolders with a menace I never imagined on his sweet face. In my visions, his anger was always on my behalf. He'd commiserate with me about my shitty job, the dicks at work, and he'd nod along with a cute frown creasing his forehead. Then one of us would break the tension with a silly joke or kiss.

I don't recognize the man in front of me. He's full of bile. Hatred.

"You little *bitch*." He points toward the damage in his living room. "I hope you have the money to pay for that."

"I probably don't."

An angry flush fills Tom's face. "What the hell is wrong with you? How many times do I have to tell you to stay the fuck away?"

My back hits the wall. "At least a few more."

He makes furious moves toward me, but Melissa grabs the back of his shirt. She moves behind Tom like a pink ghost. "Aubrey," she says, several octaves higher. "You should go."

"Come with me," I beg her. "You'll die if you don't leave!"

Tom's gaze falls on me. "What did you say to my wife?"

My muscles tense. I move instinctively backward, more afraid than I've ever been in my life. The man in my dreams would've never harmed a woman. He was wonderful—their lives were supposed to be perfect. All those hours watching them, and I didn't see what Tom was doing to his wife.

I didn't know.

Gripping a chair, I slide it between Tom and me. "Melissa's spending the night at my place. We just want to leave."

"That's not happening." Rage ripples across his face. "She stays. You go."

I never appreciated how massive his six-foot frame was until now. The two of us don't stand a chance if it comes to a fight, and he won't let me go with Melissa.

What do I do?

I could abandon Melissa to this hell. It's not my job to save her from herself, or from the man who's slowly bleeding her to collect every penny she's worth. We have to live with the choices we make—good and bad.

Once I was willing to kill Melissa to have Tom.

Now I'll do anything to keep her alive.

"I'm not going anywhere."

In his rage, he knocks over a chair. "Get the fuck out, or I'm calling the police."

"I already did," I tell him. Behind him, Melissa's hand flies to her mouth. "They're on their way, and they'll have questions for you."

I hold my breath as Tom stops several feet away from me. For a moment his gaze is appraising, and then his lips stagger into a smile. "Liar."

"It's over, Tom. I know everything."

The chair rips from my hands as Tom tosses it aside. "Another delusion, Aubrey? A little fantasy in that demented head of yours? No one believes a word that comes out of your mouth."

"But they'll believe your wife when she says you've been poisoning her."

He lunges for me. I leap away, sprinting to the kitchen. My feet skid on the tiles as I grope the counter for a weapon, seizing the handle of a cast-iron skillet.

"Aubrey, no!" Melissa's horrified tones echo throughout the house. "This is crazy. Put it down."

Amusement briefly flickers across Tom's face. "Yes, put it down before you get hurt."

My biceps strain as I lift the skillet. "I saw what you did at the grocery store!"

He grips the island standing between us. "What, now shopping's a crime?"

"Don't play dumb. You've been swapping her supplements. You lied about the cancer. You've done everything in your power to make your wife sicker. You want her *dead*."

"That's—that's *ridiculous*." White-faced and furious, Tom presses his shaking lips together.

"I saw you do it!"

Tom looks at Melissa, a pained grimace stretched across his face. "You don't believe this garbage, do you?"

Trembling head to foot, she lifts her shoulders in a shrug. "I looked at the receipt. And the pills in the bag."

"So you think I'm trying to kill you?" he says incredulously. "Seriously?"

"I'm not saying I believe her! I'm saying—I have doubts."

"Doubts," he repeats acidly. "After everything I've done for you. The countless hours researching and I don't know how many goddamn times I cooked dinner. Every day I'm a slave at work while you sit here and do nothing. And you believe this psycho before your own husband?"

"If Aubrey is right..." Melissa clenches her fists. "I'm taking everything to the pharmacy. They'll identify exactly what they are."

"Unbelievable," he rages. "You are un-*fucking*-believable!"

Bingo. I smirk. "Were you going to contest her will before or after she died? I'm guessing after. You're not as stupid as you look, although leaving that email in your inbox was a pretty dumb move."

The outrage melts away as he approaches Melissa, who looks sickened. "Babe, I was worried, that's all. You gave me a huge scare."

My legs tense, ready to spring. "Can you forgive him for meeting with lawyers when your daughter was dying?"

He slams his fist into the marble. "That doesn't make me a murderer!"

She shakes her head, lips moving soundlessly. "This can't be—"

"Melissa, it's not too late." It's important that she understands this. "You can turn this around and be healthy again. You don't have end-stage cancer."

"No." Tears stream down her thin face. "Don't say that! It's not true."

I shout over Tom's protests. "He wants you to fucking die!"

Adrenaline shoots into my chest as Tom makes furious strides toward me. He grabs my collar, half-dragging me to the door.

"Melissa!" I yell. "You have to believe me!"

But Melissa looks like she's incapable of making decisions.

She slumps to the floor, moaning the same word over and over, "*No.*"

"I'm throwing her out! I've had enough." I stumble as Tom shoves my back. "Stop fighting me, or I'll hurt you."

This is my last chance. I twist around, looking for her. "What about your kids? Don't you want to get better for them?"

"Shut the fuck up," Tom hisses.

Colors and shapes whirl past as Tom throws me forward. I lose my balance, shoulder crashing into the mahogany door. The force reverberates all the way to my elbow. Tears spring in my eyes as I gasp with the pain.

"You hurt her." On her feet, Melissa gapes at Tom. "What is the matter with you?"

Gritting my teeth, I claw myself to a standing position as Tom aims a vicious punch inches from my face. "She made me do this."

I slip out from under him, limping back to the kitchen island. He grabs me and yanks so hard my arm socket makes a sickening pop. I crash into the wall. My scream is knocked from my lungs.

"Tom!" Melissa's whip-like voice lashes Tom's skin. "*Leave her alone.*"

Gasping, I seize Tom's distraction to crawl toward the island.

Fists clenched, he faces Melissa. "She's out of her fucking mind."

I lift myself upright. "Not about this!"

Tom lets out a sound like a wounded animal before seizing a chair and throwing it at me. The wood crashes into the marble. I duck as it clatters over my head, smashing to the ground.

Melissa's scream sends a thrill to my heart. "Stop it!"

But Tom is beyond reason. "All I've done is for our family! Yes, I emailed that lawyer. Can you blame me? Our child almost died because you were too self-absorbed to notice how sick Stacy was."

"What?" Melissa takes a step back as though struck by his words.

"It was always about *you*. Your cancer. Your fucking delusions!" Tom stops abruptly, his face rapidly turning red.

"Delusions—what are you talking about?" Her lip trembles as she glances from me to her husband. "*Tom*."

"You remember how many doctors we went through? They all said the same thing, but you refused to accept they were right."

"I—have—cancer!" Melissa screams.

"No, you don't!" Tom's voice roars through the house. "You've never had cancer, you crazy bitch, but you'd rather die than live the beautiful life we built together. I tried to tell you that you were wrong, but you didn't listen. So I thought, *fine*. If she wants to die, I'll help her."

Melissa's mouth opens with a silent scream.

"I made the right choice," he says, eyes narrowed in malevolence. "My kids won't be raised by a lunatic obsessed with her failures. They need stability."

"I'll murder my wife for the sake of our children." My laughter rings throughout the house. "Yeah, you're the picture of mental health."

A projectile launches at my face, and I duck just before the blur shatters on the wall behind me. Screaming, Tom leaps for me. I slip on a piece of ceramic as I sprint around the island.

Frantic, Melissa beats her fists on the wood. "Stop! Tom, stop right now!"

I turn to see Tom seizing the handle of a knife. He lets out a howl of rage and races toward me. Stunned, I watch him swing the blade in a wide arc. I duck. The metal strikes the marble, gouging a deep line.

Melissa screams. "STOP IT, TOM!"

Hysteria bubbles in my mouth as he grabs a glass, launching it at my head. I whip to the side, hearing the crash behind me. Heart jammed in my throat, I sprint down the hallway and focus on placing as much distance between us as possible. One blow and I'm dead. I can't let him anywhere near me.

Lungs burning, I seize a frame from the wall and hurl it in his direction. A loud curse tells me I hit my target, and then I dash toward the door. His footfalls grow louder, his shadow almost swallowing mine.

Too close. I glance over my shoulder. Tom swings the knife, aiming for me but smashing picture frames instead. Glass showers the floor.

"Aubrey!" Melissa screams at the top of her lungs. "Out here!"

I round the corner, heading in the direction of Melissa's voice. She stands next to the front door, which is wide open. Any second, Tom will catch me with a terrible blow, and it'll be all over.

"Keep running!" Melissa moves away to collide with Tom, who trips over her body.

I glance at the tangle of limbs as my lungs scream for air.

Tom shoves her. Melissa claws at him, sinking her nails into his skin. Her yell splits the darkness as Tom beats her aside, and then he steps over her, toward me.

I stumble over the threshold and onto the damp grass. My legs tremble with every agonizing step. I need to keep going. He'll kill me.

"Tom, stop!" Melissa's screams echo down the block. "Aubrey!"

For her sake, I hope it's quick.

I look for her, but she dashes into the darkness. A bitter taste rolls my tongue back. At least she won't have to see me die. Christ, I didn't want this.

My breaths come in ragged gasps as I crash through rose thorns into the neighbor's yard. Tom follows steadily, knife clenched in his hand. He's taking his goddamn time. Wearing me out. It won't be long before my legs give out, and then a sharp pain will dive into flesh. My lungs seize the moment I burst into the driveway. I collapse, gasping for breath as Tom's shoes scrape the pavement. The blade floats inches from my eyes.

The knife pricks my throat. "You should have stayed out of this."

I roll on my back, staring at his silhouette. "Shut up and kill me, you coward."

The garage lights flicker, illuminating Tom. His silky blond hair falls around his face, resembling for a moment the man I fell in love with. His pale eyes glow. They'll be the last thing I see before I die.

The blunt edge of the knife sinks into my throat, cutting my air. My vision mists over. Blackness creeps across. If this is dying, it's agony. I claw the metal choking me, but he presses down.

A dark shape looms behind Tom. I watch its shadow grow. Am I dead already? The pain's still here, slicing my lungs. I can't be gone, so what is that? It floats in a distorted bubble of gray as it rolls forward soundlessly. I blink, and the tears melt away, giving me a clear image of a car's fender.

"What the—" Tom drops the knife.

The Tesla catches his knees. He doubles over the hood, grimacing. As though in slow motion, Tom turns around to see a wall behind him. His scream cuts off short. The car rams into his midsection with a sickening crunch. I stare at his twitching legs.

What just happened?

Gasping, I crawl underneath the maze of machinery. The pavement scrapes my knees and wrists. I collapse next to the tire and claw myself to a standing position. Slowly, I blink black dots away and take in the horrible sight in front of me.

The Tesla pins Tom's body against the buckled garage door. Red-faced, incapable of making sound, he gropes the hood. Tom's hands slide over the metal, his bloodshot eyes trained on the windshield. It lasts a few seconds, and then he slumps over.

Dead.

33

MELISSA

Tom's gone. Three months now.

Sometimes I feel him around me. His ghost walks the shadows of my house, and if I close my eyes, his stubble scrapes my cheek. I lie awake most nights. My therapist tells me I did nothing wrong, but I feel like a murderer.

It took weeks of group therapy, one-on-one counseling, and anti-psychotic pills to get where I'm at today. Psychotherapy addressed my somatic delusions. It took weeks of painstaking hours at the therapist's office before I believed her.

I'm not sick. At least, not in the way I thought I was.

A year ago, my stress levels were so high they were manifesting in different ways. Managing a company took all my attention, and I'd just moved to a very expensive part of the city. The sky-high mortgage, two kids, and the mounting guilt of not being able to provide sent me into a spiral of depression. I was vomiting daily. My thoughts were choked with paranoia. For a year, I didn't sleep. There was always so much to do, and I couldn't handle it.

I couldn't feel guilty if I had cancer.

My therapist says I believed what I wanted to believe as a defense mechanism. It was only too easy for Tom to nudge me in the right direction. All he had to do was reinforce my delusions, and he did.

Sometimes I catch myself feeling for lumps in the shower.

My insides rot as I climb the steps to Santiago's Hospice, catching a glimpse of my fuller figure in the glass windows. Healthier figure. Remarkable what a difference a few pounds make. I wish time had been as kind to Aubrey.

I meet the bubbly receptionist with a box of donuts, which she accepts with a wide grin. They're a gentle reminder to treat Aubrey with special care. Given what I pay this place, she better be treated well.

"She's in her room," Mary tells me, sneaking a cake donut onto a napkin. "Thanks so much."

I beam at her. "Enjoy them!"

After everything, I couldn't bear to see Aubrey waste away at a state hospice. She doesn't have anyone else except for a former neighbor who drops in to keep her company. After I sold the house, my savings were more than enough to cover her monthly expenses.

I walk across terra-cotta tiles, passing leafy ferns and tasteful artwork. I love the way they decorate this place. Everything's bright and upbeat, so unlike the gray hallways at the state hospice.

I rap on Aubrey's door and wait for her muffled response. "Come in."

I stroll into a sunshine-yellow room with a cheerful,

impressionist painting hanging on the wall. Aubrey sits up in bed, propped up by a bunch of pillows. An orange cat sprawls over her lap.

Her face cracks with a grin. "Hey, Mel."

I slide the tin of ginger snaps on the table, leaning over the mattress to hug her. It's like embracing a bag of bones. She's gotten worse over the last couple months, but her spirits are up. They always are. "What are they giving you through that IV? Ecstasy?"

Aubrey laughs, her eyes as brilliant as they were when I met her. "I don't know. All I do is sleep all day." Her voice brightens. "I think I'm getting better, though. My hair's growing in a little thicker."

I take a seat, fighting to keep the smile on my face. "Yeah."

She pops open the lid of the tin, grabs a cookie, and takes the smallest of bites. "So how are the kids?"

It breaks my heart to watch her wince and put it aside. "They're adjusting...I guess. It's going to be a while before things settle down. I've only just got them back, so, we'll see."

The rehabilitation hospital I checked myself into was a sixty-day program. My mom had the children all to herself for two months. If I could, I'd wipe dealing with Tom's extended family and the funeral from my memory.

Aubrey frowns. "They don't know what happened, right?"

My fingers twist in my lap. "They think it was an accident, but Grayson's been asking questions. Eventually, they'll find out. And then they'll hate me." Sighing, I glance at the flat-screen TV that plays a rerun episode of *South Park*.

Aubrey sniffs loudly, and I turn around to see tears streaking down her face. "What happened?"

"Sorry," she whispers. "I'm so sorry."

"For what?" I'm bewildered. "Honey, you don't have to eat if you don't want."

She covers her eyes, shaking her head. "I'm sorry I tried to kill you."

A chill spider-crawls down my spine before I remember the tumors. Aubrey gets like this sometimes. The nurses warned me to take anything she said with a huge grain of salt. It's also why they keep a close watch on her. She's prone to thinking she's fine when she's not.

I pull her hand away from her face. "Forgiven. I promise."

Her dark eyes widen into saucers. "How's that possible?"

"You didn't mean it. Otherwise, I'd be gone."

"I did," she says in earnest. "I had a whole plan."

Smiling, I pat her shoulder. "It's okay."

"What about Amit? I killed him, Melissa." She sucks in a shaking breath. "He came to my house and collapsed while we were arguing. I could've called an ambulance, but I let him die."

Another fiction. "You did call one. Remember?"

Agitated, she pushes herself back. "Yes, but—"

"There's no point dwelling on the past, Aubrey. You're a good person. It was just a fantasy."

"Not all of it." She frowns, her eyes scanning the sheets as though trying to separate the threads of truth. "I don't know. I'm confused."

"Right hand to God, you didn't kill anyone. If anything, I'm the one who should feel guilty."

"Do you?" She licks her lips. "I mean, do you ever think about him?"

I sit back in the chair. "Every day."

There won't be a moment in my future where my heart doesn't ache for everything I lost.

"I don't see him anymore," she says, wistful. "Since he died it's like he disappeared."

I can't imagine apparitions of my dead husband would be a good thing. "That's probably best."

"I still don't know how much of it was real, but I'm seeing someone else now."

Did I hear her correctly? "You have a boyfriend?"

Aubrey beams, nodding. "And he's incredible. His name is Jack, and he's a suit from Wall Street. We met here, of all places. He was hanging out in the lounge after visiting his grandmother, and we started talking. One thing led to another—"

I gape at her catlike grin. "You had sex in this place?"

"God, no." Aubrey laughs, grabbing her phone from the nightstand. "But we added each other on Instagram. Look, this is him."

A gallery of a dark-haired, olive-skinned man splashes across the screen. "Wow, he has a gorgeous smile."

"I know."

Jack has probably never set foot in the hospice, but I grin at her. "So he's flying in?"

She shakes her head. "No, I'm meeting with him as soon as I get out of here."

My chest tightens at the hope in her voice. She's not getting out. The nurses told me she wouldn't last much longer. "How will you do that?"

"Oh, I have a plan. Jack's waiting for me. His family is dying to meet me, and they're all old-school Italians, so I'm wondering if I should bring a bottle of olive oil." She suddenly yawns, her eyelids drooping. "I'm so tired."

A lump rises in my throat, but I swallow it down. She won't see me cry. I don't want her last months to be filled with pain, even if I know this man and his promises aren't real.

What's the harm in it? "I'll let you rest. I hope I can meet Jack someday."

"Yeah." She brightens. "I've told him all about you. He said you're welcome to visit us anytime."

I stand from the chair, squeezing her knee. "All right. Sleep well."

"He's waiting for me," Aubrey murmurs, sinking into her pillows. "Need to go to him."

Her eyes flutter as she whispers about her Jack, looking like a shrunken girl surrounded by white blankets. She's so small, almost childlike.

Her wistful smile tugs at my heart. "Goodbye, Aubrey."

————

THE IMAGE of Aubrey in that hospital bed follows me all the way home, which is only fifteen minutes away from the hospice. My cheeks are wet by the time I pull into the driveway. I steel myself with a few breaths before leaving the car. I head up the winding path to my new house.

After I sold the San Francisco property, I downsized my life with a mortgage I knew I could handle for years and moved to Walnut Creek. The kids adjusted to the smaller space, and having Mom nearby meant she could babysit more often. It hasn't been the easiest transition, especially for Grayson. He was very close to his dad.

Sighing, I walk through the threshold. I gaze into the darkened hallway, but no one comes. There's no stampede of feet. Swallowing my bitterness, I shove my purse into the closet and head into the living room. Mom sits on the carpet with the kids, playing a game of Monopoly.

I wave at them. "Hey, I'm back."

Stacy grumbles a response. Grayson manages to hold eye contact for a brief second.

Progress.

With a groan, Mom rises to her feet and dusts off her capris. "Hello, sweetie. How is she?"

"The same." I graze Stacy's head, tousling her hair. "She's on her way out."

"Aren't we all." She shoulders her purse. "Well, the kids had a nice day. We played some board games and walked to the park. Dinner's in the Crock-Pot. It should be ready by six."

"Thank you so much." I bump my cheek against Mom's, kissing the air. "You're a lifesaver."

"Of course. Anytime, baby." Mom pulls back, eyes shining. "Grandma's leaving! Be good, kids."

They echo goodbyes as Mom leaves, the door swinging shut behind her. Grayson glances up as I join them on the carpet. "Who's winning?"

He swipes the plastic homes off the board. "No one."

Stacy yells in protest. "Stop!"

"Game's over." Throwing a withering look at me, Grayson stomps toward his bedroom. I clean the mess. Then I seize the laptop from my office and sink into the couch next to Stacy. Opening Cocoa, I gaze at the Swift code I wrote down last night and make alterations. My fingers fly on the keyboard, coding processes for a new app I'm developing. Strictly a side project. It'll be a fitness app that syncs macronutrients with the workout and daily calorie data. Eventually I'll add meal planning to suggest recipes with a person's specific macronutrient diet. This will take too long to program myself, but I need to wait until I'm better. For now, I lose myself in the sprawl of code, stopping occasionally to stroke my daughter's hair.

This is how I used to be before I lost myself.

An hour later, an earsplitting chime breaks my concentration. I grope for my phone in the couch cushions. The screen blinks with a name.

Santiago's Hospice.

I accept the call. "Hello?"

A woman's frantic tones fill the speaker. "Hi, is this Melissa Daughtry?"

"Yes." Please don't tell me she's dead. "What is it?"

"It's Aubrey. She's gone."

The air leaves my chest. "Oh. Was it peaceful?"

"No, Mrs. Daughtry. She's *gone*. We can't find her."

III.

I'M STILL HERE.

Tom isn't.

I don't know why I write about him anymore. They say he's not real, that our love was a figment of my broken cancer brain. Even if we did have something, he's gone to a place my letters will never find. Did I imagine Melissa crushing Tom with his Tesla—or was that another glimmer of psychosis?

I'm not sure, but I'm so over Tom.

He is the reason I am alive. For that I owe him gratitude, but he hurt me more than he helped me. I thought he made me whole. Instead, he fractured me. I realize that now.

He and I were a mistake from the beginning.

You and I aren't.

You warm me like the sun.

What Tom gave me is a candle to your brilliance. My love for you is restless, whipping tides. It is endless. I am exploding with this feeling. I will fight for you. Die for you. Strap bombs to my chest—do anything I can to make you mine.

They keep saying my love is madness, but I know my truth. It's here, behind my ribs, beating a steady beat for you. I'm in love with your name. Jack. It's strong and masculine. I can't wait to whisper Jack in the shell of your ear. You said you felt the same way about me.

I might die before I get to you, but that's okay. As long as I'm headed toward you, I'll die happy.

See you soon.

Love always,
    Aubrey

ACKNOWLEDGMENTS

This book wouldn't have been possible without my writer besties: Jess, Kat, and C. Thank you. I owe you so much for painstakingly going through earlier drafts. Thank you, Christine, for your wonderful editing. I'm indebted to Kevin, who made this amazing cover on such short notice! Last but not least, thanks to my boyfriend for supporting me throughout my career. Love you, babe!

ABOUT THE AUTHOR

Rachel Hargrove is a 30-year-old from Montreal, Canada. She earned a BA in English and Comparative Literature at San Jose State University and worked as a data analyst in a biotechnology company. When she turned 26, she left her career in tech to write fiction full-time. Rachel now lives in Seattle.

Rachel's next novel, *My Sister's Ashes*, will be released in May 2018. She is represented by Jill Marsal of Marsal Lyon Literary Agency. Rachel can be reached at admin@rachelhargrove.com